If only

and he just the son of an outlaw!

But she'd seen his smile, and apparently taken it for condescension. "You think it's funny, don't you?" she fumed. "That I would want to do something besides sit and sew all day! Ohhh! Men like you make me so angry—!" She whirled away from him. "Well, good *night* to you, Rede Smith. I shall leave you to your insufferable dreams of male glory!"

Addy turned on her heel and began to stalk out of the barn, but he didn't want her to go away angry at him, so he reached out and caught her by her wrist.

"Now, Addy, there's no need to get your feathers all ruffled—"

"I'm sure *you* don't think so," she snapped, trying to wrench her wrist loose, but he held it fast. "Let me loose, you arrogant sidewinder!"

But he couldn't...!

Dear Reader,

Harlequin Historicals is putting on a fresh face! We hope you enjoyed our special inside front cover art from recent months. We plan to bring this "extra" to you every month! You may also have noticed our new look—a maroon stripe that runs along the right side of the front cover and an "HH" logo in the upper right corner. Hopefully, this will help you find our books more easily in the crowded marketplace. And thanks again to those of you who participated in our reader survey. Your feedback enables us to bring you more of the stories and authors that you like!

We have four incredible books for you this month. The talented Shari Anton returns with a new medieval novel. *Knave of Hearts* is a secret-child story about a knight who, in the midst of seeking the hand of a wealthy widow, is unexpectedly reunited with his first—and not forgotten—love. Cheryl St.John's new Western, *Sweet Annie,* is full of her signature-style emotion and tenderness. Here, a hardworking horseman falls in love with a crippled young woman whose family refuses to see her as the capable beauty she is.

Ice Maiden, by award-winning author Debra Lee Brown, will grab you and not let go. When a Scottish clan laird washes ashore on a remote island, the price of his passage home is temporary marriage to a Viking hellion whose icy facade belies a burning passion.… And don't miss *The Ranger's Bride,* a terrific tale by Laurie Grant. Wounded on the trail of an infamous gang, a Texas Ranger with a past seeks solace in the arms of a beautiful "widow," who has her own secrets to reveal.…

Enjoy! And come back again next month for four more choices of the best in historical romance.

Sincerely,

Tracy Farrell, Senior Editor

THE
RANGER'S BRIDE
LAURIE GRANT

HARLEQUIN®

TORONTO • NEW YORK • LONDON
AMSTERDAM • PARIS • SYDNEY • HAMBURG
STOCKHOLM • ATHENS • TOKYO • MILAN • MADRID
PRAGUE • WARSAW • BUDAPEST • AUCKLAND

ISBN 0-373-29150-7

THE RANGER'S BRIDE

Copyright © 2001 by Laurie A. Miller

This edition published by arrangement with Harlequin Books S.A.

Visit us at www.eHarlequin.com

Printed in U.S.A.

To Christoval, Texas, home of my grandparents, the late John Lee and Sally Hill. When I'm writing about a small town in Texas, I'm thinking of the time I spent there as a child. And always to my own hero, Michael.

Chapter One

Texas, 1874

He looked like an outlaw on the run, she thought, with his lean, sun-bronzed, beard-shadowed cheeks that hadn't seen a razor in at least two days, his wide-brimmed hat pulled down low enough so he could see, but no one could really see him. She couldn't determine whether his eyes were brown or as black as his soul inevitably was.

Or maybe he wasn't an outlaw, but a gunslinger, a man who made his name by the speed of his draw. There was no gun belt around his waist, but the battered saddlebags he kept on his lap looked heavy and lumpy enough to conceal a pair of Colts. His long legs intruded into space in the crowded stagecoach that was rightly hers, causing her to sit slightly sideways so their knees didn't bump. Sitting sideways, however, forced her either too close to the big sweaty man who kept giving her avid sidelong glances, or the weary-looking old woman who hadn't said a word all the way from Austin. It was too hot on this early June midday to sit too close to anyone.

What would either an outlaw or a gunslinger be doing on the stage that ran between Austin and Connor's Crossing? Wouldn't such a man have his own horse and keep to himself, except when he was robbing or gunslinging or whatever such men did?

Perhaps, though, she was wrong about the man slouched opposite her on the swaying seat. God knew she had been wrong about men before—especially about her husband, Charles Parker. *Ex*-husband, she reminded herself. After the divorce she'd had her surname legally changed back to her maiden name, so it was time she remembered to think of herself only and always as Adelaide Kelly. It was imperative that no one in Connor's Crossing ever discover that she was—*gasp*—a divorced woman. If they did, the respect that had been automatically extended to her as the widowed niece of the late Maud and Thomas Connor would automatically vanish.

Charles—her gambler ex-husband took himself way too seriously to refer to himself as *Charley*—was nothing like the man seated across from her. A head shorter than the enigmatic stranger and fanatically neat, Charles would never have appeared in public without the benefit of a shave. He would smell of bay rum, and his watch chain, a wedding present from Adelaide, would gleam across his brocade waistcoat—or it would have, if he hadn't lost it in a game of monte. He'd get it back, he had assured Addy. By that time, though, she no longer believed his promises.

Addy knew now Charles had sniffed out the information that her family had money before he'd ever asked for that introduction three and a half years ago. But at the time, her head had been so turned by his fervent courtship that she had been deaf to her father's skepticism and blind to Charles's faults. It was only after she was Mrs. Charles Parker that she'd discovered that her husband had no assets of his own to speak of and that he'd only married her to get ahold of hers. The honeymoon had barely begun when he'd started going through her bank account at such an alarming pace that Addy's father had counselled Addy to leave him. "It's the only sensible thing to do, Adelaide, dear," her father had said.

However, Charles was always promising he'd make it up to her if she just continued to have faith in him. Addy would see—he'd settle down and become a diligent employee at her father's shipping firm and an excellent husband. But there was always another game, and he'd need to borrow her diamond and ruby earbobs as a stake. Oh, not that she'd need to fear their loss, for he would win *this* time.

She'd have saved time and heartache if she had left him early on, but pride prevented her from admitting her mistake. So she'd stayed with him for three years even after her inheritance was gone and they'd lost the house her parents had given them for a wedding present. There followed a succession of rented rooms, each one dingier than the last.

The last straw had been when he'd filched her plain gold wedding band off the nightstand while she was bathing and had lost it at poker. She'd gone back to her parents then, and allowed them to pay for her divorce. After all, it was not only the sensible thing to do, it was the only thing left to do.

But she couldn't stay in St. Louis, Addy had decided. However glad she was to be free of Charles, a divorced woman was still a pariah in society. No, she needed to start over somewhere new.

Her widowed Aunt Maud had written offering her a home with her in Connor's Crossing. Addy, who had visited there as a young girl and remembered both the house and locale fondly, accepted with gladness and relief. She would have to work for a living, but she had discovered, during those hard times with Charles, an unexpected talent as a seamstress.

She'd been packing to leave St. Louis when word arrived of Aunt Maud's unexpected death. She had left Addy her house and its small acreage in Connor's Crossing, on the Llano River on the western edge of Texas's hill country.

Addy had lived in Connor's Crossing for a few months now and had been accepted without so much as a ripple of suspicion, for her aunt and uncle had been liked and respected. Today she was returning to the town after a brief trip to Austin, where the selection of fabrics and sewing notions for sale was plentiful.

Suddenly, the stranger across from her straightened in his seat, interrupting her recollections. Lifting the heavy leather flap that kept out most but not all of the road dust, he peered outside, his eyes narrowing as the brilliant afternoon sunlight bathed his lean face. He was unaware of the obvious displeasure of the derby-hatted drummer next to him, who had been peacefully snoring until the lifted flap flooded him with blinding sunlight, and the bony middle-aged woman on his other side, who'd been whining about a migraine all morning.

Angling his head, the stranger peered around curiously. Addy could not see out the stage window because of the way he was holding the flap. He kept it shut on her side, but she supposed she should be grateful, for at least the dust wasn't coming in on her. But the stranger stared out for so long with a vigilant, narrowed gaze that she finally asked, "Sir, is something wrong?"

It was the first thing she had said to him. A lady was not supposed to speak to a man to whom she had not been properly introduced, even if they were traveling many miles in the same uncomfortable small box.

He sat back and let the flap fall back in place before he answered. "Nope, not that I can see."

She didn't believe him, for he had shown no interest in their whereabouts heretofore.

"Oh. Well, did you *hear* something, then?" she persisted.

"Just wanted to have a look at the countryside, ma'am."

She studied him for a moment; then, giving up on getting the truth out of him, said, "Excuse me, sir," to the florid-faced big man sitting next to her and leaned forward to lift her side of the flap.

Rede Smith took advantage of her momentary distraction to appreciate the sweet line of her bosom as she bent from a trim waist to look out the stage window. He'd been covertly looking at her ever since she'd climbed into the stagecoach just ahead of him in Austin. He'd first been transfixed by the graceful sway of her silk bustle, but that was before he had been able to get a good view of her classic oval face with its soft, lush lips, pert little nose and round, green eyes.

He was careful not to leave his gaze on her long enough that she noticed. He had no desire to make her uncomfortable. There was already a wariness about her that didn't subside except for a brief period when she had fallen into a doze, just outside of Round Mountain. Then he had let his eyes drink her in and savor her rosebud lips, the slenderness of her neck, the rich chestnut hair that framed her forehead and was evidently caught up at her nape in some sort of a twist.

He wished he had been sitting next to her, instead of across from her. Then he could have stolen closer while she slept. It would have been torture to feel the length of his thigh against hers, but still damn well worth it.

Rede, there's just no use putting yourself through that for a lady. Ladies had no time for a man like him, a man with no permanent home and with a job that could put him on the receiving end of a bullet at any time. A lady wanted a man who was settled, with a little bit of land and maybe a thriving business to boot. A man who didn't feel he had something to prove. A man who had not been already disgraced by the last name he'd been born with—a name his mother had changed as soon as she'd finally left James Fogarty.

He hadn't answered the lady truthfully when she'd asked him what was wrong because he could not have said what had made him uneasy and given him that prickling along his spine. He'd been unable to identify its cause as he'd gazed out over the rocky landscape of the Texas hill country. He had seen nothing unusual—not even the telltale flash of metal that could indicate the presence of horsemen hiding in ambush.

He preferred the flatter terrain of farther south—it was harder for Indians or white rascals to hide in that country, where the tallest things in it were scrubby mesquite and knee-high clumps of prickly pear. Anything or anyone could hide in this rolling country of wide, juniper- and mesquite-covered hills and limestone outcroppings.

For the hundredth time he wished he wasn't in this swaying, rattling box, and had his good roan gelding under him. But he'd known he had a better chance of sneaking into the area without the news reaching the Fogartys if he wasn't seen riding into town on his roan. Word had a way of spreading fast, as if the wind whispered the news.

"Three Mile Hill," the woman murmured as she let go of the flap and sat back on her seat. "I'll be home soon."

She had a pretty voice, Rede thought. Not high and shrill, or mannishly low, but pleasantly pitched. Not twangy-Texan, either, though it wasn't nasal or clipped like a Yankee's. She'd been raised somewhere else, somewhere in the Midwest, he guessed. He wished he could ask her, but knew he wouldn't.

"You live in Connor's Crossing?" the big man between her and the window asked her, exhaling down on her so gustily that a loose tendril at her forehead fluttered for a moment.

Rede saw her nostrils flare involuntarily, and guessed she had gotten a potent whiff of the man's beer-and-onion scented breath. But her smile was polite as she nodded.

"Well, ain't that nice," the big man said. "Happens that's where I'm headed. Gonna set up a business there. Mebbe I could come callin' sometime, mebbe take you drivin', soon's I get me a rig and a hoss."

"I'm sorry, but I'm a widow," she said, with a meaningful glance at her clothing.

Rede had been so intent on the sweet curves of her body, he hadn't noticed she was dressed in half-mourning, a gray dress banded in black. Such shades indicated the death had been some time ago, didn't it? Several months, or was it a year or more?

He wondered how she had felt about her husband. Had she been devastated by his death? Did she still grieve? A man couldn't judge by her answer to the big smelly man—most women would have used any excuse not to have that one come calling.

Rede felt a flare of anger, not only that the man had been such an insensitive idiot, but also, he recognized, because the man had made overtures to the very woman Rede wanted himself. A part of him already thought of the woman as his.

If only things had been different. *Idiot.*

But not as bad an idiot as the big man. He couldn't imagine the green-eyed woman would have consented to let the malodorous big man call on her even if he'd been the only gent left in Texas.

"Sorry, ma'am," said the other man. "I jes' saw you were wearin' half-mournin', and I thought maybe it'd been long e..." His voice trailed off, as Rede purposefully intercepted his gaze and narrowed his eyes in warning. "Sorry," he mumbled.

"Ain't this the road the Fogarty Gang used to rob

the stage along, back before the war?'' the drummer asked just then.

The woman's eyes widened with alarm, and her face paled. Rede longed to slam his elbow into the skinny drummer's ribs hard enough to make him lose his dinner, just for frightening her.

"But I heard they hadn't been robbing stages around here for years,'' she said. "Ever since—''

"They haven't,'' Rede said flatly, wanting to banish the furrow of worry from her forehead. "Not since m— since Jim Fogarty was hanged.'' *My father. My father died at the end of a choking rope—years ago.*

James Fogarty's execution for the killing of a stagecoach driver should have taught the rest of the gang a lesson, and it had—for a while. They had lit out to the wild Pecos country for several years. But recently they'd been inching back to their old locale, the limestone-studded hills of central Texas.

"Harrumph. They better keep their eyes peeled and the shotgun ready,'' the drummer said, jerking his head to indicate the driver and the stagecoach guard riding up on top.

A lot of good that would do, if the Fogartys wanted to rob this stage, Rede thought, watching the color slowly ebb back into the woman's face.

He wondered what her name was. Something prim and fancy, he thought. Not harsh, like Harriet, or dowdy-sounding, like Ethel.

Elizabeth, he decided. He wondered if she went by Beth or Liza.

Then all hell broke loose.

Chapter Two

A rifle cracked suddenly from somewhere behind the stoop, followed closely by a sharp cry from the stagecoach driver. Addy heard a thud, then suddenly the team of horses was plunging off the road at a full gallop.

The thin woman with the migraine screamed.

"Bandits! The driver's shot!" cried the shotgun guard. Addy could hear him scrambling around on top. No doubt he was struggling to grab the dropped reins while still holding the shotgun. Had the thud she'd heard been the sound of the driver's body hitting the road?

The drummer yanked up the leather flap. "We're 'bout to be held up!" he shouted.

Many things happened at once. The stranger grabbed for his saddlebags, thrusting a hand into one and coming out with the Colt revolver Addy had suspected was there. The older woman on Addy's left began to whimper in chorus with the other woman across from her.

Addy was sick with fear. She felt a scream bubbling up inside herself, but the knot of terror in her throat wouldn't let it out. She wanted to look out the window, but bullets whizzed past and she knew it wouldn't be wise.

"Get down on the floor!" the stranger ordered Addy and the old women. Then, when the old woman seemed frozen to her seat, he yelled, *"Do it! Right now!"*

Addy heard him cock his gun, and for a single panicked second, she thought he was in league with the outlaws. Then she decided it was more likely he was trying to get a clear shot at the robbers and didn't want the two women in the line of fire.

"Get down with me, ma'am!" she cried, pulling at the resisting old woman's hands. "He's just trying to help us!" But the woman yanked her hands out of Addy's, clenched them into a fist at each ear and screamed.

"Whip up those horses there!" she heard the big man yell to the man on top. "We can outrun—"

He never finished his sentence. There was another loud *crack,* and suddenly he slumped over across Addy. She couldn't tell where he was hit, but a warm crimson fountain instantly bathed Addy, running down her cheek in a warm, sickening flow.

It was too much. She felt a black mist descend over her, and suddenly there was nothing.

The buzzing of flies at her ear woke her, how much later Addy had no idea. She only knew there was an enormous weight lying against her back, hampering her breathing so that she couldn't take a full breath. Her nostrils were full of the horrible coppery stench of blood.

She could feel no rise and fall of breathing from

the body lying against her, but just to be sure, she took hold of the wrist dangling over her back and felt for a heartbeat. None. The big man who had leered down at her so recently was dead.

Struggling against the horror that was welling up into a scream—which might put her in danger if the outlaws were still around—Addy forced herself to listen, to concentrate on something else besides the corpse partially pinning her down on the stagecoach floor. None of the other passengers remained inside. Where were they? Were the outlaws still outside?

She could hear no voices, neither outlaws calling out orders nor those of the passengers. Nothing but the humming of the flies and the endless soughing of the hot summer wind as it echoed around the limestone hills. Holding her breath so she could hear better, though, she could hear the soft tearing sound horses made as they cropped grass.

Where was everyone else? Were they all dead, too? Would someone shoot her the moment she showed her face outside the coach?

Determinedly, she pushed and wiggled until she had worked herself out from under the dead man and stealthily lifted the flap, pushing herself up just enough to see over the edge.

The hem of a fluttering skirt on the grass was all she could see.

Pushing open the door, she stood at the door for a minute, peering out at the scene before her.

The outlaws were gone. Five bodies lay in the dusty road—the shotgun guard, flat on his back, the old woman, lying on her side as if napping, the drummer, sprawled in an ungainly heap as if he had been kneeling, the thin middle-aged woman who'd had the migraine, looking like a puppet whose strings had been cut, and finally and most horribly, the man who had been sitting opposite her in the stagecoach. He lay prone, his arms outflung in the dirt.

Stifling a moan of anguish, she ran to each of them in turn, finding in each a fatal bullet wound either in the chest or the head.

Addy left the stranger's body until last, knowing that when she proved to herself he was as lifeless as the others, she would very likely succumb to hysterics. For then she would be truly alone.

She was so shaky she couldn't be sure if his chest was rising or not. The back of his shirt was streaked with blood. What would she see when she turned him over?

When she took hold of his shoulder and pulled him gently back toward her though, she lost all hope. Blood spread over his shirtfront like a horrible scarlet blossom. No one lived after being shot through the heart.

And then he groaned.

Addy, who had been crouched over him, fell back on her extended elbows.

He groaned again. He was alive! But for how long?

"Mister! Can you talk to me? Wake up! Where are you hit?" Addy cried. His eyes flew open even as he tried to wrench away from her, then settled back with a grunt.

"Easy, now, easy!" she soothed him. "I'm not one of the outlaws! Seems like they're gone now. I need to know where you're hit," she said as she pushed back his rawhide vest and began to unfasten his shirt.

She saw him relax fractionally at her words.

"F-Fogartys," he muttered.

"You mean you think it was the Fogarty Gang that did this?" she questioned him, as she reached the last button. "Weren't you the one who said they hadn't been operating around here since their leader was hanged, years ago?"

He opened his eyes again and looked at her, but she couldn't tell what he was thinking. She just knew that the eyes she'd thought might be black were brown, but the deepest shade of it she'd ever seen.

Wrenching her gaze away from those fathomless pools, she pushed aside his shirt.

The bullet hole was higher than she'd expected, just over his collarbone. It must have gone in higher than the lung. That's why he still lived, then. But if the bullet was still in him, he could die of blood poisoning. Reaching down his back, though, she felt a larger, bloodier wound in the back of his shoulder, and breathed a sigh of relief. The bullet had apparently exited there.

He'd shuddered even at her gentle touch, but now the stranger's eyes drifted shut.

"We've got to get you some help," she said urgently. Then, when he seemed reluctant to reawaken, Addy shook him by his left upper arm.

That brought instant results.

"Judas priest, woman, let go! That hurts like fire!"

Looking down, she saw a bullet hole she'd missed before in the cloth of his sleeve. Easing the shirt down from his shoulder, she saw another wound in the fleshy part of his upper arm. Probing the muscle with careful fingers, she could not find a second hole. That bullet must still be in there.

A horse whinnied behind her, and Addy darted a look over her shoulder, half expecting to see the outlaws had returned to finish them off. But it was only one of the team, still hitched to the stagecoach.

"Fogartys...they'll come back...." he muttered.

They had to get out of here, and get him to a doctor, but how? It wasn't as if she could carry him, and from the pallor beneath his sun-bronzed face, he sure couldn't walk the two miles to her place.

There was only the stagecoach—and of course she'd never driven one. The body of the dead man was still inside it. But what other choice did they have?

Addy touched the man's other shoulder to rouse him. "Mister, we've got to get you out of here, get you to some help," she said, nervously eyeing the horizon lest the outlaws come galloping over it.

He didn't open his eyes. "Everyone's dead...."

She nodded, though she knew he couldn't see her. "Yes, everyone's dead, except you and me."

"Just...witnesses. 'Sposed to be me...."

She didn't know what he meant by that, and at the moment, she didn't care. "Look, we're going to have to get you into the stage. That big man who was sitting next to me is lying dead in there, but I can't move him, and neither can you."

He shrugged, a movement that instantly made him groan in pain. "I've been around dead bodies before." He opened his eyes, and pierced her with his dark gaze. "You ever driven a stage team?"

She fought the urge to laugh hysterically. "No, of

course not. But looks like I'll have to try, doesn't it?''

His mouth twisted wryly. "Don't think I could climb up on top if I had to...."

"No, of course not." She squared her shoulders. "Well, you're going to have to help me get you to your feet."

He'd closed his eyes again. For a moment he was so still, she thought he'd passed out; and then he reached inside his vest and fumbled at something for the longest time.

"Whatever you're trying to find can wait," she said. "We need to hurry and get you to a doctor."

Opening his eyes again, the man shook his head. "No doctor..." He held out his hand, the one that had reached inside his vest. His fingers were folded around something. "Here—put this...on one of the men. The shotgun guard."

Her eyes locked with his, Addy allowed him to drop the object into her hand. Its hard coolness told her it was metal before she looked down.

When she did, Addy was startled to see it was a lawman's badge. She squinted in the strong afternoon sunlight. It was the badge of a Texas Ranger.

Her eyes flew to his face. "You're a *Ranger?* I thought..." She shut her mouth before she could say, "I thought you were an outlaw or a gunslinger," but his raised brow and the wry twist of his mouth told her he'd guessed exactly what she'd been thinking.

He was too pale, and the sun above, too fierce. She had to get him to shelter. "Well, never mind. I'll do as you said." Later, she would find out why he wanted her to make it look as though the dead shotgun guard had been him.

Addy avoided the sight of the dead guard's staring eyes, but couldn't help flinching as she pierced the blood-caked cloth with the pin of the badge.

She came back to find the Ranger struggling to his feet, his left arm dragging. He swayed, and she was just in time to put her shoulder underneath his arm to brace him.

His face had gone gray with the effort, but his gaze was direct as he spoke. "From what you said earlier, sounds to me as if you live a ways outside town?"

Puzzled, she nodded. "About a half mile this side of Connor's Crossing. We're just a couple of miles away."

"That'll do. You can take the bullet out there."

"I can't remove a bullet— I'm no doctor!"

"Lady, there's men lookin' t' kill me, and they will if it gets 'round that the doctor's been called to tend some fellow wounded in a stage robbery. I reckon if you don't care about that, you can take me on into town."

"Well, of course I don't want you killed," she protested. "But don't you see, I can't..."

"Look, lady, whatever you decide is fine by me," he snapped. "I don't have the strength to stand here and argue with you. Let's just get out of here, all right?"

Startled at his tone—and embarrassed that she'd forgotten how much blood he'd lost and how much pain he must be feeling—she nodded.

He gave her a wan smile. "Sorry, I didn't mean to bite your head off. If you can hold the horses steady, I think I can climb in."

The leaders shied and sidestepped nervously, obviously smelling blood as he drew near, but Addy went to the head of the nearest one and held its chin-strap, murmuring soothing nonsense to it.

Addy watched the Ranger take hold of the side of the coach with one hand and grab the window frame with the other, uttering a barely muffled groan as he did so. She wished she could be in two places at once so she could hold the horses and help him somehow. He more or less fell inside, landing on the seat with a thud and a smothered curse.

"Okay, lady, I'm set," he announced from within. "You ready to drive?"

"As ready as I'll ever be," she called back, then said, "Addy. My name is Addy—Adelaide Kelly."

He made no answer.

She stared over the empty road again, but saw nothing but a jackrabbit pausing to nibble some gramma grass.

Chapter Three

She'd probably never be hired as a driver for the stagecoach company, even if she wanted to be, but she wasn't doing too badly, Addy decided. It helped that the team was an obedient, willing foursome who seemed to appreciate having a human controlling them again.

She had to steer to the left when they'd come across the body of the murdered stagecoach driver around the bend in the road. As the coach passed around the corpse, Addy said a prayer for the dead driver and for the other slain passengers she'd left behind. She'd have to let the sheriff know what had happened as soon as possible, so he could have the bodies brought in for burial.

But first she had to see to the wounded Ranger. She'd heard nothing from within the coach since they'd left the scene of the attack. Had he passed out from pain during the long bumpy two miles to her house? She would soon see. She turned the coach off the main road and into the rutted path that led up to her house.

Reaching the front of her house, Addy threw the

brake on the coach, then clambered down and tied the reins to the porch rail. The two leaders were going to devour the primroses in her flower bed, but that was the least of her problems after what had happened.

Just as she opened the coach door, the Ranger pushed his hat back off his face.

"How are you doing?" she asked, her eyes roaming over his blood-soaked shirt, looking for signs of fresh bleeding.

"Well, the company wasn't the best," he said, with a sardonic nod toward the dead man still lying crumpled in a heap on the floor of the coach. "And that's got to be the bumpiest section of road in the whole state of Texas. I felt every rock the wheels rolled over. But I reckon I'll keep."

She had to admire his grit. "Let me help you out," she said, extending a hand. "We'll get you into the house and I'll put you to bed."

Distracted by his haggard face, she hadn't chosen her words with any special care, but apparently he wasn't in too much pain to tease.

"Why, that's the best offer I've had in weeks, Miss Adelaide Kelly," he drawled, managing a wink. "Just wish I was in good enough shape to take advantage of it."

She felt her temper flare, even as the flush flooded her cheeks. "If you *were,* you wouldn't be coming into my house, let alone my bed, sir. But for the grace of God, you might be lying dead out there with the others!"

He sobered instantly. "Sorry, Miss Adelaide. I didn't mean any lack of respect to you or to them. I reckon I'm purely giddy-headed, realizin' how lucky

I am that hombre who aimed to kill me was such a rotten shot and didn't bother to check afterward to see if I was breathin' or not.''

Addy figured she owed her survival to a similar piece of luck. Drenched in the dead man's blood and partially covered by his body, she'd probably looked dead to the outlaws, too.

"It's probably the loss of blood making you giddy-headed," she replied tartly as she fitted her shoulder under his uninjured one. "Come, let's get you inside."

"All right, but don't let me put you outa *your* bed, Miss Adelaide," he insisted as he raised his foot to the first stone step. "Surely you have a sofa or a truckle bed or something. Even just a pallet on the floor."

She didn't answer him. He'd have to use her bedroom. Getting him up the stairs to the spare bedroom was out of the question, in his condition.

They passed the room at the front of the house that had once been her aunt and uncle's bedroom, but she had transformed it into her shop. There was a rack along one wall full of bolts of fabric, but their bed was piled high with scraps of fabric, cards of buttons, a case full of spools of thread, and rolls of lace and ribbon trim. It was to this room that the misses and matrons of Connor's Crossing came to get alterations done or new dresses made in the latest styles from *Godey's Lady's Book.*

Addy had taken over a room off the kitchen for her bedroom. It was small, but had the advantage of facing northeast, making it cooler on hot summer evenings.

He closed his eyes on the steps leading up to the

porch, letting her guide him. Aware of his tightly
clenched jaw and the groans he tried to stifle, she
moved slowly down the hallway, passing through the
kitchen and into her room.

He sagged against her just as they reached the bed,
and she had no choice but to let him down right on
top of the calico quilt.

"I'll go get some water so I can clean up those
wounds," she announced as she picked up his booted
feet and placed them on the bed.

Ashen-faced, he didn't answer. Addy wondered if
he had passed out again.

After she had returned and cut away his ruined
shirt, and had begun washing the dried, clotted blood
away from his upper chest wound, though, his eyes
fluttered and opened again.

"Am I too rough?" she asked. "I'm sorry."

"No, don't worry, you have a real gentle touch,"
he replied. And she did. She was far gentler than
George McDonald, his Ranger company captain,
would have been. Nevertheless, though he'd never
have admitted it to her, each stroke of the damp cloth
was like a blast of flame. He knew what she was
doing was necessary—if she didn't cleanse the
wounds, he had a worse chance of dying of blood
poisoning.

A groan escaped him, however, as she helped him
to turn so she could wash the larger wound in the
back of his shoulder where the bullet had exited. He
felt her hesitate, so he muttered, "Go ahead and finish," then set his jaw and held on to the mattress
until she was done.

Once she had eased him onto his back, he concentrated on her face, willing the pain to recede. She

was so pretty, despite the streaks of blood on her
cheeks and neck and the smudge of dirt on her cheek.
Her hair had mostly escaped the knot at the back of
her slender neck, but its disarray gave her a wild,
wanton look that was quite opposite, he guessed,
from her normal appearance and personality. She'd
be pretty as a silver dollar with her hair up and wearing a dress that wasn't stained with a dead man's
blood. He guessed she had totally forgotten—if she'd
ever noticed—the sorry state of her clothing.

He watched her tear strips from an old, well-worn
man's shirt to make a bandage, then realized, by the
self-conscious way she worried at her full lower lip
with her teeth, that his staring was making her uncomfortable. But he was damned if he could stop.
After all, it kept his mind off the fiery ache above
his collarbone.

"What's your name?" she asked suddenly.

He hesitated. Could he trust her not to tell even
one person when she went into town about his presence here?

"You gonna tell anyone I'm here?" he asked.

She looked mildly indignant at the question. "For
now, no— I know you said it was important not to.
Though I can't see how it would hurt for the sheriff
to know you're here. Surely he'd be your ally in
capturing the Fogartys."

Miss Adelaide Kelly would probably be surprised
at just how often a sheriff could be hand in glove
with desperadoes, he thought. "Some small-town
lawmen flap their jaws too much," he said. "I don't
want to bet my life on whether this one does or not
while I'm lyin' here weak as a poisoned pup."

"Sheriff Wilson doesn't strike me as a gossip,"

she said, coloring a little, "but I'll respect your wishes."

Something about the way she defended the man was a bit too enthusiastic, and his heart sank. Was she sweet on the sheriff?

He supposed he owed her honesty, after she'd brought him to her house and put him in her own bed—he'd guessed it was hers by the flower-sprigged wrapper and hat that hung from hooks on the door. "It's Rede...Rede Smith," he said.

"How do you spell it? R-E-E-D? Or R-E-I-D?"

"R-E-D-E. It's short for Redemption," he admitted sheepishly. "I guess you could say my ma had a Biblical bent when it came to names." *To make up for my father's lawlessness.* She'd taken the surname of Smith to hide their connection to the outlaw who'd been her husband.

Rede wondered what Miss Adelaide Kelly would think if she knew the leader of the band of killers who'd attacked the stage today had been his uncle, his father's youngest brother.

"Redemption Smith," she said experimentally. "A bit of a mouthful, isn't it? I see why you go by Rede."

He liked the sound of his name on her lips. "Rede will do. Or just plain Smith."

Her nose wrinkled at his last sentence. "I'm not calling you Smith. Sounds like I'm some rich lady and you're my butler. I suppose I should properly call you *Mr.* Smith."

"Please, call me Rede. Can I call you Miss Addy? Adelaide's kind of a mouthful, too. And it's too stuffy a name for a pretty woman like you," he added, purely for the pleasure of seeing her blush again.

Which she did, enchantingly, though she tried to put on a severe expression to counter it. "Horse-feathers," she sputtered, after a moment. "I suppose it's all right for you to call me Miss Addy. Most of the town calls me that or Miz Addy. Since I was widowed," she explained.

He nodded obediently.

"But you needn't think that means I'll stand for any monkeyshines from you while you're here, Rede Smith."

Again, he nodded, trying to look lamblike.

"Which will be for as brief a time as possible, is that clear? I'm a respectable widow with a business to run, which will be difficult enough while you're here. Just as soon as you're well enough to ride out of here, you'll be leaving, is that understood?"

This wasn't the time to tell her he'd decided this was the ideal place to stay, not only while he recovered, but while he looked for the Fogartys' hideout.

"Yes, ma'am," he said, with all the meekness he could muster. Judas priest, but she was even prettier when she was riled, if that was possible.

"And now I had better get that bullet out of your arm, before you get blood poisoning," she said. "I'll just go and get a knife—"

The thought of her digging that bullet out made him queasy all over again. Ignoring the pain that lanced through him at the sudden move, he took hold of her arm before she could step away from the bed.

"Not just yet," he said. "I mean, it's gettin' pretty late, isn't it? You'd better go report the attack so someone can go out and pick up those bodies before the varmints get to 'em.''

"I suppose you're right," she said, looking down at his hand.

Reluctantly, he let her go. "Remember now, when they ask you about the dead folks, tell 'em Rede Smith is the one lyin' out there with the star on his shirt.''

She shuddered. "But how would I know he was Rede Smith? We didn't all introduce ourselves while we were traveling. I couldn't tell them the names of the others. If I just knew *your* name, it would make it look as if we were...well, carrying on a flirtation or something. And I'm a respectable widow—I have a reputation to maintain here," she told him tartly.

She had starch all right, Addy Kelly did.

"All right, just be sure and mention you noticed the man was wearin' a Texas Ranger badge.''

She nodded her assent, started to walk out of the room, then suddenly asked, "Who wants you dead, Rede? Why don't you want anyone to know you're alive?''

"The Fogartys. The same bast— Excuse me, ma'am, the same outlaws that attacked the stage today.'' He'd been trying to come into the area secretly, to find their hideout before they knew he was here, but somehow the word had gotten out.

Which meant someone in his Ranger company had talked. He'd have to find out who that was, preferably before the company joined him to capture the Fogarty Gang. It could be that one of them had just babbled too much while drunk. He didn't want to think that a Texas Ranger could be bribed.

She seemed to want to discuss it further, but he

wasn't ready to trust her that much yet. "Are you up to drivin' that stage into town?" he asked, to divert her.

Addy nodded. "I think so. I—I don't like to think of that man lying dead in there, right in front of my house."

He was glad she felt that way, because that meant the sheriff wouldn't be nosing around here right when Addy was about to dig that bullet out.

His stomach clenched all over again at the thought. "Say, Miss Addy, maybe you'd better buy some whiskey while you're there. Sure would be easier to stand you operatin' on my arm if I could get good and drunk before you start."

"Now how am I going to explain a sudden fondness for whiskey?" she demanded.

He hadn't thought of that. Good Lord, was he going to have to go through this ordeal sober?

He must have looked as uneasy as he felt, for she smiled. "Don't worry. Fortunately for you, there's still some of my uncle's supply here. My aunt didn't dispose of it when he died—I think she used to sip it herself. There's one bottle left. You want it now?"

Rede shook his head. He didn't know how long it'd be before she could start her digging, and he'd have a better chance of passing out and avoiding the pain if he drank a whole lot of it right before she started.

He'd drink the whiskey while she was boiling the knife before she went to work on him. He didn't know why it was, but from what he'd seen, a wounded fellow just seemed to do better when the bullet-digging instrument was boiled first.

"Oh, Miss Addy—before you leave, will you

bring in my saddlebags?'' he called after her retreating form. "They're still inside the coach. My pistols and gun belt are in 'em." Since he was still alive, he figured, he might need them again.

Chapter Four

If it hadn't been for the tragedy that had necessitated her driving the stagecoach into Connor's Crossing, Addy would have been amused by the reaction that greeted her as the coach rolled onto Main Street after crossing the bridge over the Llano River.

Dogs barked and scurried out in pursuit of the stage. A pair of ladies strolling onto Main Street— ladies she recognized as two of her best customers— stared in slack-jawed amazement, one of them dropping her parasol. The town ne'er-do-well, lounging outside the barbershop, turned to run inside—no doubt to tell the barber what he'd seen—and ran right into the support pole holding up the roof that jutted out over the shop. As the horses trotted farther along Main Street, cowboys loitering outside the saloon shouted questions at her and the news of a woman driving the stage to patrons inside.

Addy ignored them all, determined not to be delayed. She wanted to tell the story only once. Approaching Miss Beatrice Morgan's trim cottage, she spied a towheaded, freckle-faced boy of five staring between the slats of the white picket fence. It was

Billy, the sheriff's son, whom Miss Beatrice looked after during the day while his widowed father served as Connor's Crossing's sheriff.

"Billy!" she called, "run ahead and find your father for me, will you? Tell him to come to the jail, that I need to speak to him right now!"

If he had no prisoners to guard, Sheriff Asa Wilson spent little time in his office at the jail. Usually, at this time of day, he was ensconced in the general store playing checkers, but there was no guarantee of that, and Addy didn't want to spend valuable time looking for him. She was eager to turn the coach and its dead passenger over to him as soon as possible so that she could get back to the wounded Ranger in her house.

Still paying no attention to the questions called out by every soul she passed, Addy had just reined in the team in front of the jail and was setting the brake when Asa Wilson catapulted out of the general store with Billy on his heels.

"Miss Addy! I thought Billy had lost his mind when he told me you were driving a st— *Dear God, what's happened to you? You're all bloody! Are you—are you shot?*"

Belatedly, she gazed down at her dress and saw the blood that had dried into dark-brown splotches and streaks across the front of her bodice and skirts. Dear God, indeed! But her appearance was of no concern to her right now.

"No, Asa," she said, as she took hold of his hand and allowed him to help her down. "I'm unharmed. But...I'm afraid we were robbed back there." She gestured back up the road that led past her house into town.

"Wilson, there's a dead man in here," called the barber, who had apparently been peering inside the coach while she spoke. "He's all shot up."

Asa's eyes flew to her face, and he seized her other hand.

Addy nodded in confirmation, feeling her knees starting to turn to jelly now that she had accomplished her mission of bringing the coach—and the news—to town.

"Th-that's how I got so bloody," she told him, aware that more than half the town was clustered around the coach and hearing every word. "I was crouched down in the floor of the stage…and he fell over on me."

A buzz arose from the crowd at her words, but over it she could hear Asa murmuring, "Dear God," once again.

"You could have been killed," he added in a hoarse whisper. "Oh, Miss Addy, I knew I shouldn't have let you go by yourself!"

Her eyes dropped, uneasy at the naked devotion in his eyes. His kindness and caring made her feel guilty. Ever since she had come to town and made his acquaintance he had always been a gentleman. He'd said he understood that she couldn't return his feelings just yet since she had only been a widow for half a year. But she couldn't think about the way she'd been deceiving this good man, not now.

"Asa…there's five more people dead out there, about three miles out, where we were attacked. The driver, two women—"

"Women?" someone cried. *"They killed women?"*

Suddenly feeling more weary than she ever had in

her life, she nodded and went on. "Another man who was a drummer, and the sh—" She shut her mouth. She had almost said, "the shotgun guard." Quickly she corrected herself and told the lie. "And a Ranger."

"There was a *Ranger* aboard? They killed a *Texas Ranger?*"

"Where was the shotgun guard? The stage company usually has a shotgun guard riding up top with the driver."

"I—I—" Addy stammered. Was her lie to be exposed so easily? She thought fast. "The Ranger was riding up on top...I guess he was acting as the shotgun guard?" Then she thought it would be best to mix in as much truth with her lie as she could. "The stagecoach driver was killed first, and he fell off the top. Then I think the—the Ranger grabbed the reins and tried to fire back at them...but they caught up and then the man...inside there—" she shuddered as she gestured at the interior of the coach "—was shot and fell over on me. I guess I must have fainted, for when I awoke and managed to get out from under...the body—" she closed her eyes, and her shudder was not the least put-on "—I found everyone else lying dead outside the coach."

"Sweet heaven," someone muttered.

"Sounds like the Fogarty Gang," someone else said.

"Didja see their faces, Miss Addy? Any of them buzzards?" someone else asked.

Addy shook her head. "Not really," she said, though the image of a face half-concealed by a red bandanna as he stuck a pistol in the window flashed through her brain.

She shut her eyes again, suddenly feeling more than a little dizzy. She swayed.

"Miss Addy, didja—"

"Shut up! Can't you see she's about to swoon?" snapped Asa. "Back away, gentlemen, back away. I'm gonna take Miss Addy inside so she can sit down where it's cooler." Asa Wilson inserted an arm bracingly around her and guided her firmly but gently toward the door of the jail. "You men, stick around," he called over his shoulder. "We're going to have to form a posse—and if someone can drive a buckboard out there, those bodies have to be brought in for identification and proper burial. Oh, and Miss Morgan, would you have any smelling salts with you?"

"Oh, dear me, no," Addy heard Beatrice Morgan say. "But I could run back to my house...."

Beatrice Morgan was a plump old maid of perhaps sixty years who had already come to Addy once for the making of a new black bombazine dress. Black was all she seemed to wear, though who she was in mourning for was a mystery to Addy and the rest of the town.

"No smelling salts, Asa," Addy protested. The stinging scent of hartshorn always nauseated her.

"Never mind, Miss Morgan, perhaps it would be more helpful if you'd come in and be with Miss Addy," Asa said. "A feminine presence, you know...*just* Miss Morgan," he said, as a handful of Connor's Crossing ladies moved to follow them. He pushed open the door and ushered Addy and Beatrice Morgan inside.

It felt good to sink into Asa's big chair while he bustled about, pouring Addy a drink of cold water from the pitcher he always kept on his desk. The cool dimness of the jail office was restorative, too, after the heat of a Texas summer afternoon.

"Here, my dear, let's elevate your feet on this," Beatrice said, lifting Addy's feet and shoving a stack of unread newspapers underneath them. "Addy," she whispered, "surely we had better loosen your stays, too? Sheriff," she called in a coy voice, "would you please step out while I...ahem!...assist Miss Addy to breathe better?"

Addy had no need for tight-lacing and had had about enough of Miss Morgan's fluttering, well-intentioned though it was. She opened her eyes. "Never mind, Miss Beatrice, I'm breathing just fine, truly I am," she said with as much firmness as she could muster.

Beatrice Morgan looked disappointed. "Well, if you're sure, dear."

Asa Wilson cleared his throat. "Well, Miss Addy, I'll be leaving for a little while anyway. I've got to go out there now and organize a posse. I won't be gone any longer than it takes to capture those no-good bas— Pardon me, ladies, those outlaws," he amended. "In the meantime, Miss Morgan can stay with you here. And then I'll take you home in my buggy."

Addy knew there wasn't a chance in a million that the outlaws would still be in the area, but she didn't want to deflate his pride by arguing with him. She couldn't stay here, though, not with the wounded Ranger awaiting her return!

"But it could take you hours to find their trail and capture the outlaws, and then you'll be much too busy guarding them to be worrying about me, Asa—

though I thank you for your concern, of course. I'm feeling much better, truly I am," she insisted. "Let me just sit here for a few minutes, and then I'll just walk on home—"

"You'll do no such thing," Beatrice said, clucking disapprovingly. "It's out of the question for you to be alone tonight. After your grueling ordeal, you need the company of another woman. You'll come to my house and stay the night. You'll have a hot bath while I wash the bloodstains out of that dress, and you can wear an old wrapper of mine while it dries."

"I'm much obliged, Miss Morgan," Asa said, looking relieved as he strode to the door. "Miss Addy, you do just what she says. I'll call on you there in the morning."

If it hadn't been for the presence of Rede Smith at her house, Addy would have been tempted to allow Beatrice to take her to her home and fuss over her. Addy had already been invited for supper twice and knew that Beatrice Morgan was a legendary cook, and she was sure she would feel much better for a bit of the kindly older woman's pampering. But she had to get home to the Ranger. Every minute she delayed increased the Ranger's chance of developing fatal blood poisoning.

"But I'm afraid I can't—"

The sheriff let the door slam shut behind him, a man on a mission of justice.

"Miss Beatrice, I appreciate your kindness," Addy began, "truly I do, but I'm fine. I'll just walk on home. I have so much to do—"

"Addy Kelly, all that stitching can wait. You've had a dreadful shock. Walking on home by yourself, indeed! You wouldn't make it five yards beyond the barber shop! If you won't come to my house, I'm coming to yours!''

Oh, dear, now she had truly made things worse. She could just picture Beatrice Morgan discovering the wounded man in her bedroom!

She could see there was no use arguing with the determined spinster. But the excitement appeared to have taken a toll on the old woman, for she looked suddenly fatigued. That gave Addy an idea.

''Miss Beatrice, I suppose you're right,'' she said meekly. ''I shouldn't think of going home right now. In fact, I'm suddenly so tired I can't even move beyond this jail. I think I'll just go lie down in there for a few minutes,'' she said, pointing to the cot in one of the jail's two cells. As soon as I've rested, we'll walk down to your house, all right?'' She wasn't worried about using the same cot on which lawbreakers slept. The cells rarely had occupants, and Asa was so fastidious that the whole town teased him about having the sheets laundered after a cell had been occupied.

''Now you're sounding more sensible!'' Miss Beatrice crowed triumphantly. ''You do just that! I'll sit right here and wait. Don't you get up a single moment before you're ready.''

As soon as Addy rose and moved toward the cell on the right, she plopped herself down in the same chair Addy had been sitting in. Already, the plump older woman's eyelids were sagging over her watery, pale eyes. ''I'll be right here, dear,'' the older woman murmured.

Addy made a great show of settling herself down on the narrow cot, yawning elaborately while she said, "I declare, I'm suddenly so tired…don't let me fall asleep, Miss Beatrice…."

Beatrice Morgan's eyes had already drifted shut.

Addy lay on the cot in the jail cell, listening to the horses' snorting and stamping of hooves, the creak of leather and the jingling of spurs and bits as the men of Connor's Crossing prepared to ride in pursuit of the Fogarty Gang.

It took about half an hour, but finally they were ready and Addy heard Asa Wilson call, "All right, men, looks like we're ready to move out. Sooner we hit the trail, the sooner we catch those no-account bastards and bring them to trial. Now, there'll be no talk of lynching, is that clear?"

Dear Asa, Addy thought. As upright and steadfast as the day was long. He truly believed that he and his little Connor's Crossing posse were going to come upon the outlaws, milling around out there among the hills, just waiting to be caught.

Asa was a good man, and Addy was fond of him, and even fonder of his little boy Billy. Billy's mama had died two years ago during a cholera epidemic, and Addy knew Asa wanted to give the boy a mother again. And so Asa had decided he was in love with Addy, and perhaps he really was. But Addy knew she didn't love Asa, and probably never would, and that her assumed widowhood functioned as a sort of shield from his ready devotion. She realized that when the year was up since her husband's supposed "death" she was going to have to either accept the proposal of marriage Asa would undoubtedly offer, or admit that she didn't love him.

She also knew that all it would take to discourage Asa Wilson was the truth—that she was a divorced woman, not a widow. Shock would widen those clear blue eyes, and then he would look sad. He would say he understood, and of course he would not trouble her with his attentions again. And he would never tell anyone in town that she had deceived them all in order to retain their goodwill, and that she was no honest widow, but a woman who was beyond the pale of respectability—who had actually *divorced her husband.*

Addy couldn't tell him, or anyone, the truth. No one must know that her former husband still lived back in St. Louis—assuming, of course, he had not fallen afoul of some liquored-up gambler who caught him cheating at cards.

All sound had died away outside. Carefully, moving slowly to minimize the rustling of the straw-stuffed mattress beneath her, she sat up and then tiptoed to the shuttered window.

By the desk, Beatrice Morgan snored, her mouth slackly open, her head sagging on her thick neck.

The shutter creaked on its hinges as she pulled it open, and Addy froze, but the old woman did not awaken.

Cautiously, she peered out.

The streets were deserted for as far as she could see in either direction. The stagecoach had been moved down the street and parked in front of the undertaker's shop, no doubt to make removal of the big man's body easier. Someone had unhitched the four horses that had pulled it. She couldn't see the livery from here, but she was sure the horses had been put into the corral with hay and water and would remain there until the stage company claimed them.

She had to leave Asa a note, or he'd worry, and perhaps come looking for her at her house. She'd better include Miss Beatrice too, who would be distraught when she woke to find her gone. Careful not to make a noise that would wake the still-snoring woman, Addy grabbed a wanted notice lying on the desk and a stub of a pencil, turned the stiff paper over, and wrote:

> Dear Asa and Miss Beatrice,
> Thank you for your kindness. I've gone on home, as I'm sure I'll be more comfortable in my own place. I'm going to go to bed as soon as I get there. I'll be fine, don't worry. I'll see you both tomorrow.
>
> > Gratefully,
> > Addy Kelly

Then she tiptoed to the back door and stealthily lifted up the latch and let herself out. So that no one would see her, she would go down the back street, which connected up with the main road at the edge of town. Once she crossed the bridge over the rocky-bedded Llano, it was just a short walk to her house.

Chapter Five

The house was quiet—much too quiet—when Addy entered it. Dear Lord, had his wound somehow started bleeding again? Had Rede Smith bled to death?

The thought pierced her with guilt for having left him, even at his direction and for so brief a time. Addy hurried down the hall and through the kitchen to the back bedroom.

"Judas priest, woman, where have you been?"

Rede Smith was sitting up in bed, propped up by her two feather pillows, his color pale but no paler than when she had left him.

She let out the breath she'd unconsciously been holding.

"It took considerable cunning to escape a woman like Miss Beatrice Morgan, I'll have you know," she informed Rede tartly, and then explained how the sheriff and the old woman, determined to coddle her after her ordeal, had conspired to keep her in town.

He frowned as she described Asa Wilson's concern for her.

"Don't worry," she said, assuming he was just

worrying about the bandits' trail getting cold, "he didn't remain any longer than he had to, once he'd gotten the facts and seen to my welfare. He's already out there with a posse, looking for the Fogartys. It *was* the Fogarty Gang, you think?"

He gave her a baleful look. "I don't *think,* I'm sure of it," he said. "You didn't tell him about me, did you?"

She was already exhausted from the day's events, and his scornful tone sparked her ire. "No, I most certainly did not, though it felt despicable to be lying to that good man, not to mention the whole town—telling him the Ranger was dead, when you're lying right here in my bed!"

She felt herself blushing at what she had said, and hoped he hadn't noticed, but of course the Ranger missed nothing.

He scowled. "What's the matter, is the virtuous Widow Kelly the sheriff's secret sweetheart? Are you afraid he'll find me here and think he has a rival?"

Her temper reached the flashpoint and ignited.

Hand raised to slap his face, Addy took one step toward the bed before she realized what she was about to do and stopped dead in her tracks.

Addy saw in his eyes that he fully realized her intention, and wanted to die of shame. She took a deep shaky breath. "I won't do it. I won't slap a wounded man, though you richly deserve it after what you just said."

He looked away first, scowling again. "I'm sorry. It's none of my business who visits your bed, *Mrs.* Kelly," he said stiffly.

"No one—" she started to say, and then stopped herself. He was right. It was none of his business.

Let Rede Smith think Asa Wilson was her lover, if it would keep him from behaving improperly toward her. He didn't have to know Asa was the last man who'd make an ungentlemanly move toward a woman he thought was a six-month widow and whom he considered a lady. But if she expected meekness out of Rede Smith now, she was doomed to disappointment.

"Are you a good liar?" he demanded. "Did they believe you?"

"I think so," she said, striving for a level tone. *Oh, you don't know how good a liar I am, Rede Smith. I've been living a lie ever since I came to Connor's Crossing.*

"All right, good. I need you to get this bullet out, now that you're back. And I'll take that whiskey now, if you don't mind," he added.

Addy bristled anew at his brisk tone, and again when she had brought in the bottle and a freshly washed glass, only to hear him say, "I need you to boil whatever knife you're going to use for several minutes."

She started to bark back a sarcastic reply, then saw the apprehension that lurked within his dark gaze. Rede Smith was worried about how he'd react to the pain of having that bullet removed. The realization rendered him more human and made her stifle her stinging retort.

"Certainly." She turned on her heel and left the room.

It took her half an hour to get ready. She had to light a fire in the stove, pump a kettle full of water, set it to boiling, and after selecting a knife she normally used for paring fruit, boil it for several minutes. While she waited she washed her hands thoroughly, using the lye soap she used on laundry days.

By the time she returned to her bedroom, carrying the kettle with the aid of two clean cloths, the whiskey had apparently mellowed his mood.

"Will this do, do you think?" she said, holding the kettle so he could see the paring knife in the still-bubbling water.

He darted a glance at it in the steaming water, then quickly back at her. "I guesh sho—*so*," he said, his exhaled breath sending a cloud of whiskey fumes in her direction.

He was apparently aware that some of his words were slurred. "Shorry—I mean, *sorry* I was so gr-grouchy, Miz Addy. I r-reckon I'm not lookin' forward to this little bullet-huntin' exspedition we're 'bout to go on."

His face was flushed, his dark eyes dulled. She glanced at the liquor bottle, and saw that he'd drunk over half the contents of the bottle, which had been nearly full. Heavens! It was amazing he was still conscious, let alone talking.

"I can understand that," she said.

He sighed, and said in a resigned tone, "Well, le'sh get thish over with, then," he said, and sank back in the bed. "D'you have anyshing—*thing* I can bite into?"

She stepped over to her chest of drawers, pulled out one of her handkerchiefs and rolled it up, but when she stepped back to the bedside, his eyes were closed and he was breathing deeply and evenly. She hoped he was unconscious from the prodigious amount of whiskey he'd drunk so fast, and that he wouldn't come to until she was done.

She reached inside the pocket of the apron she wore and brought out the lump of lye soap. Dipping one of the clean cloths with which she had carried the hot kettle into the hot water, she rubbed it over the lump of soap until the cloth was soapy. Then she used it to cleanse the remaining dried blood from around the wound's edges. He winced slightly when she rubbed hard at a stubborn clot, but otherwise did not stir.

Once she had cleansed a wide circle of skin around the raw red edges of the arm wound—making it ooze a trickle of blood, she noted—she touched the flesh gingerly, feeling for the spent bullet within.

For a moment she could feel nothing, but then she closed her eyes and palpated his upper arm again, using just the ball of her index finger, exploring a widening circle around the arm. Finally she found it—a hard lump about half an inch beneath the surface of the back of his arm. She sighed in relief that she would not have to probe blindly with her make-shift scalpel. But the wound was awkwardly situated. How was she to get to it without standing on her head?

After a moment, she tucked Rede's hand, palm up, under his head, which exposed the posterior of his upper arm perfectly. Movement of the wounded arm made him flinch and mutter something unintelligible, but once she let go of the arm, he seemed to sink back into insensibility.

She turned to retrieve the knife.

But the water was still too hot to dip her hand into. Crossing the room, she raised the windowsill and dumped most of the water onto her kitchen garden below. A couple of radish plants might never be the same, she thought, but it couldn't be helped.

Now she could reach the knife. Using the other clean cloth to pick up the still-hot handle, she moved back to the bedside, her insides churning within her.

Gently bred *ladies* did not do such things. Extracting a bullet was a job for a doctor, or at least a tough frontier woman, not Adelaide Kelly of the St. Louis Kellys.

But he didn't want her to call a doctor or anyone else. He believed it was important for his presence here to remain a secret. If the bullet was not removed he might very well develop gangrene and die. So it was up to her.

Uttering a prayer that God would help her do this without causing him too much pain, she bent to her work.

Her first tentative slice into his skin brought him yelping up off the bed, both fists clenched. "Whaddya think you're do—"

She sprang back, but before she could say anything, his bloodshot gaze focused on her and he muttered, "Oh. 'S you, Miz Kelly. I…'member. G'wan, finish it."

She darted close and threw him—much as one would throw a hunk of meat at a vicious dog—the handkerchief she'd gotten out for him to bite. He thrust the rolled square in between his jaws, closed his eyes, and replaced the hand of his wounded arm underneath his head. He gestured with his other hand that she was to go ahead, then grabbed hold of the bedpost. Gritting her teeth and holding back the sob that threatened to choke her, she did just that.

Five minutes later, drenched in perspiration, she straightened, her bloodstained fingers clutching the bloody, misshapen slug.

"I got it, Rede," she said softly. "It's out."

He opened bleary eyes and sagged in the bed, letting out a long gusty breath.

"Quick, pour the rest o' that whiskey over my arm," he growled, closing his eyes and setting his jaw. He flinched as she obeyed, but made no sound.

She had done it. The room spun, and she leaned on the bed for support. Then she felt his hand on her wrist.

"You did real fine, Miz Kelly," he said. "Thanks. Now maybe you better sit down. Oh, an' you might oughta open up s' more whishkey. You're lookin' a mite pale."

Rede lay in Adelaide Kelly's bed, hearing her rooster crow and watching dawn gradually light the square of glass opposite his bed. The ache in his arm—and the matching throb in his head due to the whiskey he'd drunk the evening before—had awakened him an hour ago.

He'd been a fool to think that he could steal back into the area by taking the stage. He should have just taken his chances riding in—traveling under cover of darkness, perhaps, and making cold camps in gullies. Now, because someone had had loose lips, five innocent people were dead. And the sixth had had to dig a bullet out of him and was going to have to play hostess while he laid low here and recovered.

The whiskey had made his memories of last night fuzzy around the edges, but he remembered enough that he could still picture her bending over him, her pale, sweat-pearled brow furrowed in concentration as she clutched the paring knife that had eventually rooted the bullet out of his flesh.

She'd done a hell of a job, he thought, for a refined lady who'd obviously never planned on performing surgery. Captain McDonald couldn't have done any better, and he sure as hell wouldn't have bothered apologizing up and down for each and every twist and turn of the knife, as Addy Kelly had done. Yessir, she had grit, Addy Kelly did.

But she did do one thing better than his captain: snore. He'd camped out plenty with the Rangers' commander when they'd been in pursuit of outlaws or marauding Indians, so he should know, and Addy Kelly could outsnore all of his company any night of the week.

Possibly it was the uncomfortable position she had slept in, Rede thought, eyeing her sympathetically. She hadn't left the room but had passed the night in the chair next to the bed. She was there still, her head resting against the wall, her hands clasped together in a ladylike primness that was entirely at odds with the buzzing noise coming at frequent intervals from her mouth.

Sometime during the night she'd left him long enough to wash up and change out of her blood-stained dress and into a violet-sprigged wrapper. She'd let her hair down and braided it, and now the thick chestnut plait hung over the curve of her breast.

All at once she gave a particularly rattling snore. It must have awakened her because she blinked a couple of times, then shut her eyes again and still sitting, breathed deeply, stretching long and luxuriously.

The action stretched the flowered cotton across her breasts, and he luxuriated in the sight. Lord, but he loved the shape of a woman not wearing a corset.

Something—perhaps the groan of pleasure he had not succeeded in altogether smothering—must have alerted her she was not alone, for Addy's eyes flew open and she caught sight of him watching her.

She uttered a shriek and jumped to her feet.

"Whoa, easy, Miss Addy," he murmured, and put out a hand in an attempt to soothe her. He tried to relieve her embarrassment by making a joke. "I don't look that frightenin', do I?"

He watched her face change as she reoriented herself.

"No! That is…well, you *do* look a bit haggard…but I expect that's natural after what you've been through! I'm sorry—I couldn't think where I was!"

"That's natural, too," he assured her. "A day like yesterday would buffalo anyone." He knew she couldn't feel very rested after sleeping in a chair, but no lady wanted to be told how tired she looked.

Addy blinked as if surprised by his understanding.

"Did you…that is, *are* you having much pain?" she asked.

He remembered to shrug with just his uninjured shoulder. "Well, I wouldn't say I feel like running any races," he admitted. "But it'll get better."

"I should examine your wounds."

He lay still while she pulled back the makeshift bandage, trying not to look at her while she bent close to him so she wouldn't be self-conscious. He couldn't help but breathe in her womanly scent, though. She must wash with rosewater.

"How's it look?" he asked when she straightened again.

"Well, I'm no doctor, but it looks all right to me…as well as can be expected the very next day, anyhow," she said, then laid a soft, cool hand on his forehead. "Good. You don't seem to have any fever, either." Then she added brightly, "How about some breakfast? Bacon, eggs, biscuits?"

The thought of anything fried hitting his still-queasy stomach made that organ threaten to revolt. "No thanks, Miss Addy. Just coffee, if it wouldn't be too much trouble."

"Oh, come now, you need good, nourishing food to recover your strength," she coaxed. "It's really no trouble, and I *am* accounted a good cook, if I *do* say so myself."

He could tell nothing less than the truth would discourage her. "Miss Addy, I don't reckon you've ever drunk an excess of whiskey before—"

"No, of course not," she interrupted, startled. "I don't even know what it tastes like."

He pretended he didn't hear her. "The thing is, the headache a fellow gets afterward kind of deadens the appetite. Really, coffee's the best thing you could give me, ma'am."

"All right then, coffee it is," she agreed, looking sympathetic. "Just give me a few minutes—"

Just then a knock sounded at the front door.

Chapter Six

The knock came again, harder this time.

"Yoo-hoo, Addy! Are you there, Addy?"

"Pretend you're not here!" Rede whispered.

Addy wished she could do just that. The very last thing she needed this morning was one of Beatrice Morgan's long, chatty visits.

"I can't!" she whispered back. "If I don't answer, she'll think I'm still sleeping and come around and knock at the back. *She might even look in a window!*" she said, pointing frantically at the two low windows, one to the left of the foot of his bed, the other facing the foot of his bed. The lantana bushes on the side of the house would probably keep Beatrice from getting close to the first window, but she could easily look in the back one. And if she did, the old woman would be able to see Rede Smith sitting up in Addy's bed, even through the sheer muslin curtains.

"All right, but get rid of her!" Rede growled, gesturing toward the sound.

She glared at him before turning to dash down the hallway. She called, "I'm coming!" in hopes of keeping Beatrice from starting to go around to the back.

How dare Rede Smith try to order her around in her own house? She didn't intend to encourage Beatrice to stay long, but being polite was the very least she could do after sneaking out on the older woman the way she had yesterday.

She was barely in time. Beatrice was just stepping off the porch when Addy threw open the front door.

"Why, there you are! I was just fixin' to go 'round to the back," the old woman said. "Sleep late, did you?" she said, eyeing Addy's creased wrapper and braided hair. "I shouldn't wonder, after all that commotion yesterday!"

"Yes, I'm afraid I did," Addy admitted. "Sorry to take so long getting to the door."

After bustling back up onto the porch, Beatrice shook a plump finger at Addy. "You were a naughty girl yesterday, not to let me know you were leaving. The next thing I knew, Asa Wilson was shaking me awake! I was so worried about you!"

Addy had to smother a smile at the picture the woman painted. It must have been hours later by the time Asa had returned—no wonder the old woman was ashamed to have been caught dozing.

"I *am* sorry, Miss Beatrice. You looked so tired, and were sleeping so soundly I didn't have the heart to wake you. Didn't you see my note?"

"Harrumph," the old woman snorted. "As if a *note* could make me rest easy about you. And you look awful, Addy Kelly. Perhaps you should rest in bed today. Why don't you let me stay here and look after you?"

"Oh, thanks, but I couldn't possibly go back to

bed," Addy said quickly. "I'm fine, Miss Beatrice, really. I'm expecting customers today. But why don't you have a cup of coffee with me? I could bring it out on the porch, and we'll enjoy the sunshine—"

"I'll take the cup of coffee, and thank you, Addy, but I've been 'enjoying the sunshine' all the way here, and it's already hot enough to wither a fence post out there," she said, pointing at the sun-baked road. "So I'll drink it in your kitchen." Without waiting for an invitation, she let herself in.

Addy worried the whole time Beatrice sat in her kitchen that Rede would make some noise that would betray his presence. She was achingly conscious of him lying in the bed just on the other side of the thin wall between the back bedroom and the kitchen, waiting while the old woman chattered about every inconsequential thing that came to her head.

An hour passed before Beatrice at last rose to go. Addy was just letting her out the front door, when she heard hoofbeats.

She looked up and saw Asa Wilson reining in his bay gelding. Tarnation! Now it would be even longer before Rede got his promised coffee.

Remembering that she was still wearing just the violet-sprigged wrapper, she quickly snatched up a black crocheted shawl from the peg by the door and threw it around her.

"Sheriff, maybe you can talk some sense into her head," Beatrice Morgan said, pausing by his horse as Asa dismounted. "I told her she needs to rest in bed today and she won't listen to me. But perhaps *you* can exert some—ahem!—*influence* with her, Asa," she said in a coyly insinuating tone.

Addy felt herself coloring at the implication.

Clearly, Beatrice Morgan had discerned Asa's ado-
ration for Addy and assumed the feeling was mutual.
She probably figured Addy and Asa were just waiting
for Addy's year of mourning to be up before they
declared themselves.

"Asa, I'm *fine*," she said firmly. "Just tired, naturally, after yesterday. I—I couldn't sleep very
well."

"Well, of *course* she couldn't, Asa," Beatrice
Morgan interjected, before Asa could speak. "My
heavens, it isn't every day of the week a gently bred
lady is nearly murdered and has to drive a stagecoach
with a *corpse* inside it to town!"

Asa gave Addy a rueful smile before taking his
hat off to Beatrice. "I'll surely do that, ma'am."
Then he reached into his saddlebag and brought out
a couple of wrapped parcels, and Addy remembered
the fabric, patterns, laces and other sewing notions
she had purchased in Austin and brought with her on
the stage. She had entirely forgotten about retrieving
them yesterday.

"I found these on the top of the stagecoach," Asa
said, holding out the parcels, "and assumed they
were yours. There were some bolts of cloth, too, but
I'll have to bring them out another time when I have
the buggy."

"Thanks, Asa. It was good of you. And don't
bother about bringing the rest. I can always hitch up
Jessie and come for them."

"Oh, it's no bother, Miss Addy," he assured her.
"But right now, if you'll allow me, I need to talk to
you some more about the outlaws' attack."

Beatrice started to follow them, obviously eager to
hear the horrid details, but Asa put out a hand. "I

wouldn't dream of detaining you, Miss Beatrice. Miss Addy and I will just sit out here on the front porch, so we won't need a chaperon.''

"But—"

"I promise not to stay too long, Miss Beatrice," Asa said, and this time Beatrice got the hint.

"I'd about given up on this," Rede said, when Addy finally handed him the long-awaited coffee.

He was sitting in a chair next to the window, and the curtains were drawn. They had been open when she'd left the room.

"You shouldn't be up. What if you had started your wounds bleeding again?" she scolded, figuring he'd arisen as soon as she'd left the room to shut the curtains.

He glanced at his shoulder and arm. "I didn't."

His matter-of-fact tone was a splash of cold water on her worrying. "I'm sorry you had to wait," she said as she handed him the mug. "I got rid of them as soon as I could without acting suspicious, but I know it must've seemed like forever."

He took a long sip, then closed his eyes for a moment. "This was worth the wait." He took another sip, then barked out, "What'd the sheriff have to say?"

Addy shrugged. "The posse didn't find them. When they got to the site, the outlaws' trails led off in several different directions. They followed each, but eventually each trail petered out, either at the river or on stony ground."

"Your sheriff surely didn't expect them to be hanging around the bodies, counting their loot, did he?"

"He's *not*—" she began hotly, then stopped herself from reacting to Rede's needling. "No, of course not—Asa's not an idiot, Rede. But I'm sure he was hoping to be able to trail them to their hideout."

"He won't find it," he said, staring out the window rather than at her. "No one ever did before. The reports always indicated that they seemed to vanish into thin air."

"And you think *you* can, if no one ever could before?" she challenged, still irritated at his scornful attitude.

He nodded. A half smile played about his lips.

Suddenly she was very conscious of still wearing a wrapper and her hair still lying on her shoulder in its night braid. "Well, if you're sure you don't want any breakfast and think you'll be all right for a little while by yourself, I have chores to do."

He nodded. "I reckon I'll be right here," he said with a wry twist to his lips.

An hour later, she had washed, dressed, and been out to the barn, where she scattered some feed for the chickens clucking in the yard. Next she poured out a measure of oats for Jessie and curried the horse while Jessie munched on them, then turned her out to pasture.

Stopping in the small vegetable garden just in back of the house, Addy picked some black-eyed peas and salad greens, holding them in her apron as she made her way back to the house. She cast an eye at the sun, which was almost directly overhead. Just about time for dinner. She decided she'd stop in the springhouse for a jar of cold water, then mix up some corn bread to serve with the peas and greens.

She'd checked on Rede, and found him dozing, and was just mixing up the corn bread dough when she heard the sound of a buggy halting out front.

Oh dear, another interruption, Addy thought as she hurried to the front of the house after pulling the door to her bedroom quietly shut. *Who could that be?*

An imperious rapping greeted her ears. "Mrs. Kelly!"

Addy recognized the booming nasal twang of Mrs. Horace Fickhiser, the wife of the mayor. Olympia Fickhiser was the self-appointed social arbiter of Connor's Crossing and the mother of sixteen-year-old Lucille. The girl fancied herself a belle, but unfortunately she took after her short, thickset father and had too dumpy a build for true elegance.

Forcing a smile onto her face before opening her door, Addy said, "Good morning, Mrs. Fickhiser, Lucy. What can I do for you?"

"Lucille!" Olympia Fickhiser corrected Addy frostily in an overloud voice. "I did not name her Lucille to have it shortened into something so common, Mrs. Kelly."

"Oh, Mama, she's forgotten, I can just tell!" cried the girl, a pout forming on her Cupid's-bow mouth.

"Have you forgotten we were to pick up Lucille's gown for the cotillion today? I certainly hope it's completed. It would be *most* inconvenient if you haven't finished it."

Fortunately Addy had completed the gown before her trip to Austin, but after what had happened yesterday, she *had* totally forgotten they were to pick it up today. But she was not about to admit that to Olympia Fickhiser.

"Naturally *Lucille's* gown is ready, Mrs. Fick-hiser," Addy said smoothly. "All but the waist seam, which is only basted. I always leave that till the last minute, because that measurement has a way of changing, even for the best of us. Lucy will need to try it on, so come on in, ladies."

Lucy must have been stuffing herself with sweets again, Addy thought, for she looked at least two inches bigger around the middle.

"Well, I suppose we should spare some time for this," Mrs. Fickhiser allowed.

Addy led the way into her sewing room in the front of the house and took down the gown of lavender peau de soie with a white lace trim and a white bow over the bustle. Stepping behind the three-paneled screen to assist Lucy out of the dress she had been wearing and into the new one, she saw that her guess had been right. The bodice that had fit perfectly a week ago was now straining at the waist seam.

"I'm going to have to let out the waist just a little bit," Addy called out to Olympia Fickhiser. "Don't worry, it won't take but a few minutes, so I can do that while you wait," she added, sighing inwardly at the thought of delaying dinner even longer. Since the Ranger hadn't wanted any breakfast, she hadn't bothered to eat anything herself this morning, and now her stomach was growling.

"Nonsense. Just tighten her laces a bit more!" Olympia ordered in her wake-the-dead voice. "Lu-cille, I *told* you you shouldn't have consumed that entire lemon pie!"

Lucy's face went brick red with embarrassment, and Addy felt sorry for her.

"All right," Addy called, but she had no intention of complying. The stocky girl was already so tightly laced she could hardly breathe.

Catching Lucy's eye and putting a finger to her lips, Addy undid the back buttons, then moved to the laces at the back of the corset, but instead of tightening them, she loosened them just a bit.

Lucy gave her a grateful, conspiratorial smile.

After serving Mrs. Fickhiser the rest of the coffee and Lucy a glass of cold water from the springhouse, she set to work on the waist seam while the mayor's wife chattered nonstop.

"You had quite an ordeal yesterday, didn't you?" the woman asked, then, without waiting for an answer, droned on. "No wonder you look so fatigued. I'm certain you didn't sleep a wink last night! Imagine, surviving because a dead man fell over on you! How ghastly! Why, if that had not happened—you could have met with a Fate Worse Than Death," she intoned. "Didn't I warn you it was dangerous to travel alone?"

"But Mama, what could be worse than dying?" Lucy asked, her round face all innocence, but there was mischief in her eyes.

"Never you mind!" Olympia snapped.

"Well, I wasn't exactly *alone*," Addy felt compelled to point out. "There were several other passengers…but perhaps we should speak of something else?" she said, darting a meaningful glance toward Lucy.

Olympia's lips thinned, but she could hardly argue that the murderous assault on the stagecoach was a fit subject to discuss in front of her daughter.

"Of course," she sniffed. "I merely meant to express sympathy. To change the subject, then, did you happen to hear of the couple that *dared* to try to buy the lot across from the mayor's manse? No, of course you did not. This took place, I believe, while you were gone to Austin.''

Only Olympia, Addy thought wryly, would refer to her own house as a *manse.* ''Were they not suitable in some way?'' she inquired, keeping her eye on her needlework.

''Unsuitable?'' the mayor's wife crowed. ''Why, that's the understatement of the year, Mrs. Kelly! They had moved here hoping that no one would know what the woman—I shall *not* call her a *lady*—really was. But my sister in Houston—that's where they came from, Houston—wrote and warned me.''

''Do you mean that the woman was a criminal?'' Addy inquired, wondering if what Olympia Fickhiser was about to say was any more fitting a subject for an innocent young lady's ears than murder had been.

''My dear Mrs. Kelly, perhaps not in the eyes of the *law,* but certainly in the eyes of decent folk. The woman had been *divorced,*'' Olympia Fickhiser intoned in a stage whisper behind her hand.

Addy flinched at the distaste in the woman's voice. If Olympia Fickhiser even suspected the truth about *her,* she would gather her skirts and sweep out of Addy's house, telling everyone in Connor's Crossing that the widow Kelly was actually a fallen woman whom no decent lady should patronize.

''But even if the woman had been divorced, weren't they a married couple, or did I misunderstand?'' she asked mildly.

''Supposedly, though one only has their word on that,'' Olympia Fickhiser muttered in an acid voice.

"I sent them running from Connor's Crossing with their tails between their legs, I can tell you!"

Addy, imagining how the couple must have felt, said nothing.

"But surely you can understand why I could not possibly bring myself to tolerate such a scandalous couple living across the street from my innocent daughter, can't you?" Her tone indicated Addy's answer had better be yes, if she hoped for continued business with the mayor's wife.

Addy would have loved to say that Lucy would probably be better off living *with* the supposedly scandalous couple than with such a judgmental woman as her mother, but she could not afford to. The disapproval of a pious busybody like Olympia Fickhiser could make Addy's living on her own in this town financially impossible.

"Of course I can see why you would feel that way," she hedged. It was women like Olympia Fickhiser who would have made Addy's life in St. Louis hell after her divorce.

And what on earth would Olympia do if she knew Addy was harboring the Ranger in her bedroom, a man she had just met on the stage yesterday?

As if to echo her thoughts, just then a *thud* sounded from the back of the house, followed by a muffled sound that Addy thought might be a groan.

"What was that?" Olympia demanded suspiciously. "Is someone here?"

Good Lord, had Rede fallen out of bed? Addy leaped to her feet, throwing the gown on the chair she had just vacated.

"No, of course not," she called over her shoulder. "I was moving a stack of books to my bedroom when you came, and it sounds as if they've fallen over. Let me just check—''

"But that second noise—it sounded like a cry of pain."

"I thought so, too, Mama," Lucy said, obviously eager to get back into her mother's good graces by agreeing with her.

"No, I'm sure you're mistaken," Addy assured them, eager to run to the bedroom, her mind full of visons of Rede hemorrhaging from a reopened wound while Olympia Fickhiser babbled on. "It's an old house, and it makes all sorts of odd noises, especially in hot weather like this."

"Nonsense, this house isn't that old. Your uncle built it only ten years ago." It appeared that the mayor's wife had every intention of following her back to the bedroom.

She *had* to get to Rede, but she had to stop the woman from coming with her! "I—I—I hesitate to tell you this, Mrs. Fickhiser," Addy said desperately, "for I'm sure you'll think it's too silly for words, but my aunt wrote me that she'd seen the ghost of my uncle in the house. Of course, I don't believe such a faradiddle, but my family is Scots-Irish, and you know how fanciful the Irish can be...."

Mrs. Fickhiser turned as white as the lace trim on the high neckline of her dress. "I—we have to be going," she said, rising unsteadily to her feet. "You may deliver the dress when you're finished with it."

Addy watched out the window as Olympia Fickhiser, her daughter in tow, ran out the front door and into her waiting buggy.

She could barely suppress a groan of her own. Now the mayor's wife would tell everyone the seamstress's house was haunted, or if she feared to appear foolish, that Adelaide Kelly was mentally deranged enough to believe it was!

But she couldn't worry about that now. She had to find out what had caused the loud thud in the back bedroom.

Chapter Seven

Addy came bursting into the room, her eyes wild and anxious, calling, "Rede, are you all right? I heard a noise—" She stopped short when she spied him sitting on the bedside chair, his feet propped comfortably on the bed.

"Sorry, Miss Addy. Didn't mean to alarm you none. I was just a mite clumsy the first time I tried gettin' up, and knocked the chair over on the floor. It hurt some, makin' sure I didn't go over with it." He put a hand on his ribs, hoping to engage her sympathy, but her expression didn't change. "Is that loudmouthed old biddy gone? I could hear every word she said, clear back here. I swear she could talk the hide off a longhorn bull."

Her green eyes kindled and her lips tightened. "You shouldn't have gotten up without help anyway, Rede Smith! You're lucky you didn't fall and tear open your wound! And that 'loudmouthed old biddy,' as you call her, is one of my best customers—or *was*," she corrected herself while glowering at Rede. "Now she probably won't ever come again, and she'll tell everyone in Connor's Crossing I'm demented, and then no one else will have their dresses made here, and I'll either starve to death or have to beg my parents for my fare back to St. Louis—''

Rede held up a hand. "Now, just hold your horses! What on earth are you talking about, Miss Addy? Why will they think you're demented? And why are you goin' to starve to death?"

Some of the fire died from her eyes. "I—I jumped when I heard the thud, fearing you'd fallen or something," she began. "That got Mrs. Fickhiser suspicious, and she demanded to know who was here. I tried to...cover up...by saying a stack of books I'd been moving must've fallen over, but she didn't act like she believed me, and..." Now she bit her lower lip and twisted her hands together, looking away from him.

"And what?" he demanded. Lord, had Addy Kelly already given away the secret of his presence to the woman with the biggest mouth in the town?

"And I...oh, heavens, you're going to think I'm such a silly goose... I implied it might be the ghost of my dead uncle."

He stared at her, realizing he'd read embarrassment as guilt. He threw back his head and let out a hoot of laughter. "You told her your house might be *haunted,* yet you want to blame *me* for ruinin' your business?"

She stiffened. "I didn't say it was haunted, just that my aunt had told me that she had seen the ghost of my uncle in here. Oh, it was a complete lie, of course—my uncle was much too kind a man to frighten my aunt by appearing like that—but it was the first fib that popped into my head. I suppose I'm not a very good liar. It was wrong of me to blame you.''

He started to grin at the admission, but then he realized Addy wouldn't have to be lying about anything if he wasn't here hiding out at her house.

''I reckon it's probably better for a person not to be a good liar,'' he murmured. ''But what kind of business are you in?'' he asked, curious.

''I'm a seamstress,'' Addy told him, raising her chin a little as she said it. ''I sew dresses and do alterations. That's the reason I was in Austin—buying supplies I couldn't get at the mercantile here.''

''And you run your business out of your home? Why don't you have your shop in town?''

''I inherited *this* place, not a place in town,'' she said, a bit defensively. ''I can't afford to rent a shop in town—at least not yet,'' she added. ''It's not so far beyond town that people mind coming here—or at least, they didn't, until I convinced Mrs. Fickhiser the place was haunted, or that I was crazy.'' Her brow furrowed in obvious anxiety.

''Your late husband didn't leave you very well off, I take it?''

Rede was sorry as soon as the question left his lips. Her mouth tightened again, and she looked down at her lap.

''I'm sorry, Miss Addy,'' he said quickly. ''It ain't any of my business.''

She raised her head, meeting his gaze squarely. ''Indeed it isn't. But since you asked, no, Charles did not leave me very well off. And I have not been in Connor's Crossing very long. So I do depend on my good reputation to get my business established and keep it going.''

"Miss Addy, next time someone comes I'll be so quiet you can hear a hummingbird's heartbeat," he promised, his hand over his heart. He was trying to make her smile again; and she started to, but then she got that worried look again.

"Well, hopefully you'll be well enough to leave before too much longer," she said briskly. "How long before you'll be able to ride?"

"Oh, a few days," he said, deliberately vague. He'd wanted to extend his stay, using her place as his base of operations, but it sure didn't look like it was going to be easy to talk her into that. And that was too bad, because from what he'd been able to determine, Addy Kelly's house was perfectly situated—far enough out of town that folks didn't drop by without a reason, near enough to keep in touch with the news. And once he'd found the Fogarty hideout, Connor's Crossing was surely big enough to have a telegraph office he could visit to summon his Ranger company.

He'd just have to convince Addy she had nothing to fear from his continued presence. *But first, Rede, you'd better convince yourself.* If he was allowed to stay, it was going to be awfully hard to keep his hands off the tempting young widow.

Just then he heard the distinct growl of her stomach.

Addy pressed a hand against her middle and blushed. "Excuse me! I was just about to fix dinner when Mrs. Fickhiser came—now it must be the middle of the afternoon! Could you eat a little something, Rede?"

Rede's queasiness had long since left him, and he could eat more than "a little something." In fact, he was now so hungry he could eat a horned toad backward, but he didn't think it was polite to say so.

"Yes ma'am, I reckon I could."

Two days later, Jack Fogarty rode into the hideout scowling—a bad sign, his men knew from past experience.

"Thought you said you saw the Ranger's body when you rode back to look, Chapman," Jack Fogarty snarled. Fogarty had been on a reconnaisance trip to Connor's Crossing and swore as he pulled off the fake gray beard he wore as a disguise whenever he went into town.

Chapman, crouching over a pot of beans, stopped stirring and squinted up at the outlaw leader as the rest of the gang gathered around to listen. "I *did,* boss," he insisted. "He had a Ranger badge on, right enough—just above the hole in his chest. What's wrong?"

He never saw the swift fist that knocked him flat on his back, but when he opened his eyes, Fogarty's angry face was scowling down on him.

"You damned fool! He warn't no Ranger!" Jack Fogarty shouted down at him. "I went t' claim the body at the undertaker's in town, on behalf a' the grieving widow in Llano, I told 'em—*only to be told his carcass had already been taken away!*"

Chapman blinked. "Already been taken away?" he echoed. "By who?"

"By his *real* wife—who said he was a shotgun guard, not a Ranger, and the undertaker told me she was right puzzled as to why her man had that Ranger badge pinned on his shirt. The undertaker was lookin' all squinty-eyed at me, so I figgered I'd better hightail it outa there before he pointed me out to the sheriff.''

Fogarty's voice was ominously quiet now, and Chapman felt a flicker of alarm. The leader of the Fogarty gang had been known to shoot a man for less cause than a mistake like this.

''So how would someone get a Ranger's badge on his chest that wasn't a Ranger?'' Lew, one of the other outlaws, asked.

''That's just what I'm wonderin','' Fogarty growled, a murderous glare in his eyes.

''Sounds like someone wanted folks to *think* the Ranger was dead,'' the man said carefully, keeping an eye on Fogarty.

''Especially us folks,'' someone else muttered.

''Yeah, especially us,'' Fogarty said, as if to himself. ''Which means that Ranger we heard was on that stage is still alive.''

There was silence around the campfire as the outlaws considered the idea.

''You reckon we got double-crossed, Jack?'' Clete Fogarty, his younger cousin asked.

Fogarty stiffened. ''What d' you mean?''

Clete shrugged. ''You was told the Ranger'd be on the stage. What if the fella that tol' you so was lyin'?''

''He wouldn't dare.''

''What's t' stop 'im?'' Clete retorted, careful to keep his voice nonchallenging.

Fogarty grinned and jerked his head meaningfully at the bony-thin woman who sat mending his shirt in the sparse shade of a mesquite tree, just out of ear-shot. ''Mary Sue, yonder. She just happens t' be my informant's wife, ain't she, Chapman?''

Chapman had been the only other one in on the secret, and now he puffed out his chest with pride—and secret relief that Fogarty no longer seemed angry at him. "That's so," he told the others, eyeing the female who was Fogarty's sole possession.

"I figger he don't want nothin' t' happen to his wife, even if she is a mite...wayward," Fogarty said of the woman he'd enticed to run away with him. "He knows her life wouldn't be worth two bits if he lied to me—or his neither."

The casually uttered words cast a chill on the group, and they looked away from Fogarty's expressionless eyes.

"So you're sayin' the Ranger had to have been on that stage," Chapman said.

Fogarty nodded, rubbing his chin, which itched after wearing the fake beard. "I don't remember seein' a badge on any a' the men we shot that day, come t' think on it. Lessee, there was the driver that we plugged first," he said, counting on his fingers, "that other fella on top that turned out t' be the shotgun guard, that skinny little fellow with the derby hat..."

"Hoo-whee, I 'bout busted a gut when that silly li'l hat flew up in the air when you plugged 'im, boss!" one of the men snickered.

Fogarty's jaw clenched. "I'm so glad I could amuse ya, Thompson," he snapped. "Now, if we could stick to the subject—"

"There was that big fella dead on the floor a' the coach," Thompson said, eager to get back in the outlaw leader's good graces again. "You know, the one that fell over the woman? Mebbe we got 'em both with the same slug, ya think?"

"Jack, I d-d-don't f-f-figger *he* was the R-R-

Ranger, noways," Walt Fogarty, Clete's brother, said with his usual stutter. "A b-b-big tub a' l-l-lard like that!"

"But as I remember, there was one other gent on the stage," Fogarty mused.

"Yeah—some dark-haired tall fella," Chapman said. "Looked like a drifter. I shot 'im in the chest."

Fogarty gave him a measuring look.

"Did ya? Did you check t' see that he was dead when I sent you back for a look-see? Did you check all of them?"

Full of nerves and resentful that he'd been sent on this task, and eager to be safe back at the hideout, Chapman hadn't done more than glance at each of the corpses. They'd sure as hell looked dead enough to him. He couldn't admit that now, naturally. "'Course I did. They was all was dead, all right."

"So...that leaves that wiry little fella with the derby hat who coulda been the secret Ranger, Chapman? Is that what you're sayin'?"

Too late, Chapman saw the chasm yawning in front of him. He'd have done better to admit he hadn't checked the bodies very closely.

He shrugged, ice closing around his heart.

"You're sayin' the man *I* shot while you were pluggin' the other fella was the secret Ranger?" Fogarty persisted. "The one whose skull I let daylight into?"

The others chuckled uneasily.

"Or maybe it was the big fella whose blood was puddlin' on the floor—*or maybe even one of them women was really a Ranger dressed up like a gal, and wasn't dead!*"

Chapman took a step back. "Boss, I don't

know…I sure *thought* they was all dead, 'specially the one I shot—''

Fogarty whipped out his pistol and killed Chapman while the other man was still making excuses. Once a man lied to Jack Fogarty, he would never trust him again.

''Next time I want you fellas to be sure,'' he told the others, who stood slack-jawed and wide-eyed with horror at the sudden killing of their compadre.

Chapter Eight

"Time for your dressing change," Addy called as she swept into the room.

Two days of being confined to the small room had made Rede as restless as a caged cougar. "You sound awfully cheerful today," he accused, scowling at her over the remains of his breakfast.

Addy blinked, then smiled tolerantly in a way that made him want to clench his fists. "Is that a crime, Ranger Smith?" she inquired with raised brows as she sat down by his bed, a freshly ironed bandage in hand. He felt her studying him.

"'Course not. So why are you so happy?"

"What dressmaker wouldn't be, after getting the job of making not only Sally Renfrew's wedding gown, but those of all four of her attendants *and* her mother?"

"Who's Sally Renfrew?"

"*Only* the daughter of the area's most prominent rancher." Addy fairly sang the words. "I guess this means Olympia Fickhiser either didn't say anything about my ghostly uncle," she said with a wry chuckle, "or the Renfrews don't care about her tales.

And the wedding's not till fall, so I have plenty of time.''

"Good for you. Guess that'll keep the wolf from your door for a while," he growled, and immediately wanted to take back what he'd said, or at least, the *way* he'd said it. His restlessness had made him cranky. But Rede couldn't be as carefree about the passage of time as Addy was. Every day he had to hole up here, unable to do anything but eat, sleep, and have his dressings changed, was a day the Fogarty gang continued to run free—and he was further than ever from bringing honor back to his name.

He had to admit that Addy's cooking was wonderful—the food she prepared was the sort of thing a man dreamed of during the monotony of beans cooked over a campfire and washed down with coffee. Because of the nourishing food, the long hours of sleep, and Addy's nursing, he was getting stronger each day—but he was nowhere near ready to ride out in search of the Fogartys' hideaway.

And Addy's nearness was becoming a torment. After all, he hadn't had a woman in a long time— even a saloon girl. And a lady like Addy Kelly was about as far from a saloon girl as Rede could imagine.

Ever since he'd grown to manhood, Rede's mother had urged him to find a good woman and settle down. After her death a couple of years ago, and still a bachelor, Rede had joined the Rangers. Now he avoided meeting "good women"—ladies—like the plague. It was unfair to ask a lady to wait around for him when he was apt to be away for endless weeks chasing bandits and marauding Indians. He never knew when he'd be home—or when a bullet from a

Comanche or an outlaw could put an end to his life. What gently bred female would want a man like that, anyway?

In the past, he had resorted to saloon girls if his needs became insistent enough, and if his Ranger company happened to be near enough to a town big enough to have a saloon or cantina. But purchased caresses had never done anything for the loneliness of his soul.

"Why don't you just unbutton your shirt, Rede, and we'll change that bandage?" Addy said as she bent toward his shoulder.

He caught a whiff of the rosewater essence she always seemed to wear, and his body came fully, painfully to life. Suddenly the room seemed to be closing in on him, bringing her much too close.

"No," he managed to say.

"No? But Rede..." She looked at him again. "Rede, what's wrong? Are you...aren't you feeling well?"

The note of alarm in her voice shamed him. He was feeling grouchy as a devil made to sit through a Sunday sermon, and here she was thinking he'd had a relapse.

"Miss Addy, I know you've got to be careful about not lettin' my presence here be known and all, but d' you think we could do this dressing change out in the kitchen?" *Anywhere, but in this room where I'm already sitting on your bed and pulling you down onto it is all too easy to imagine.* "I'm startin' to feel like I'm in a prison cell," he added, gesturing at the walls. "I can move real fast back into here if we hear anyone come."

Addy looked startled at the comparison of this

room to a cell, then thoughtful. "Why yes, I suppose that would be all right," she murmured. "I'm not expecting anyone else today, anyway. Do you need some help?" she added, offering him her arm. "Or should I get my uncle's cane?"

It was bad enough to be having these heated fantasies about Addy Kelly, without her treating him like a damn invalid! What he *needed* was to have the pain gone from his chest and arm, so he could ride away from here before the respectable widow Kelly found out just how her presence affected him!

"No, I can manage," he said, getting to his feet and pretending not to see the proffered arm. After all, he'd moved between the bed and the chair several times a day. Surely it couldn't be that much farther to the kitchen just beyond the door.

By the time he lowered himself into one of the chairs at the kitchen table, though, his chest wound was throbbing and beads of perspiration had broken out on his forehead.

"Now then," Addy said briskly, setting down the bowl of water and the towel and acting as if she hadn't seen how stiffly he had moved. "If you'll just slip off the shirt..." She waited while he slowly shrugged out of the borrowed shirt and helped him push it over the back of the chair.

Then she bent over him to unroll the dressing that looped under his arm and back over his shoulder several times. It had held the pad of cotton cloth close to his chest.

"It's not sticking to your skin any more, Rede," Addy announced in a pleased tone as she carefully peeled the square pad away from the chest wound. "And it's looking much better—much less red and angry. Let's have a look at your arm, too.'' A moment later, she had unwrapped the roll of cloth from around the arm wound. Eyeing that wound, she announced its progress toward healing as well.

The simple, clean smell of her hair, coiled in a knot at the nape of her neck, wafted up his nostrils as she began to gently wash the arm wound with a clean rag.

His groin tightened in response. He closed his eyes as he imagined reaching out with his uninjured arm and putting his hand on the back of Addy Kelly's head, pulling her toward his waiting lips. And then...

Immediately she stopped washing, and he heard her indrawn breath. ''I'm hurting you,'' she accused herself. ''Oh, Rede, I'm so sorry! I didn't think it would still hurt so—''

''No, you're not—'' he tried to assure her.

''You don't have to be polite, Rede Smith! Your eyes were squeezed shut as if you were in pain, and—''

''Honey, you're *not* hurting me,'' he said quickly, then realized what he'd called her. *Hellfire!* It was too late to retreat now! ''At least, not in the way you thought.''

Knowledge widened the pupils of her eyes and deepened the surrounding green of her irises as hot color crept up her cheeks. ''Oh. I...see....'' She took a step backward. ''I suppose that's just another sign you're on the mend,'' she said with determined lightness after a moment. Avoiding his eyes, she busied herself with patting the area dry, then winding the strip of clean bandage around his arm.

''I reckon,'' he muttered in agreement, and wished proximity was the sole explanation. He knew that even if he could leave her home today, though, and never see her again, he'd never forget this woman, and not just because she risked her own life to save his. Those green eyes, that soft mouth—they'd haunt his dreams the rest of his life.

It seemed to Rede that Addy hurried through the dressing change after that. Then she invented a need to go into town for certain sewing supplies she claimed to have run out of, and after heating a bowl of soup for him, left him with the promise that she'd be back soon.

Addy was just leaving the mercantile, carrying the white thread and a packet of pins she hadn't really needed when she nearly collided with Lucy Fick-hiser, who was running down the plank walkway as if pursued by demons.

The mayor's daughter was flushed and her eyes suspiciously bright, as if she were trying very hard not to cry.

"Oh! Excuse me, Miss Addy!" she apologized, and was about to take off again when Addy reached out a hand to detain her.

"Oh, Lucy, how good to see you!" Addy said, deliberately using the girl's nickname since her mother was apparently not with her. "I was just looking for an excuse to go back in and have some of Mr. Herman's wonderful lemonade, but I hate to sit there by myself. Why not come in and have a glass with me? My treat," she added, when the girl hesitated. "To thank you for all the business you and your mother have given me."

Lucy took a deep breath. "All right, I'd like that,

Miss Addy. I'd wanted to talk to you anyway, but my m—'' she broke off and looked away.

Addy didn't know, but she could guess. Olympia Fickhiser had probably told Lucille they would have no further dealings with Adelaide Kelly. Insanity, after all, might be catching. She pretended she hadn't guessed what Lucy had been about to say.

"Now," said Addy when they had sat down in the back of Herman's mercantile, where there were four small tables, "You said you wished to talk to me?" She really wanted to ask the girl what she had been upset about, but knew that would have to be Lucy's idea.

"Oh, it wasn't anything special, really," the girl said with elaborate casualness while the mercantile owner was setting down glasses of his lemonade. Then, once he had retreated behind the counter at the front of his store, she said, "I...uh...I was wondering if you'd ever seen him?"

"Who?" asked Addy, honestly mystified.

"The ghost, of course! Your uncle! Since he...became a ghost, that is." She sighed. "That's so interesting, having a ghost in the house! Nothing ever happens in *our* house," she added in obvious disgust. "Mother never lets it."

"Why no, I haven't," Addy said, amused, but keeping a straight face for Lucy's sake. "As I said, I'm not sure I even *believe* there's a ghost. I just felt honor-bound to mention it, since your mother was so concerned about that—that noise we heard, that day you were there for your fitting. I *did* find a stack of books had fallen over, by the way."

Lucy looked disappointed, then skeptical. "But

there was a thud, then a groan. Books don't make a *groaning* sound when they fall over, Miss Addy."

But a wounded man trying to do too much did. Addy shrugged, then changed the subject, hoping Lucy wouldn't persist with her probing. She supposed the girl couldn't help being nosy, with a mother like that. "Would you like some cookies to go with your lemonade? Mr. Herman had some up front, two for a penny," she offered, then wished she had bitten her tongue instead when the girl's face turned a muddy red.

"My mother said I wasn't to touch any more sweets until my waist was seventeen inches," she muttered miserably.

Addy's heart went out to the girl. With stocky Mayor Fickhiser as her father, she'd probably never achieve a seventeen-inch waist! Didn't Mrs. Fickhiser realize there were more important things in life?

"I shouldn't have tempted you, then," Addy apologized. "If it's any comfort to you, Lucy, many girls go through a 'puppy fat' stage that they outgrow a little later. I know I did."

The girl's jaw dropped open, and she eyed Addy's present willowy figure with open envy. "*You* did? Oh, Miss Addy, you sure don't look like you ever went through that stage!" For the first time a spark of hope lit her pale eyes, but then misery seemed to wash over her again like a wave.

"By the way, Lucy," Addy began carefully, "when I was leaving the store a few minutes ago and nearly ran into you, you looked rather distressed. Is there anything I could help with?"

The girl looked startled, and her lower lip quivered. "Henry told me he liked me, and asked if he could sit with me at the church social."

Addy had no idea who Henry was, but she asked, "Don't you like him?"

The girl nodded as moisture gathered in her eyes again.

"Then surely that's a good thing? Where's the problem?"

"My mama said I couldn't associate with him because his father runs the livery. She says he's *beneath* the daughter of the mayor. I had just come from telling him that when—when I nearly ran into you, Miss Addy."

Anger at Olympia Fickhiser's petty snobbery flooded Addy, though of course she couldn't let Lucy see it. But what could she safely say?

Fortunately, Lucy didn't wait for her to speak again. "It's not fair! He's the only boy in town who doesn't tease me about...well, about being a little plump," she said, blushing again. "He thinks I'm just fine like I am! And Henry's got ambition," Lucy continued. "He doesn't plan to work at the livery all his life. He's finishing his schooling, so maybe someday he can start a newspaper."

"He sounds like a nice young man," Addy said. She knew who Henry was now—a lanky, towheaded beanpole of a youth she'd seen in church, sitting with his equally lanky father, Henry Jackson, Sr. "You might just have to be a little patient, Lucy. If he's the young man you say he is, he'll win your parents' respect sooner or later."

Lucy's face brightened. "Oh, do you think so, Miss Addy? I sure hope you're right!"

Addy nodded, relieved she'd managed to say

something that had given the girl hope. How lucky she had been, as a girl who'd been "a little plump" herself, to have a mother totally unlike Lucy's!

"Miss Addy, I'd better get on home. Thank you for the lemonade…and for listening. And for calling me Lucy!" she added with a giggle.

She'd better get on home herself, Addy realized, and left the mercantile. She couldn't hide in town forever. She was going to have to figure out how to keep her distance from Rede Smith while he was staying in her house, yet still tend to his wound, she thought as she passed the barber shop.

"Miss Addy! Whoa up, there!"

Chapter Nine

Recognizing Asa Wilson's voice, she turned around to wait for him.

"Howdy, Miss Addy," he said, his cheeks still pink from the shave he'd just received. "You're lookin' mighty pretty today."

"Why, thank you, Sheriff," she said, wishing she could feel as thrilled by his obvious pleasure at seeing her as he seemed to be.

"You in a hurry to get home? I need to ask you about that man you said was a Ranger."

Unease flickered within her. That man you *said* was a Ranger—that implied doubt. She felt a surge of guilt within her because of the lie she had perpetrated, at Rede's insistence.

"Well, I am rather in a hurry, Asa. I have a sewing job to finish, and I just walked into town to get some thread," she said, holding up her parcel. "Besides, I really don't know what else I can tell you."

"No problem, I can walk you home," the sheriff replied, unaware that this was exactly the opposite of what she wanted. She certainly didn't want Asa coming into her home with Rede there, even if he had gone back into her room!

"Oh, there's no need to trouble yourself," she said quickly. "I can certainly spare you a few minutes, Asa. I'm as interested as you are to see that the outlaws are brought to justice, though I don't see how I can help."

But Asa was not to be dissuaded. "Oh, I reckon I shouldn't be talkin' to you on such matters out here in the street. It's no trouble for me to walk you home, Miss Addy. In fact it'd be my pleasure. And if you'll just let me fetch those bolts of cloth you bought in Austin, I can bring those with me."

Tarnation, she had forgotten all about the fabric she'd bought on her trip! Addy stifled a sigh. Any argument she made now would only appear suspicious. She would just have to hope he would ask his questions on the way, and say goodbye at her front porch. She nodded her assent, and followed him to the jail. Then, once he was loaded down with the bolts of cotton, silk, and wool batiste, they strolled down Main Street, and over the bridge across the Llano.

"River's really down," he said, looking down at the thin trickle of water over its limestone bed.

"I'm told it always is, by summer, unless there's really been a good rain," she replied politely, wanting to scream at the courteous inanity of their conversation. "Uh...you said you had a question?" Addy prompted, when Asa seemed in no hurry to speak. She wanted to get it over with.

"Mmm-hmm, though I surely do apologize at havin' to bring it up at all, Miss Addy. I know how anxious you must be just to forget about the whole thing.''

Forget about the whole thing, as if it had been merely an inconvenience! Impatience with Asa swept through her. Asa Wilson was a pleasant man, but a bit obtuse at times.

"I doubt I could ever just *forget* about it, Sheriff,'' she said tartly. "I've never seen a dead body before, let alone five of them.''

"Of course, of course,'' he soothed. "I just meant, I knew you wouldn't be wantin' to talk about it. But the undertaker told me somethin' that really does have me puzzled.''

A prickle of apprehension raced down her spine. "Oh? And what was that?''

"He said when the family of the dead man—I mean the one that you said was a Ranger—came to claim his body, they were real surprised to see that badge among his effects. Said they didn't know anything about him being a Ranger. In fact, they were certain he'd never been one, and would never have considered being one.''

Addy's pulse accelerated within her as she pretended polite interest. "Is that right? Well, that's certainly mysterious that he was wearing that badge, isn't it? Maybe he'd just joined?''

"And maybe there was another man on that stage,'' Asa suggested, "someone you might've forgotten about, in all the confusion? Someone who might've managed to crawl away afterward? After all, the interior of a Concord coach could hold nine people if need be.''

While her mind raced, Addy allowed herself to look as if she were struggling to remember. If she admitted now that there had been another man in the coach that she hadn't mentioned, would it appear that she'd been holding back information, or just that she had been a flutterhead and forgotten the fact?

Much as she despised appearing a scatterbrain, Addy took the excuse Asa had given her and let an expression of surprise steal over her features. "You know, I had forgotten! There *was* another man! He got on at the last station, while they changed teams!"

"What did he look like?" asked Asa, suddenly intent. "Could he have been a Ranger?"

Addy shrugged. "I don't know," she said. "I never really got a good look at him. He rode up on top."

Asa rubbed his chin. "Riding up there, seems like he would've got shot right along with the driver and the shotgun guard."

Logically, he was correct, but having said what she had, Addy could only shrug again. "Maybe he bears a charmed life, I don't know. All I can tell you is he wasn't there when I managed to crawl out from under that dead man in the coach." She affected an elaborate shudder, hoping to get him to drop the subject.

Asa, however, didn't seem to notice. "But even supposing he managed to play dead until the Fogartys rode off, why would he pin his badge on a dead man?" He blinked. "Unless…"

Hoping she could head Asa away from the truth, she infused all the crossness she could muster into her voice. "Sheriff, really! You seemed determined to make me relive every horrible second of that day!"

Asa had the grace to look ashamed. "I'm sorry,

Miss Addy. I didn't mean to, honest. I guess when something just doesn't add up, I just want to worry at it like a dog with an old shoe. Forgive me?'' he begged, just as they reached her house.

He was giving her his most winning smile, and while it didn't have the power that Rede Smith's rare smiles did, she knew she should let him off the hook now.

"Of course. Don't give it another thought,'' she said. "Thank you for walking me home, Asa.''

She turned to go in, but she wasn't to escape so easily.

"Now, if you don't invite me inside for a glass of your lemonade, Miss Addy, I'll know you're still angry,'' Asa murmured.

She stared up at him. "No, I'm not still angry, Asa, of course I'm not, but I have a lot of work to do,'' she protested. Dear God, she couldn't let him come in! What if Rede was still sitting in the kitchen? Not for the first time, she wished Rede had agreed to accept the sheriff's help, so she didn't have to be so deceptive!

"Aw, you work too hard, Miss Addy. Why don't you let yourself relax a little?''

It was on the tip of her tongue to retort that if she didn't, she wouldn't have any way to support herself, but she didn't want to sound any more waspish than she already had.

While she was hesitating, trying to think of a more convincing reason to bid him goodbye, he said, "You wouldn't send a man away thirsty on such a hot day, would you?'' He glanced upward mock dramatically at the sun overhead.

He had her there. It *was* hot. It would be downright uncivil if she refused him a cool drink.

"All right," she said, pretending to give in gracefully, "I won't send you away thirsty, but after that I have to get down to business."

"I won't stay long, I promise, Miss Addy."

She opened the front door. "Have a seat in the parlor, here, and I'll go get the lemonade," she offered, as they entered the house. At least, if she served him here, she'd be keeping him in the front of the house. Rede had yet to progress that far from the back bedroom.

"No, I wouldn't think of havin' you wait on me like that, Miss Addy," Asa said. "I'll just come on back to the kitchen with you. It's cooler, anyway, shaded by that big old cottonwood."

She tried not to look panicked as she accepted the inevitable. If they found Rede still in the kitchen, Rede would just have to explain his presence and her reason for lying. After all, Asa and Rede were on the same side, and Addy was sure Rede would catch the Fogartys faster with the sheriff's help than on his own!

"Well, all right, Sheriff, come on back to the kitchen, then," she said, pitching her voice a little louder than necessary to give Rede warning of their approach if he'd been napping.

Nerves on edge, she heard the quiet shutting of the bedroom door, but a quick glance at Asa's face showed no change. Apparently he hadn't heard anything.

"Would you mind going out to the springhouse to get the pitcher, Asa? I left the lemonade out there to keep cool. Asa—?'' she repeated, when she saw he had stopped dead.

He was staring at the shirt that still hung over the chair where Rede had placed it to get it out of the way while she changed his dressing.

She froze as Asa stepped forward and picked up the shirt between his thumb and forefinger.

He turned and held it out to her. ''Miss Addy, whose is this?'' His bland face had clouded with suspicion.

She hoped she didn't look as guilty as she felt as she uttered a little laugh. ''That old thing? It's my uncle's,'' she said truthfully. ''I…uh…wear it sometimes when I work out in the barn,'' she said. ''Keeps my good clothes clean.''

Asa's face cleared. ''Oh, of course. I forgot you still had that mare of your uncle's.''

Gratefully, she took refuge in the topic. ''Yes, Jessie. I don't need to hitch her up to the carriage very often, but once in a while I go ride her out over the hills.''

''Well, maybe you'd better not do that until we catch those outlaws,'' Asa said. ''I wouldn't want you to meet up with them. I'll just go out and get that pitcher.''

She forced herself not to go check on Rede while Asa walked out to the springhouse, and busied herself instead with setting out a pair of glasses and some cookies.

But just as Asa was raising the glass of lemonade to his lips, the sound of approaching horses made him pause.

A moment later she was greeting Dick Brooks, Asa's deputy.

"Figured I'd find you here, Sheriff," he said. "Barber said you headed this way with Miss Addy." He nodded toward her. "Knew you'd want to know right away—them Fogartys has been at it again. Hit the bank in Loyal Valley an hour ago. Their sheriff sent us a telegram sayin' they was headed this way."

Asa rose quickly, shooting Addy an apologetic glance. "I guess I wasn't meant to enjoy your lemonade or your company, Miss Addy. Reckon we'd better mount up and see if we can ride out to meet 'em."

"I thought that's what you'd say, Sheriff," the deputy responded with a grin. "That's why I brought your bay along."

"Good thinking, Dick. Miss Addy, I'll see you later," Asa murmured, as he followed the deputy to the door.

"Asa, shouldn't you form a posse? What if you did come across the Fogartys, and it was just the two of you?"

The sheriff smiled indulgently at her. "There isn't time, Miss Addy." And then he was gone.

She stood staring at the door, still smarting a little at Asa's patronizing tone. He might just as well have told her not to worry her pretty little head about it! Did he think she would admire him all the more for his bravery? *Men!*

"He'll never catch them," a voice said behind her.

Addy whirled and found Rede leaning against the doorway, still bare to the waist, his powerful, weather-bronzed chest in stark contrast to the white bandages covering his wounds.

She felt her pulse accelerate into a bumpy gallop.

"How can you be so sure?" she snapped, annoyed

at the casual way he strode past her to the chair and picked up the shirt, his muscles flexing as he shrugged back into it again.

"The Fogartys'll split up long before they come close to Connor's Crossing," he responded, the corners of his mouth turning up slightly as his eyes locked with hers.

Addy hated the way Rede's half smile made her heart turn over as Asa's wholehearted grin never had, but she was perversely miffed on behalf of Asa. "You just don't want a small-town sheriff to arrest the gang before *you* get the opportunity to," she accused.

Still with that infuriating ghost of a smile, he murmured, "Slim chance of that."

"You can't be sure," she retorted, and maddened by the way his presence still affected her, despite the fact he had covered his chest, added, "and I'll thank you to keep your things picked up, so I don't have to try and explain what a man's shirt is doing in my kitchen!"

Now his lips spread into a full, cocksure grin. "Afraid you'll lose your suitor before your year of mourning is up, Miss Addy?"

His effrontery made her breathless with fury. "Of course not! I *told* you Sheriff Wilson means nothing to me! I was merely trying to protect the secret of your being here—a secret I never thought was necessary—at least from him! If you had any sense, you'd let me tell Sheriff Wilson you were here, pool your knowledge about the Fogartys with him, and catch those outlaws that much sooner!"

He looked like a big, black cat as he stalked toward her. "If I had any sense," he said, "I wouldn't do this."

Before she could figure out what his intention was, he had pulled her close with his right arm and was kissing her with a thoroughness and expertise that left her breathless—and wanting more. He gave it to her, gently parting her lips with his and invading her mouth. She could only sag against him for a moment until the dizziness passed, but when she tried to draw back and slap him for his audacity, he danced out of reach.

She felt a flare of satisfaction at the way the sudden movement made him wince. "If you *ever* do anything remotely like that again—" she began.

"You'll run screaming to the sheriff," he finished for her. "I'm sorry, Miss Addy. It's just that when you get mad, your eyes glow like green emeralds. I never could resist a green-eyed woman."

He'd said just the right thing to fuel her anger. "Well, I suggest you learn. Because I *will* 'run screaming to the sheriff,' as you so condescendingly put it. Not to protect any relationship with him, mind you, but my good name. As I've indicated before, I'm not a loose woman, Rede Smith."

Oh no? her conscience accused. *Then why didn't you want his kiss to end? Why did your legs go weak and your brain fill with visions of you and Rede going further than just kissing—much further?*

"I never said you were," he retorted evenly. "Or thought it. But for a second there, it didn't seem you minded all that much."

His words struck her like a shower of little, stinging pebbles, sharp-edged with truth. She opened her mouth to retort, but nothing coherent would come out. ''I—''

He waited, patient as a big cat who had cornered his prey, while she struggled for words. *I didn't mind it all that much,* her heart cried. *In fact, I'd really love it if you would put your arm around me and kiss me again.*

He took a step forward, as if he had read her mind. And then came the knock at her front door.

Chapter Ten

Rede spent a restless night, tossing and turning. His chest and arm wounds stung like fire. But it wasn't the pain that kept him awake, it was wondering what would have happened if a customer hadn't arrived and knocked on the door, just as he'd been about to embrace Addy Kelly again.

She'd been afraid of it, but she'd wanted it, too—that much had been plain to Rede from the luminous quality of her gaze and her half-parted moist lips. And he was nearly sure there had been a flash of disappointment across her face when they'd been interrupted.

He'd fled into the bedroom—his cell, as he was beginning to think of it—and paced, while Addy spent an interminable time up front in her shop with a passel of bridesmaids for that rancher's daughter's wedding. Even though the nuptials were six months away, apparently they'd been so excited about it they couldn't wait one more day for their fittings. He had been able to hear them giggling and chattering clearly, even at the back of the house.

Addy had been silent and withdrawn over supper

and had then excused herself to do some work in her shop. He'd left the door open, hoping she'd look in on him before she sought her bed. But just as the fireflies were coming out, he'd heard her quietly going up the stairs, though, and all had been silent after that.

The sun rose, but he heard no noises overhead to indicate that Addy was stirring. Evidently she'd had a tough time sleeping, too. Finally he gathered his strength and made his way out the back door, heading straight for the barn. While it was early enough that customers wouldn't be dropping in, he wanted to have a closer look at the sorrel he'd glimpsed grazing in the pasture behind the barn.

Addy finally found him in the barn, reaching across the stall door and scratching Jessie's ears while the mare placidly munched on hay.

"I've looked everywhere for you!" she announced, cross from the worry his disappearance had caused. Then she felt herself flushing under the impact of his sidelong gaze. How ridiculous she sounded—like a fretful mama.

"Looks like you found me."

"But—but what are you doing out here? You shouldn't be walking so far—at least without me to help you!"

"I'm feeling much stronger today, Miss Addy. I figured it was time I stopped actin' like an invalid." His gaze shifted away from her. "Nice mare," he said, nodding at Jessie, who at this moment was nuzzling the Ranger's hand for more petting.

"That's Jessie. She was my uncle's," Addy said, watching the way his fingers stroked the mare's glossy red neck. She couldn't block the involuntary thought— *How would it feel to be stroked by that hand?*

"I need you to help me saddle her." It was a statement, not a question.

"Saddle her?" she echoed. "For what? You're not strong enough to leave here yet—" A thought suddenly came to her as to what he meant. "Surely you don't think you're taking my Jessie when you do?" When she'd brought Rede to her house, she'd looked forward to the day he would ride away, but she hadn't gotten around to figuring out just how he'd do that. He couldn't imagine she was just going to tamely hand over her horse, could he? Or did he have the power, as a Texas Ranger, to commandeer the animal?

He held up a hand to stop her flood of argument. "Easy there, Miss Addy. I didn't mean permanently. And I know I'm not strong enough to leave yet."

She told herself the relief she felt was just because they wouldn't have to argue about Jessie.

"I need to get my strength back, so I just want to go out for a ride. While it's still early, and you don't have anyone nosin' around here," he added. "I'll head away from town so no one'll see me, and I'll come back by way of the pasture. If you leave a dish towel hangin' from the knob of your back door, I'll know you have a customer, and I'll stay in the barn."

"I'm sure it's still too soon for you to be trying such a thing," she insisted, knowing she sounded mulishly stubborn.

"Look, Miss Addy, I need to get ready to do what I came here for—to track down the Fogarty Gang."

There was an earnest pleading in his eyes that softened her heart even while she wondered at its fervency. *Why* was this so important to him?

She sighed. "All right." He'd be stiff and sore tonight, and it would probably set back his recovery, but there was no convincing a man like Rede to take the easy road.

"You'll be careful, won't you? You won't stay out too long? And you'll be careful to check whether I have a customer before you come back in?" she asked, hands on her hips.

Grinning like a boy who'd just been let out of school early, he placed a callused finger on her chin. "Don't you worry, Miss Addy. I'll be quiet as a deaf mute's shadow."

Ridiculous how his lightest touch made her quiver inside.

That night, he admitted being dog-tired, but far from suffering a relapse, he seemed buoyed by his ride on Jessie. "She sure is a nice little mare—willing, eager to please, pretty, with a lope smooth as silk. I couldn't help thinkin' of the colts she'd throw if she was bred to my roan. With his speed and fire and her looks…" He shrugged then as if he realized how unlikely it was.

Surprised at his turn of thought, Addy was just about to ask him more about his own horse when he shook his head as if to clear it of such daydreaming. "If it's all right with you, I'd like to borrow Jessie again tomorrow and go a little farther," he announced. "Maybe practice some target shooting to work the stiffness out of my arm. You have some empty tin cans I could use?"

Addy nodded and pretended great interest in the

seam she was sewing. Before long he'd pronounce himself well enough to leave her house. Then she'd likely never see him again. And that was good, she reminded herself firmly. Despite the fact she had only lent him the use of the back bedroom, he now strayed all over the downstairs—except during hours in which she might expect customers, of course.

The house seemed to have shrunk with Rede's occupation of it. His presence announced itself in a dozen little ways, from the cup of coffee that sat half-consumed on the table to the extra laundry she was doing. Everything she did was influenced by his needs, especially the need to keep his staying here a secret.

She didn't mind those things, she realized suddenly. Since she had brought Rede into her house, she had felt more happy and alive than she had since the days Charles Parker had subjected her to that whirlwind courtship.

Though Rede had kissed her with great passion yesterday, he had done nothing before or since that indicated he wanted to *court* her as a man courts a woman he has tender feelings for. So it would be foolish indeed if she let herself miss him once he'd gone.

Once he'd left for good, the only way she'd ever hear of him again was perhaps if the Fogarty Gang was captured nearby. Then Addy's life would go on as before, a quiet struggle to make a living, maintain her respectability and keep hidden her status as a divorced woman.

In a few months, when it had supposedly been a year since her husband's ''death,'' she could put off half-mourning. And Asa Wilson would probably start courting her openly—until she felt obligated to tell him the truth.

Then he would politely bow out of her life, and that was when she would see the true Asa Wilson. If he was really the kind, trustworthy man he appeared, she would continue to be seen as the respectable widow, Mrs. Kelly. If he wasn't, he'd let slip what she had told him, the whispers and sly nudges would begin when she went into town, the ladies would shun her as a fallen woman, while the men would start showing up on her doorstep on flimsy pretexts....

The next day, Rede stayed away even longer, not returning until she was fixing supper.

"How was your target practice?" she called out to where he was washing up at the pump. Her eyes studied him, alert for signs that he had overtired himself, but finding none. Despite her uncle's hat, Rede's face had been kissed by the sun today, and the reddish-bronze color made his dark eyes even more compelling.

He grinned, seeming rather pleased with himself. "I'm proud to say I haven't totally lost my touch," he called back, and she sensed he was understating the case out of modesty.

"Well, come in to supper," she said, trying to ignore the way her pulse sped up under the influence of that grin. "I've made chicken fricassee."

"Mmm... I hope you made plenty. I warn you, lady, I'm hungry as a wolf in a drought."

It was an apt comparison. There was something wolfish in the way his dark eyes swept over her as he came toward her up the steps. Even while it made her a bit nervous, it also made her wish she could be clad in something besides black, white, gray and lavender!

Over supper, he told of shooting the tin cans she'd given him so full of holes there was little left but the rims. Then he asked about her day. But there was little of interest to tell him—how fascinating could it be to a man of action like Rede that she had cut out the bride-to-be's gown or let out a few seams to accommodate a young matron's advancing pregnancy?

"Miss Addy," Rede said, suddenly intruding into her thoughts, "I was just wondering…"

"What?" She swallowed her bite of biscuit, wondering what he had in mind.

He shifted in his chair. "I—I'll understand if the answer is no," he began. "I mean, I know my presence here has been a burden to you." He held up a hand to fend off her polite evasion. "It's kept you from livin' like you normally do, and it's exposed you to risks."

Addy couldn't deny that, so she nodded, meeting his gaze. "There's no harm done so far."

"I'm glad of that. I want to propose something, but before you object, I hope you'll hear me out."

She indicated her willingness with a slight inclination of her head.

"I'll be well enough to leave here in a couple of days."

"No!" The pain in her heart allowed a sharp cry of protest to escape before she could stop it. "Rede, you can't be serious! I think it's way too soon!"

"I don't. You've been wonderful to me, Miss Addy, but I wouldn't have been able to coddle myself near this long if I was out on the trail with some other Rangers."

She waited, numbly waiting for the ache to blossom fully, unable to imagine what he meant to ask her. Nothing about his leaving required her permission, after all.

"I'd like to stay on a while."

Addy blinked at him in confusion. "But you just said—"

"I said I'd be *well enough* to ride out of here. And I will, if you want me to. But it would be better if I could remain here, borrowing your mare, and using your place as my camp, so to speak. It'd be just till I find out where the Fogartys' hideout is—then I can notify my Ranger company to help me bring them in."

Suddenly she felt as if he'd been playing her like a well-tuned fiddle. He'd known all along he wanted to stay, but he'd seen her for the vulnerable woman she was and knew she would protest his going—even if she'd done it out of concern for his wounds.

"What would you have done if you hadn't gotten shot and come back here with me?" she snapped. "Find some other lonely widow to hole up with? Someone who'd cook for you and keep you from having to sleep on the hard ground?"

His surprise appeared genuine, surprising her. "It's not like that, I swear it. I won't lie to you and say I mind sleeping in your soft bed every night, Miss Addy…"

She felt the flush rising up her cheeks. Damn him for using those words, for the way those dark eyes caressed her as if she'd been sleeping in it with him!

"I'm used to making camp and eating tinned beans for supper every night," he continued. "And if the stagecoach hadn't been attacked and all, that's what I'd have to have done—a 'cold camp,' though—a campfire would tell 'em I'm out there, you see. And it's possible the gang's gotten wind of the news that that dead 'Ranger' is no Ranger at all. So they'd be lookin' to find and ambush me.''

''They could do that anyway, while you're out riding my mare,'' she argued.

''Yes, but there's a whole lot less chance they'd catch me unaware when I'm out looking for them, wide-awake. I admit, I *am* concerned about my reactions bein' a hair slower because of these wounds—especially if they find me nappin' on my bedroll.''

The image of the outlaws sneaking up on Rede, catching him at a helpless moment and slaughtering him made her shudder, even while she tried to hold on to her anger.

''You wouldn't need to give up your bed to me anymore. I'll stay in your barn, Miss Addy. There's an empty stall next to Jessie. You'd hardly see me,'' he said persuasively, even as his dark eyes challenged her to accept. Then the devil danced in them as he added, ''You could even invite your beau Sheriff Wilson over for supper, and he'd never suspect.''

That did it, she thought.

''And it's my duty as a law-abiding citizen, I suppose?'' she said stiffly.

''I'm not saying that.'' His voice was level. ''I said you didn't have to do it. But if I'm able to capture the Fogartys, the whole state of Texas would have reason to be grateful to you—though it's understandable why you might not want anyone ever to know I'd been here.''

She said nothing while she tried to squash the

fierce joy that raced through her. Rede wasn't leaving yet. She'd still be seeing his wolfish smile and hearing his voice in the evenings.

"Very well, you may stay. But it's not necessary to sleep in the barn, Rede," she said, with a wave of her hand as if it were a matter of little concern. "You could move to the upstairs bedroom, where I've been staying since you've been here, and I'll move back in there." She nodded her head toward the back bedroom.

"I think I better stay out in the barn, Miss Addy." His eyes locked with hers. All at once she was very aware of him as a man, a man who had come to her house wounded and in pain, but was now fast recovering his capabilities. And his appetites.

Addy drew a shaky breath and looked away, knowing he was right. It would be too tempting for both of them, knowing the other was just a flight of stairs away. "All right, I suppose you're right. I was just trying to be…hospitable. After all, sleeping in a barn isn't very…" She shrugged. "Well, you know."

Addy was aware of a stinging disappointment. She knew he wanted her; his eyes and his kiss had told her that much, but perhaps he didn't want her enough to risk entanglement with her. Knowing she was a *lady,* and not the kind of woman a man like Rede could just enjoy sexually, then ride away from, he'd apparently concluded the momentary pleasure of bedding her wasn't worth the potential complications.

"It'll be fine," he assured her. "It's out of the wind and rain, and compared to some places I've slept, a stall is practically a palace." He smiled wryly. "And it'll be better this way, so I can come and go as I need to without takin' the chance of your customers spotting me."

"Oh. Of course," she said. "But you'll come in for supper, if you're here?" she asked. "I—I'd like to hear how the search is going, of course."

He smiled. "I'd like that."

Chapter Eleven

Rede smiled as he kneed Addy's mare into her seemingly effortless, rocking-horse lope that ate up the ground until they were well beyond the outlying ranches at the edge of town and into the limestone hills. Even though his wounds still ached, it renewed his spirits to ride over the rolling countryside on a good horse.

He slowed Jessie as they began to wind through the cedar brakes, scrubby mesquite and patches of prickly pear, dipping into the valleys and following the cottonwood-lined dry washes. Mockingbirds called from tree branches and white butterflies flitted like tiny, breeze-borne handkerchiefs among the cactus blossoms.

Would he really be able to find the Fogarty gang's hideout? He had been only four when his mother had taken him from it. All he could remember were the rocky walls of a canyon rising all around him, with horses tethered at one end, and a campfire at the other. Here his mother had done the cooking for the half-dozen Fogarty boys—James, his two brothers, and a trio of cousins—who had decided it was easier to steal and rob than it was to earn an honest living. They hadn't been above killing when they felt it necessary, either.

Rede had been born in that canyon, and its walls had been the boundaries of his existence until the night he and his mother had fled the camp while the Fogarty Gang was out on a night raid. All he could remember was inky darkness lit only by a candle flame, then the faint light of stars. They had walked through the night, reaching a town when darkness was just giving way to the dawn.

His mother had always told him she'd left because she hadn't wanted her boy to grow up an outlaw like his papa. But he didn't know what had finally given Emma Fogarty the strength to leave the man she had called ''husband'' for so long.

She didn't like to speak of those years, as if fearful that even in the sanctuary of their modest Jefferson boardinghouse rooms, someone would overhear and know she wasn't the Widow Smith, but the wife of a notorious outlaw. She'd pretended a loss of memory when, as a boy, Rede had asked where the camp had been. Had she been afraid he would leave her, rejoin his father and become an outlaw after all? He couldn't get her to say.

He'd grown to manhood without showing any propensity for lawless behavior, but she hadn't relaxed her stance. By then, though, he suspected she had suppressed the memories for so long that she truly didn't remember where the camp had been. The one thing he was sure of—it wasn't anywhere near Jefferson, the east Texas town he'd grown up in. The countryside around the town was green and lush and flat. There were no rocky canyons.

Having no property to hold him to any one place, he'd worked as a ranch hand, moving his mother to a genteel boardinghouse to a town near enough to the ranch where he worked so that he could check on her whenever he had a day off. Most of his salary went to assure that she had anything she needed.

But despite his care, his mother's health had declined and her mind wandered.

"Secret," she would say when he tried to jog her memory for some clue to the location of the hideout. "No one else can find it. Mustn't tell. Worth my life and my boy's."

"Mama," he'd said earnestly, taking her frail, blue-veined hands in his, "I *am* your boy, all grown-up. I can take care of myself now. I know the Fogartys are still out there robbing and killing, and I want to see them captured and brought to justice."

Her filmy blue eyes had gotten that vacant, staring look then, and she'd shaken her head slowly. "No, James is dead. They put a noose 'round his neck and hanged him."

"Yes, Mama," he'd said patiently, then taken out the folded, much read newspaper accounts of the Fogartys' depredations in the area. "But see? The rest of the gang is still alive. They went out to the Badlands for a while, but now they've come back here. Uncle Jack is apparently their leader now. Try real hard, and see if you can remember what the entrance of that canyon where we lived looked like, or what it's near." He'd already racked his brain for such an image, but couldn't picture anything like the mouth of a canyon, just the canyon itself.

But always, she had just waved her bony hand helplessly, and hadn't been willing or able to tell him anything of use. Each time he'd brought it up, it had distressed her more, until he had finally stopped asking. And one morning she had failed to wake up, and he could never ask her anything again.

With no reason to remain tied to any one spot after her death, he had joined the Texas Rangers, certain that someday he would cross paths with the notorious Fogarty Gang.

Among his fellow Rangers, Rede never admitted he had been born the son of the famous outlaw James Fogarty. He'd been more than a little worried they wouldn't have accepted him in their ranks if they knew. But he dreamed of the day he could bring about the capture of the rest of the Fogartys. Then, having cleansed the Fogarty name, he would feel free to take it back as his own.

He hadn't even known where to start looking for the Fogartys. Texas—even just the part of Texas that would have the kind of rocky canyon he had remembered from his early years—was enormous, and it would've been impossible to search every acre of it.

His father had been captured at the scene of a bank robbery in Salado. He had shot dead the first bank teller, who had refused to open the safe; a second one was more cooperative. Then, as they were escaping, a lucky pair of bullets fired by the local sheriff had killed James Fogarty's middle brother, Josh, then brought down James Fogarty's horse and trapped him under its carcass. His surviving brother and cousins were no fools—they'd kept going. Rede's father had been sentenced to die for the bank teller's murder and had gone to his grave with the secret of the hideout location.

Rede had gone through his mother's effects right

after she died, but then he looked again for anything he might have missed. Sure enough, he found a faded receipt for a stagecoach ticket that had worked its way into the torn lining in the bottom of her threadbare reticule. He could barely make out the printing, but at last he deciphered the words *One way fare, Connor's Crossing-Jefferson, April 10, 1854.*

The date was right. He'd been four then. It was likely that Connor's Crossing had been the closest town to the hideout, or at least the closest town big enough to be a stage stop. It was a good place to begin his search.

He'd looked on a map in the Ranger headquarters until he'd found the tiny dot on the map that represented Connor's Crossing, just on the western edge of the Edwards Plateau—a region of limestone hills in Central Texas. Eureka!

Of course, even if the Fogarty gang had returned to the area, they might not still be using the old hideout, but it was as good a place to start as any. And if the hideout's location was still a secret, what was to stop them from using it again?

It didn't seem as if he was destined to find it today, however. The rolling hills he rode Jessie over and around seemed to conceal nothing. At the top of one, however, he caught sight of a pair of high blue ridges, one lying right behind the other like rumpled muslin sheeting on an unmade bed. At the foot of the first ridge lay a long, low white formation whose regular shape made him think it a building of some sort.

He took out his spyglass from his saddlebag and focused it on the formation. Sure enough, it was a building, and the central peaked projection on its top suggested a steeple. An old mission, perhaps? It looked to be at least five miles away to the west, though, so he couldn't tell for certain in the shimmering heat.

He was more interested in the ridges than the building in front of them. *Could it be?* He listened within himself for some sense of familiarity, some faint memory to tell him that the Fogarty's hideout lay there, but there was nothing. Perhaps it had been too long.

But wouldn't the sheriff and his posse have checked the ridges out long ago, and found the Fogartys' hideout between them?

There were still a few hours of daylight left, and Rede wanted more than anything to ride over right now and explore. But he looked down at the mare he rode, seeing the sweaty patches on her sorrel hide, and knew he couldn't ask that of her. He'd already been riding her for hours, and she'd carried him willingly and without faltering, but neither of them were fresh enough to go that far and chance encountering the Fogartys. Tomorrow, he promised himself.

Reining Jessie back in the direction of a shallow creek they'd found, he allowed the mare to drink her fill and rest a while in the shade of an old cottonwood before he remounted and headed back home—*Addy's* home, he corrected himself, startled that he had indeed begun to think of the small house just outside of Connor's Crossing that way.

Keep in mind you're not going to be here any longer than it takes to put the Fogartys behind bars, he reminded himself sternly. *And tonight you're sleeping out in the stall next to Jessie's, not in the house.*

* * *

"I'm sure this isn't necessary," Addy murmured after supper as she helped him gather up blankets and sheets and his things. "I feel so—so *inhospitable,* putting you out in the barn!"

"Addy, I'm not a houseguest. I'm a Ranger," he reminded her. "I didn't plan on getting shot up, but I came here to do a job."

She blinked. Had he forgotten the "Miss?" He'd never called her just *Addy* before. "Yes...I suppose the regular rules of etiquette wouldn't apply," she said, her lips curving slightly.

He shook his head, though he wasn't sure what etiquette entailed. He was going to sleep out in the barn for the good of Addy Kelly's virtue, though he guessed she hadn't suspected it had come to that point.

"Addy," he began, to distract himself as they walked out through the gathering shadows to the barn, "When I was out riding today, I spotted a pair of high ridges west of town a few miles—you know the ones I mean? The ones with an old mission or something at the foot of the closest one?"

She nodded. "I came here to visit my aunt and uncle once when I was a girl, and I saw it—it's really not two ridges, you see, but all one rock. Like this," she said, her thumb and forefinger forming an oval. "This old Mexican who worked for my uncle told me it was called...now what was that?" Her brow furrowed. "Something in Spanish that meant 'the Oval.'"

Rede knew a little Spanish lingo; most Rangers knew at least a smattering, if they weren't exactly fluent in it, for many of their campaigns involved chasing Mexican bandits back across the Rio Grande.

"El Óvalo?" Even as he said the noun, he felt a flash of recognition, a feeling he'd heard that word long ago.

Addy brightened. "Yes, that's it. *El Óvalo*. And the mission was called Our Lady of the Canyon, if I remember right."

"All one rock," he repeated, surprised. "Sure looked like two from up on one of those hills."

Addy shook her head. "I know it does. I've seen it when I've been out riding Jessie, though we haven't gone that far away. But the man who worked for my uncle told me there's no entrance into the oval unless you're a goat or an eagle to climb up the ridge or fly over it. I remember having girlish notions of a romantic lost valley, or something of the sort." She smiled as if she thought she sounded foolish, but Rede was enchanted by the glimpse of the innocent young girl Addy had been.

How close she had come to the truth without realizing it. It was a lost valley, all right—though nothing remotely romantic had happened there. He imagined his mother had once had girlish romantic notions, but life with James Fogarty and his outlaw gang had destroyed them long ago.

Rede looked away, busying himself with hanging his saddlebags over the wall of the vacant stall next to the mare's and lighting a lantern, which he set carefully on an empty crate.

"Rede, why is this important?" she asked, placing a hand on his shoulder for the briefest of moments.

Her touch burned him like a brand. He was acutely aware of her unconscious magnetism, even while a part of his brain concentrated on the information she was giving him.

He forced himself to concentrate on what she was *saying,* though her touch had made him want to pull her down with him onto the hay. "I've been looking for a canyon the Fogartys could be using as their hideout. It's got to be in the area—they've robbed too many stages and banks around here and then vanished into thin air."

Addy looked at him intently, clearly intrigued. "Why are you so sure it's a canyon?"

Because my earliest memories are set there. But he didn't want to tell her that he was the son of a leader of outlaws and see the light shining in her lovely eyes dim to suspicion and distaste.

He forced himself to shrug casually. "Just a hunch I have. They've disappeared too fast after their hold-ups in this area."

"Well, it doesn't sound like *El Óvalo* could be the place, if there's no way inside for men on horse-back," she insisted.

"There's got to be a way inside." For he'd been there. He was surer of it every minute.

Addy shrugged. "Well, *I* couldn't say. I've been too busy since I got here just earning a living to explore that far. But the old Mexican sounded sure enough...apparently he and his friends went exploring when they were boys, and they couldn't find a way in. They even explored the mission, though local rumor had it it was haunted."

"Haunted? What did he mean?"

Addy rubbed her chin. "He said something about the bones of a murdered *padre,* and made the sign to ward off the evil eye. But Papa made him hush. He said he didn't want him giving me nightmares with his superstitiousness."

Rede smiled. He could almost see the little girl Addy had been, wide-eyed at the old man's wild tales.

"Or maybe he just wanted to keep the entrance to the valley a secret for some reason. Any chance this old fellow's still around, so I could talk to him?"

Addy shook her head. "When I came back, they told me he had died years ago." She sighed. "I wish I could do something to help you find it."

Her words surprised him, warmed him. Dangerously so.

"But you *have* helped me, Miss Addy. Just talking to you has—"

"No, I mean I wish I could ride out there with you. I feel so useless sometimes, just a female who sits and sews."

"Just a female." He had to smile at that. If only she knew how powerful an effect "just a female" had begun to have on him. He had come to think of Addy Kelly as the most beautiful and wonderful woman in the world, a woman he yearned to call his own. If only she wasn't a lady, and he just the son of an outlaw.

But she had seen his smile, and apparently taken it for condescension, for she stiffened. "You think it's funny, don't you?" she fumed. "That I would want to do something besides sit and sew all day! Ohhh! Men like you make me so angry—!" She whirled away from him. "Well, good *night* to you, Rede Smith, I shall leave you to your insufferable male dreams of glory!"

Addy turned on her heel and began to stalk out of the barn, but he didn't want her to go away angry at him, so he reached out and caught her by her wrist.

''Now, Addy, there's no need to get your feathers all ruffled.''

''I'm sure *you* don't think so,'' she snapped, trying to wrench her wrist loose, but he held it fast. ''Let me loose, you arrogant sidewinder!''

But he couldn't. He couldn't let her go, knowing she would stomp into the house, furious at him, and he would have to lie there on the straw all night with nothing more to do than think of how utterly beautiful she was when she was angry, with her eyes flashing green sparks at him, her color high on her cheeks, and her breath coming fast.

What he *could* do was pull her closer, while she was still sputtering protests, and kiss her until she couldn't fuss any more at him.

Chapter Twelve

Too late, she realized her danger. She'd spent too many days alone with this man on terms of some intimacy—and yes, a deepening friendship—as she nursed him back to health, and now he'd recovered plenty well enough to show how "insufferably male" he could be.

Rede had made it clear all along that he found her desirable. After the damage Charles Parker had done to her womanly confidence, she considered the admiration in Rede Smith's eyes to be nothing short of a miracle.

But now she was alone in her barn with him, and there was nothing and no one to stop him from taking as much as he wanted from her, no matter what *she* wanted. And they were just steps away from a bed of sorts, the blanket he'd laid over the clean straw.

If it *was* danger, why didn't it feel like it? Why wasn't she afraid? She had a split second to wonder as his mouth claimed hers, and then she was swept up in a maelstrom of sensation. Not only did she not want to argue any more, but she wanted everything he wanted. And more. She realized she was reaching the end of a journey she'd begun when she'd let her gaze linger on him in the stagecoach. Something about him had called to her then, despite the fact she'd thought he might be an outlaw.

"Rede, please, I—" She wasn't even sure what she was asking for as she allowed him to pull her into the empty stall and guide her back against the wall. The sound of Jessie's contented hay munching in the adjacent stall and the occasional rustle of the mare shifting her weight in the straw faded into the background.

"Please?" he questioned, his lips curving as he lifted them just enough from her mouth that he could speak. One of his fingers tangled in the knot of hair at the nape of her neck, loosing it. She felt her hair cascading down on her shoulders, and she didn't care. "Yes, I'll *please* you, Addy," he breathed. "I'll please you and pleasure you and show you how much 'just a female' can feel. I'll make you ache like you've made *me* ache, Addy…and then I'll make the ache go away and replace it with something much, much better…."

She wanted him. More than she craved respectability and safety from the disappointment loving a man could bring. More than life, she thought as she felt his hand reach down and cup her breast, unerringly finding the nipple through her stiff corset and stroking it to hardness. More than her next breath, she knew as his arm stole around her waist and he rocked against her, letting her feel how hard and ready he was to ease the torment that was already building inside her.

"Addy?" he breathed, before his mouth took hers again, his tongue parting her lips and going on a raiding path inside, making her quiver and her legs tremble. Her name had been both a question and a caress.

"Yes," she whispered as his fingers unbuttoned her bodice to the waist and his hand stole inside the dress to caress the top of her breast, then beneath the corset to claim all of it.

She was going to let him make love to her. Maybe it would only be this once, or maybe they would be lovers just until he'd captured the outlaw gang and left Conner's Crossing. At this moment, it didn't matter. All that mattered was that he was going to give himself to her now. When he left, maybe this giving would be enough.

She knew he'd understood her single word of assent, but he lifted his head and looked at her as if his dark eyes could read her heart. "Addy, are you sure? Are you really sure this is what you want?" he asked her.

She nodded, smiling tremulously at him, and pulled him toward the blanket. "You've made me ache, Rede, just like you said you would. You promised you'd make it better."

His eyes gleamed with heat as he stared back at her. "Yes, I did, my beautiful, wonderful Addy. But it doesn't have to be here, in the barn...." He gestured in the direction of the house. "Don't you want to go back inside, to your bed?" His words and his eyes caressed her even while he asked the question, keeping the flame burning ever hotter inside her. "I want it to be good for you, sweet lady, *so* good...."

She didn't dare wait until they walked all the way back to the house. It would give her too much time to consider the action she was about to take.

"Maybe the next time," she said as she pulled him over to the blanket and collapsed on it, urging him down with her. "Just make love to me here, Rede. *Now.*"

He followed her down and lay full-length against her, kissing her while he clutched her tightly to him. Even through their clothes, Addy could feel the extent of his desire for her. She gloried in it. *She* had the power to affect him that way. *She* did—*mousy Adelaide Parker, whom her ex-husband had called a "cold fish."* It didn't matter at this moment that he would be leaving. Once they had made love, no one could ever take the memory away.

"Addy...I've never wanted any woman like I want you now," he breathed, his voice husky as he began to unhook the front of her corset. "You're such a *lady*—so respectable...and so beautiful it takes my breath away. I can't believe you want me." One of his hands had been steadily pulling up her skirt, and now he stroked the insides of her thighs, making her move restlessly against him.

Oh, Rede, if you knew I was divorced, you wouldn't marvel that this 'genteel, respectable lady' was about to make love in the hay with you.

"Well, I do," she said, gazing up into those fathomless dark eyes in the lean, handsome face. He was beautiful himself, in a completely masculine sort of way, in the same way a lost angel is beautiful.

She loved that in spite of his obvious need of her, he was taking the time to talk to her in this intimate way. It was just as much making love as touching her. Charles Parker had never talked to her when they went to bed. He had just disrobed, told her to do the same, climbed on top of her and pushed himself into her, little caring whether she was ready for him or not.

"And why do you make it sound like you're not respectable, too?" she teased, though her own senses clamored for him to stop talking and make her fully his. "You're a Texas Ranger, for heaven's sake, a man dedicated to upholding the law. There's no more honorable breed of men in Texas."

A shadow strayed across his face, and his hand stilled its motion. "I'm just one step above a drifter, Addy. I don't have any permanent home, just the Ranger headquarters. You deserve so much more. Maybe we shouldn't do this—" He started to raise himself up from her.

Before he could go farther from her, her arms, which had been around his neck, urged him back down. "Rede, *please,* I want you. Don't stop now...."

"But Addy, honey—" He shifted so his weight was no longer over her, though they were still lying closely together, side by side.

"Rede, I understand this isn't forever. You don't have to worry that you'll have to marry me. There is only *now,* and you, and me."

His shadowed face looked more troubled, not less. "Addy, you don't expect enough for yourself. You'd have a right—"

All at once, Addy was afraid he was not going to make love to her after all. She took a deep breath, and said, "Rede, maybe you shouldn't think so highly of me. There's...there's something you should know. I'm not a respectable widow like you thought. Like I—" she looked away from his searching gaze "—like I told you I was. I'm divorced."

Levering himself up with his elbow, he sat up. "Divorced," he repeated.

His face was unreadable in the shadowy stall. Her pulse accelerated, not with passion now, but with fear.

Propping herself up on one elbow, she forced herself to look him right in the eye. "Yes, divorced. I...I lied about it when I came to Connor's Crossing so I wouldn't be treated like an outcast. You know how folks look at a divorced woman, Rede—as if she's a whore. And I wanted to make a living as a respectable unmarried woman does. So I just told everyone I was a widow." She waited, but he said nothing further. "So you really don't have to let scruples keep you from making love to me...unless you're angry at me for lying to you, that is."

He made no move to take her in his arms again. "I'm not angry," he said evenly. "Addy, you don't have to answer this if you don't want to, but...can I ask why?"

She stared at him blankly. "Why?" *Why had she urged him to make love with her, if she wanted to retain her respectability?*

"I mean, why are you divorced? What happened between you and your...husband?"

"My husband, Charles Parker—" she began. When she saw the look of confusion on his face, she added, "I took my maiden name, Kelly, back after I divorced him, you see. Anyway, he cheated on me and gambled away every cent I had. Which was considerable, since I was something of an heiress back in St. Louis."

"Were your parents still alive? Couldn't they help you?"

She shrugged. "With my pride, I wouldn't let them," she said, and heard the bitterness coloring her voice. "Not till he'd lost it all. Then, finally, I let them pay for the divorce."

"Did they throw you out of the house after that? Is that why you left?"

She shook her head. "No, they didn't throw me out. I could have stayed. But I would have been 'the *divorced* Mrs. Parker,' who 'isn't received in polite society, you know,'" she said, mimicking the society matrons' arch whispers. "Eventually the stain would have extended to my parents, and they didn't deserve that. So when my widowed aunt died here and I inherited her property, I took the chance to start over."

His eyes had left her face and were unfocused. She could tell he was taking in what she'd told him, working it over in his mind. She saw his lips thin.

"So you divorced your husband, not because you're a bad woman, but because there was really nothing else you could've done."

"I could have stayed married to him, but separated from him," she asserted. "Lots of women do. *Good* women, that is."

"That's pure foolishness," he snapped. "You're young. Why should you remain tied to a no-good man like that the rest of your life just so some biddies have nothing to talk about?"

"You're angry, and at *me,*" she breathed. "Rede, when I thought you weren't going to make love to me because I'd let you believe I was this lady of untouchable virtue, I knew I had to tell you the truth. I thought if you knew I was divorced…" She let her voice trail off, praying he would understand.

His voice was hard, cold. "You thought I'd feel

freer to take my pleasure with you, 'cause you didn't deserve to be respected,'' he finished for her with savage bluntness. "Well, you're wrong, Addy. I don't give two hoots in hell whether you're a widow or divorced or an old maid. That isn't what determines how I treat you."

"You *were* about to make love to me," she argued gently, sadly aware that there was no way he would do it now. The sensual fever that had burned between them had been well and thoroughly quenched.

"I lost my head," he retorted. "Good Lord, Addy, what if I *had* made love to you, and left you with my baby growing inside you?"

She could only gape at him, and realize that while she'd been aware such a thing was possible, it had seemed so remote a possibility that she had given it no real thought.

"I'm sorry," she said. Her fingers shook as she started to rehook the front of her corset. She felt cold all over. If only he would wrap those strong arms around her and warm her again. She had bared her soul to him and lost everything.

She had barely completed the thought when the shuffle of feet just outside the barn froze them both into stillness. Rede put a finger to his lips, but it was unnecessary, for she couldn't breathe, let alone make a noise.

"We can stay here for the night, Henry. Mrs. Kelly won't ever know, long as we're gone by dawn..."

"But Lucy, I see a light." It was a young man's uncertain voice. "Maybe there's someone in the barn."

The girl's voice had been Lucy Fickhiser's, Addy

realized in astonishment, even as her fingers shoved down her skirt, then flew over the corset hooks, refastening them. The other voice must be Henry, Lucy's young beau. What on earth were they doing out together after dark? How had Lucy evaded her vigilant mama? Frantically, she rebuttoned her bodice, aware that Rede was trying to straighten his own clothing, though he hadn't been as exposed as she had. There would be no time to fix her hair. Its disarray would make it all too clear what she had been doing.

Hearing the voices, the mare snorted and gave a soft nicker of inquiry. Then Addy heard Lucy's voice again. ''No, I don't think so. Maybe Mrs. Kelly just forgot and left her lantern in here. Come on—''

Once Lucy made up her mind, she moved fast. Addy and Rede were just standing, pulling wisps of hay from their hair and clothes when Lucy, with Henry in tow, passed Jessie's stall and stopped stockstill in the entrance of the one Rede and Addy occupied.

Chapter Thirteen

It was hard to say who looked the most astonished, Rede thought, Addy or the two youngsters staring in at them.

Judas priest. That was all Addy needed—being caught in circumstances that made it look as if she'd been intimate with a man, and a stranger to Connor's Crossing at that. And she very nearly had been intimate with him, Rede admitted grimly to himself. If her innocent teasing hadn't inadvertently brought him back to reality, the skinny youth and his buxom sweetheart might have seen a whole lot more than Addy Kelly's blush.

Addy had told him all about the burgeoning puppy love between the mayor's daughter and the son of the liveryman, and Lucy's mother's snobbish opposition to it—which was probably the exact reason they were sneaking around now.

"Miz Addy?" the stocky girl said, mouth hanging slackly in surprise. *"Wha-what are you doin' here?"*

Rede had to give Addy credit—she didn't let herself be flummoxed for long. The blood had drained from her face, then flooded back, but she gave the young woman the tart reply she deserved.

"I might ask you the same question, Lucy, and with more reason. This is at least my barn," she retorted.

Neither Lucy nor the boy seemed to have an answer. Silence, broken only by the rustle of hay caused by Jessie's shifting in the stall next door, reigned.

"Lucy, I suspect your mama doesn't know you're out of the house. Am I right?" Addy queried.

The plump girl's eyes seemed permanently trained on her high-button shoes, as were young Henry's on his own scuffed boots.

"Yes, ma'am."

"So, why were you sneaking into my barn, and talking of staying till dawn? Lucy, *are you running away from home?*" Her voice ended on a gasp.

Young Henry looked up now, his bony chin jutting forward pugnaciously. "Don't you worry none, I'm goin' t' marry her! We was goin' to get hitched as soon's we reached San Antone, honest we was!"

Rede believed the boy, for his face was as honest as it was long. But he had to agree with Addy when she responded, "That may very well have been your intention, young Henry, but Lucy's going nowhere but home to her mama and daddy!"

Rede saw the girl turn appealing eyes on her swain, who stiffened his spine and said, "Now, hold on a minute, Miz Kelly. We'll move on, but you don't have any right to tell us—"

Rede knew it was time to interrupt the youth's belligerent bluster, and clapped a hand heavily over his shoulder. "I don't believe it's proper to argue with a lady, especially one who's your elder, do you?''

The boy stared at him, measuring Rede's resolve, but Rede had no trouble giving him back stare for stare. The boy looked away first. "I guess not," he mumbled. "Sorry, ma'am."

"Why, San Antonio's the better part of sixty or seventy miles from here!" Addy exclaimed. "And just how did you plan to support Lucy if you *did* get married, Henry?"

The boy looked less sure than he had a moment ago. Rede thought he even caught a glimpse of fear in the youth's eyes.

"I dunno—cowboyin', I reckon. We thought I could earn enough to put myself through school so's I could be a newspaperman, and while I was gettin' more book learnin', Lucy could clean houses, and take in washin' and mendin'."

"That sounds fine for you, Henry," Addy said, obviously choosing her words with care, "but what if Lucy has a baby or two by the time you're ready to go to school? It might not be possible for her to earn any money then, and you'd have two or three mouths to feed. I think you have a lot of ability, Henry, but I don't think you're really ready to take on a wife and children, are you?"

Rede had watched the youth pale at the mention of the possibility of babies, but to Rede's surprise, young Henry actually looked relieved to be asked such a blunt question. "No ma'am, I reckon not," he admitted, but then added plaintively, "But we thought this way we couldn't be separated. You see, Lucy and me, we don't ever get to spend any time together. Miz Fickhiser won't let me in the house.''

"And you think eloping with her daughter is the answer? The only thing that would change is that Lucy might well be disowned by her parents. But if you work real hard and make something of yourself, by the time Lucy really is old enough to marry you, I think the Fickhisers will be proud to give you their blessing."

But Lucy wasn't ready to surrender so tamely. "But Henry, you promised we'd go through with this!" she wailed, her face beet-red.

Now Henry looked stubborn again. "Lucy, honey, I'm sorry, but she's right. I don't want you doin' without an' sufferin' because we got hitched too young."

"That's the spirit, Henry," Addy approved. "Now, why don't I just—"

But now Lucy turned on her, interrupting with, "You're a fine one to talk, Miss Addy!" Her small eyes blazed in her fiery cheeks.

"*Lucy*—" Henry protested, reaching for her, clearly embarrassed. "It ain't none of our business!"

Lucy swung away from his grasp. "After we caught you practically rollin' in the hay with this man...." Her eyes shifted to Rede. "Just who are *you*, anyway?"

Addy turned anguished, uncertain eyes on Rede, clearly not knowing what she could safely say about him and still defend herself. It was up to him.

"My name's Rede Smith, Miss Lucy," he began. "And Miss Addy wasn't—that is, she and I were not— It wasn't what it appeared...."

He was only making things worse. Lucy Fickhiser looked distinctly skeptical at his stumbling attempt at denial. He couldn't blame her; it was obviously a whopping lie for anyone with eyes, for Addy's lips were kiss-swollen and her hair was not only decorated with wisps of hay but also was cascading down her back.

"So what're you doin' 'round these parts?" Lucy demanded, and then an expression of heightened suspicion lit her eyes. *"I bet you're one a' them outlaws! One of the Fogarty Gang!"*

Rede felt like he'd been hit by a two-by-four. If only the mayor's daughter knew how ironically close she had come to the truth—he wasn't an outlaw, but of the same blood as leader and several others in the Fogarty Gang. Quickly, he shook his head. "No, I'm not an outlaw, Miss Lucy. I'm a Texas Ranger."

Addy gasped as he made the admission. It was a risk to share his secret with anyone else, but especially with these two young people. How did he know he could trust them? Both the young people goggled.

"A *Ranger?* You're really a Texas *Ranger?*" squeaked Lucy. "You aren't...you wouldn't story with me, would you?"

Rede shook his head. "No, I wouldn't lie to you. It's the truth."

"Remember, Lucy," Henry said, excitement fuelling his voice, "I told you Uncle Asa said that dead guy at the undertaker's turned out not to be th' real Ranger! I bet he's here to arrest them thievin' murderin' Fogartys, ain't you, Mr. Smith?" Henry breathed. All the belligerence had left his face, and his eyes were now glowing with hero-worship.

Rede raised his shoulders in a shrug. "We'll see. I aim to try, anyway. But it's really important that no one else knows I'm here, do you understand?

Miss Addy, here—'' he nodded toward her ''—has been kind enough to let me hide out in her barn while I recovered from the bullet wounds I got during the robbery.''

Henry's brow scrunched up. ''But why's it gotta be a secret? My Uncle Asa's th' sheriff, and I know he'd be glad t' help a fellow lawman. After all, he's been tryin' t' catch the Fogarty gang hisself!''

Rede took a deep breath, knowing he had to be tactful rather than honest. ''I'm sure your uncle's a fine man and a good sheriff, but I have my reasons. You'll just have to trust me on that. Maybe when this is all over, I can explain.''

The boy blinked, but Rede's man-to-man tone must have worked. ''Okay, Mr. Smith, I reckon we'll have to respect that. Me 'n' Lucy'll keep tight lips, right, Lucy?'' His face brightened again. ''Say, can I see your wounds? I never seen a real bullet hole b'fore!'' But Henry glanced at Lucy, whose face had taken on a distinctly greenish cast at his question, and added, ''Uh...mebbe the ladies better not see this, though....''

Addy looked amused—who did young Henry think had taken care of Rede's wounds, after all?

''Maybe another time,'' Rede said. ''Right now, Henry, I expect you'd better be getting your sweetheart home. With any luck Lucy can sneak back in before she's been missed, but if you're caught, you'll take it like a man, right?''

The boy swallowed hard, but he squared his shoulders. ''Yessir. I'll own up to it. And don't you fret none, Mr. Smith. Lucy and me, our lips are sealed.'' Without another word, he took Lucy by the hand and marched her to the door, never looking back.

But Lucy looked over her shoulder, calling, "Thanks for not makin' too big a fuss, Miz Addy, Mr. Smith."

Rede watched them go, wondering if he'd ever been as young and idealistic as the boy. Some days he thought he'd been born old.

Addy spoke behind him. "Do you think he really will take her home, Rede?" She sounded worried. "You don't think they'll just go on with the elopement, as they originally planned?"

Rede shook his head. "I don't think so, Addy— not after you took the wind outa his sails. To tell the truth, I think he was purely delighted to be told what to do. They might make a fine couple in two years, but he isn't ready yet. He just hated to turn her down, that's all."

"It helped that you appealed to his sense of honor," Addy commented, coming to stand beside him to stare out into the darkness beyond the lantern's circle of light. "You were so good, the way you spoke to him, Rede."

Her approval warmed him, but a glance at Addy told him she was still worried, however. She murmured, "Do you think both of them'll be able to keep still about you, though?"

Again, Rede shrugged. He figured the boy would go through Comanche torture now without telling about him, but he wasn't so sure that Lucy would keep her mouth shut. Despite her last words to Addy, if caught by her parents, she might seek to distract them from her own guilt by tattling that the widowed seamstress had a lover.

He was even less sure how to relate to Addy now that he'd called a halt to their lovemaking. His body still clamored at him to take her in his arms again, and say he'd been wrong, and give her whatever reassurance she'd need to lie down and give herself to him. He had no idea if her woman's body was reacting likewise—the sporting girls who'd let him buy their services had given him no insight into a woman's heart and feelings.

Her expression gave no clue. "It—it's late," she whispered. "I—I'll see you in the morning, Rede."

Rede turned away from her so he wouldn't beg her to stay. "I may head out before sunup, get an early start toward *El Óvalo*."

He heard the catch in her voice as she said, "You—you'll be careful, won't you?"

Unable to stop himself, Rede glanced over his shoulder and was startled to see the flickering lantern light reflecting off the tears gleaming on her cheeks.

He drew a ragged breath, fighting the almost overwhelming urge to cross the distance between them and kiss her tears away. "Don't," he said. "Please, Addy. I'm not worth one moment of misery to you, honey—"

She looked even more stricken. Then she whirled and fled.

Chapter Fourteen

Surprised that she had slept at all, Addy awoke the next morning to the sound of rain drumming on her tin roof.

It was such a heavy downpour she could hardly see the barn out her bedroom window, and she was conscious of a feeling of relief. Rede would not go out in that weather, so he was still in her barn, safe from the danger involved in searching for the out-laws' lair—at least for now.

Donning her wrapper and running her hairbrush through her tangled curls, she stared at the hollow-eyed image of herself in the cheval glass. He'd in-sisted he wasn't worth one moment of misery to her, and he was probably right, but the mirror revealed that she'd had a whole night full of it. She'd lain awake for hours, tortured by images of Rede being caught and shot by the Fogarty Gang, only to be pursued by those same images in her nightmares when she finally had fallen into an exhausted sleep.

She guessed the rain had awakened Rede too, and he was chafing at the delay imposed by the weather. Too bad! But while a part of her wanted to avoid him, she knew the civilized, courteous thing to do would be to take him a cup of coffee and offer him breakfast.

Minutes later, she threw her uncle's old slicker over her wrapper, placed the saucer over the cup, and made her way through the downpour to the barn.

"Rede? I brought you coffee—" she called as she pulled the barn door open, only to be met by silence. Not even Jessie's friendly whicker greeted her. Rede and her horse were gone.

A glance back over the bare, muddy ground around the barn revealed no fresh hoofprints, so she guessed Rede must have left before the rain had even started—which meant that somewhere out among the hills, he and her mare were getting a drenching.

However, the rain quit soon after she had gone back inside. Determined to keep busy, she washed her sheets and a few unmentionables and hung them out to dry. She'd have to remember to take in the undergarments as soon as the sun's heat had dried them—she wouldn't want Rede to ride in to the sight of her corset covers and stockings flapping in the breeze!

Then customers started dropping in, and Addy could only wonder, as she pinned tucks and let out seams, how Rede was faring.

Jack Fogarty didn't like loose ends. They could get a man killed—and he didn't plan on dying any other way than safe in bed at the grand Mexican *rancho* he was going to buy someday, once he had stolen enough money.

The missing Ranger represented a loose end. Once Jack Fogarty had discovered that the dead man in the

Conner's Crossing undertaker's establishment was not really a Texas Ranger, he knew that the real Ranger had to have gone to ground somewhere.

The question was *where?* It was like looking for a needle in a haystack. He'd sent the gang out in pairs to ride the hills at night, looking for a campfire that would betray the Ranger's camp. They'd found nothing but a couple of half-breed Mexicans, and when they had been disinclined—or unable—to answer the questions put to them, they'd been gunned down then and there.

He'd sent others of the gang, singly or in twos and threes, to loiter in saloons, posing as drifters and eavesdropping on the talk. They didn't worry that anyone would recognize them as part of the Fogarty Gang because during robberies, they'd always been masked.

But his spies had learned nothing. Seemingly everyone downing whiskey and beer in these little hill country saloons was local. And in any case, no one matched the description of the lean, dark-haired man on the stage—the one Chapman had lied about killing.

Not for the first time, Jack Fogarty wished he hadn't given way to his temper and shot Chapman, for the dead outlaw was the only one, in the chaos of the stage holdup, who had seen the missing man clearly. Fogarty would have liked to have questioned Chapman more closely, but now, of course, that was impossible.

Well, there was no use crying over a done deed. Chapman was dead, and they hadn't found the Ranger. Maybe the chest wound he'd sustained that day had been bad enough that he'd crawled off somewhere and died, and no one had found the body yet. Maybe they never would, if varmints had gotten to it first.

Yeah, that had to be it.

It was a rainy morning; a good time to take one last look-see in town himself while picking up the cloth Mary Sue was nagging him about. She'd wanted to come with him, but if she did he'd have to watch her every minute. He wasn't a fool—everyone knew never to trust a woman, not when she knew enough to send him to the gallows. After this many years of eluding capture, Jack Fogarty wasn't going to die like his oldest brother had, kicking at the end of a knotted rope.

As was his habit, Fogarty took a circuitous route into town, over rocky ground and down a shallow creek, so that he couldn't be tracked back to the secret opening of the hidden canyon.

He was damned if he knew why the whore needed a dress length of calico when the only people she saw were him and the rest of the boys. Women! Always wanting something more than they had!

Suddenly, as he pursued that thought, his eyes narrowed. *Maybe she wanted a new dress because one of the other men in the gang had been flirting with her.* He'd have to watch the others around the campfire at the night. She was just a whore, but she was *his*. And if someone could take his woman, he'd want to take the leadership of the Fogarty Gang next. And it wouldn't matter that several of the Fogarty outlaw gang were of his blood.

Maybe he was jumping at shadows, with this Ranger unaccounted for. Maybe Mary Sue just craved a new dress. But if someone was making eyes at his woman, he'd have to die. And Mary Sue would die, too.

He spent a couple of hours in the Connor's Crossing Saloon nursing the rotgut swill the saloon-keeper dared to charge a whiskey price for. That piss-ant sheriff was in there, too, having his dinner, and he looked crosseyed at Jack a couple of times, as small-town sheriffs were apt to do at strangers.

His scrutiny didn't make Fogarty nervous, though. From his rocky perch on the rim of the canyon, he'd seen the sheriff and his deputy through his spyglass, out searching for the gang's hideout a couple of times, but they hadn't even come close. He probably subscribed to the local belief that only a bird could get inside *El Óvalo*.

Well, he couldn't put off purchasing the damn cloth any longer. Maybe the gossip in the general store would be more useful. And even if he learned nothing there either, at least he could pick up some stinky stogies to make Mary Sue pout when he blew smoke rings in her face.

After leaving four bits on the wobbly table, Fo-garty ambled out onto the plank walkway, squinting left, then right to find the general store. He spotted it at last, across the road and past the barbershop and the bank.

The bank. The gang hadn't struck this one yet, and maybe they ought to. It looked like a prosperous enough establishment. He decided to have a smoke while he studied the place, and was just rolling a cigarette when he became aware of a conversation taking place in the narrow alleyway between the sa-loon and its nearest neighboring establishment, the bank.

"So…did your mama or papa hear you climbin' in that window last night?" It was a young man's voice, newly settled into bass, but still capable of cracking.

He heard a girl utter a throaty giggle. "I don't think so, though I swear, Henry, she did look at me funny over breakfast this morning. Said I was looking peaked and needed more sleep."

"What about your father?"

The girl uttered a snort. "His honor the mayor? Papa just glanced at me for a second and muttered something about a town council meeting, then left the house."

Fogarty smothered a guffaw. So the young pup had been poking the mayor's daughter. The boy reminded him of himself. The first girl whose favors he'd enjoyed had been a sloe-eyed *señorita,* the daughter of a Mexican *alcalde,* whom he'd encountered on one of the Fogartys' forays over the border.

Maybe the boy would make a good outlaw. He ought to see about recruiting the boy into the gang. They could use a new man, now that they'd lost Chapman.

Just then, a shout came from down the road in the direction of the livery. "Henry Junior, where're you at? They's stalls t' clean!"

Fogarty heard a thud, which suggested the boy had struck the side of the building in disgust, then the boy muttered, "You'd think those piles was goin' somewhere, the way he hollers!"

The girl chuckled. "Poor Henry! Remember, someday you won't have to work there."

Fogarty was just about to step off the plank and

into the street when the boy's next words stopped him.

"I'd sure rather go see that Ranger than go pitch...well, you know. I bet he's got some stories to tell."

"I declare, that Ranger's all you can talk about! You didn't even notice the new hair bow I'm wearin'!"

The lovers emerged from between the buildings, holding hands, too engrossed in each other to notice Fogarty.

"I'm sorry, Lucy. I *did* see it—"

"Never mind, it's all right," the girl said. Then, in an obvious attempt to spark the pup's jealousy, she added, "He *is* a rather dashing character, isn't he?" She fluttered her lashes. "I hope I can come with you when you go talk to him."

When silence followed her gibe, the girl added with a low mischievous chuckle, "Maybe we'll catch him and Miss Addy *kissing or something!*"

That sally didn't work, either. "I ain't takin' you when I go, then, if you're just lookin' to embarrass them."

"Oh, *you!*" the girl said, giving him a playful nudge. "I was just joshin'! Come on, I'll walk with you as far as the livery," the girl said. "Don't worry, Mama's lying down with a headache and Papa'll still be in that meeting—"

These *kids* knew where the Ranger was! He could hardly believe his luck, and turned toward them, trying to think quickly of a way to get them to tell him what he wanted to know without the question making them suspicious.

The lovers dropped each other's hands. He saw the

stocky girl's mouth fall open, and the light of recognition flash in her eyes.

"Why, speak of the devil, there's your hero right
there, Henry! Good morning, Mr. Smith!" she trilled.

The boy stared, his brow furrowing. "Mr.
Smith?"

Fogarty automatically took a step back. *What the
hell—? It sounded as if these kids thought he was
the Ranger!*

"Uh…I think ya got me confused with someone
else," he said. "My name ain't Smith. It's Edwards," he said. It was the usual common, forget-
table surname he assumed when necessary.

"That ain't Rede Smith," the boy said at last to
the girl. "He kinda looks like him, right enough, but
it ain't him. Sorry, mister. You're right, we thought
you was someone else." He took the girl's arm, and
they started to walk on.

Rede? Fogarty had a faint memory of his brother
James's son, the one whose mother had given her
boy that outlandish name of Redemption and then
stolen him from his father. *Was it possible?* It had
been long ago enough that the boy would be a man,
and it would sure explain why these kids thought *he*
was the Ranger! He stifled a guffaw at the irony.

"Uh, hold up jest a minute," Fogarty said quickly,
taking hold of the boy's sleeve in his eagerness.

It was a mistake. He saw that immediately in the
youth's narrowed eyes as he looked down at Fogarty's tobacco-stained fingers clutching his sleeve,
then back up at the outlaw.

"Sorry," Fogarty muttered hastily. "I couldn't
help overhearin', and I think yore talkin' about the

very man I'm seekin'—Rede Smith? Rede Smith the Texas Ranger?''

"Yes, we—" the girl began.

"*Hush*, Lucy," the boy snapped. "Remember what we promised." His eyebrows waggled meaningfully in an obvious attempt not to say the name again.

"Oh, I can understand that my—my brother Rede might be lyin' low and all, him bein' a Texas Ranger on the trail of dangerous outlaws, Miss Lucy—if I kin be so bold as to use your pretty name," Fogarty said. He winked at the girl. He knew he stood a better chance of getting her to tell what she knew than the boy, who was still eyeing him with open suspicion. "I 'preciate yore…um…*discretion*, 'deed I do. But I'm his brother, come to help him out. Fact is, I'm a Ranger, too."

"Well, isn't that nice?" Lucy said. "Henry, I think we can tell him where Mr. Smith is. He obviously *is* his brother! Why, just look at the resemblance!"

The boy ignored her. "Where's yore badge?"

"I—I left it back at headquarters," Fogarty said, "I'm here in disguise to find my brother. We Rangers…well, we haven't heard from him since he left, and we was gettin' a mite concerned."

"Don't tell him nothin'," the boy commanded. "Mr. Smith didn't say nothin' about no brother. Don'cha think he would've, if he had a brother who was a Ranger, too?" He looked scornfully at Fogarty before going on.

"But son—" Fogarty began in a reasonable voice, though he'd have dearly loved to wallop the little pissant till his teeth rattled. If only he'd encountered the two someplace besides the main street of this one-horse town!

The boy put himself between Fogarty and the girl. "We kin ask Mr. Smith if he has a brother," the boy said, his face set in stubborn lines. "If he says he does, we kin tell him you're lookin' for him. You gonna be around town, mister?"

Fogarty considered. Any further attempts at persuasion would just stiffen the boy's resistance, damn his hide. "For a coupla hours, mebbe. I have to visit the general store, then I'll be in the saloon. After that, I'll have to go lookin' for him myself. But I cain't believe yore refusin' t' cooperate with the law."

The boy's bony jaw jutted out. "So tell Sheriff Wilson on me," he dared Fogarty. "He's my uncle." He took hold of the girl's hand again. "Come on, Lucy."

Fogarty's jaw tightened. The skinny whelp better hope he didn't see him again. But maybe he'd have better luck catching the girl alone somewhere. It wouldn't be hard to make her talk.

Henry said goodbye to Lucy in front of the livery, then headed for the alley before his father could spot him. Circling back around to Main Street, he peeped through the dusty window of the general store. Sure enough, the stranger had gone in there and was studying something on one of the store's deep shelves.

Henry headed to Miss Addy's by way of the back fields, hoping to find Rede Smith and inform him about his and Lucy's meeting with the stranger who resembled him. But the barn was empty when he arrived—even Miss Addy's mare was gone. He shoulda knowed a man of action like Rede Smith wouldn't be loungin' around the barn when there were outlaws to be tracked!

Henry couldn't shake the feeling that the man who had eavesdropped on his conversation with Lucy was up to no good, and was more likely connected to the Fogartys rather than the Rangers. But how could he get word to Smith that one of the outlaws might be right here in town, sniffing around for him?

Henry hated to worry Miss Addy, but there was no other choice. He crept up to the house, hoping he'd find her alone, but he was disappointed to see that she was not alone. Beatrice Morgan was comfortably ensconced in a chair next to the seamstress's sewing machine, gabbing away while Miss Addy worked the treadle with her foot and pushed some gathered fabric under the down-darting needle.

There was no way he could go in there and say anything without arousing that nosy biddy's insatiable curiosity, but he had to leave Smith word somehow! Turning back to the barn, he went into the empty stall where he'd spotted the Ranger's rolled-up bedroll. He'd have to leave a written message— but how? He had a stub of a pencil in his pocket, but no paper.

Then he spotted the wash hanging on the clothesline between the barn and the house. Most of it was still damp, he found when he reached it, but a dainty lace-trimmed handkerchief had already blown dry in the hot sunlight. He grinned again. Miss Addy wouldn't like her washing spoiled, but she'd understand it was for a good cause.

A few minutes later Henry left, satisfied that the Ranger would understand the message he'd scrawled on the hanky he'd laid over the bedroll, even if the spelling wasn't the best.

Chapter Fifteen

About the time Fogarty had reached Connor's Crossing, Rede reached *El Óvalo*. He began his search at the abandoned mission, not because he thought there was a passageway into the canyon through it, but because it would help him recognize exactly where he had begun to look.

"*Nuestra Señora del Cañon,*" he read aloud, looking at the words chiseled into the adobe over the door of the chapel. Our Lady of the Canyon. The whitewash had faded long ago into a pearly gray, and the walls on either side of the central chapel were crumbling, giving him a view on the left into a sage-and-cactus rectangle that might have once held a productive garden, while at the back on the right, the ruin of an overhang ineffectively sheltered a small square building of the same adobe. The *padre's* rectory?

After ground-tying Jessie in front of the mission, he removed his hat, pulled his gun from its holster and cocked it before going in to search the chapel.

No door remained in the rounded archway. Some small rodent scurried past his feet as he entered, startling Rede, but his eyes adjusted to the dim light and he saw nothing to fear. His footsteps echoed in the empty chamber.

Then the odor hit his nose, a fetid smell of bat guano, and all at once his pulse began to pound in his ears. Feeling a wave of nauseating dizziness sweep over him, Rede reached out for the solid coolness of the wall to steady himself.

He had smelled that odor before. When? Had he and his mother stepped inside here on that night so long ago?

His eyes lifted to the beamed ceiling. A score of the winged rodents hung in upside-down slumber there.

He forced himself to study the beamed ceiling again, looking past the bats. The roof, surprisingly, was still intact, though even from the floor, the wood looked dry as a desert creek bed in August. The corners of the ceiling were festooned in cobwebs.

But underneath the pervasive, pungent smell of bat guano, Rede swore he could faintly smell horse droppings, though he saw no traces of it. Odd. But perhaps some cowboys had sheltered in the abandoned chapel during a rainstorm, and had been too religious—or superstitious?—to leave manure in a place that had once been consecrated.

He lowered his eyes to the sides of the chapel. The glass in the round-arched windows was long gone, or perhaps, in this hot climate, had never been there. A wan light entered through them, allowing him to see the walls, which held murals depicting the Virgin and Child, the Crucifixion, and a triumphant if Indian-looking Jesus ascending to heaven. Their colors must once have been vivid, but time and neglect had faded them so that they were now faint and indistinct.

At the side of where the altar must once have been, a headless religious statue stood, its blue-and-white-painted robes as faded as every other color in the chapel.

He saw no skeletons anywhere in the chapel. Perhaps the murdered priest's bones had been removed at last and given a decent burial, if indeed there ever had been a murdered priest. Maybe the old Mexican who had told Addy of his boyish exploration of the place had just been embroidering his tale a little.

Rede walked to all corners of the room, looking for an irregularity in the wall that would indicate a hidden passageway, but the only door led to a tiny room that must have served as the *padre*'s robing room. It was narrow, and he had to bend over to step inside. There was no way a passel of outlaws could have ridden or even led horses through that doorway, even if the passageway had been in this room—which it clearly wasn't.

It was the same story in the small square building to the right of the chapel. It held the wreck of a wooden bedframe, and a crude, hand-carved crucifix on one wall, but though Rede tapped at various places in the wall and even ran a hand over the floor for evidence of a passageway, he found nothing. Nor was there any passageway in the crumbling rock walls.

Remounting Jessie, he rode slowly around the oval rim of the canyon, looking for any irregularity in the rock low enough for a horse to enter, or a passageway near enough to the canyon that a tunnel under the rock was feasible.

There was nothing but a couple of small indentations in the limestone canyon wall so high that only a winged creature could have used it for shelter. The land abutting the canyon was no different than the rest of the country, just red dirt, cactus and mesquite.

He took his time, but in less than an hour he had reached the mission again and was forced to admit that he was no closer to finding a way into the canyon than he had been before. *There had to be an opening.*

Fogarty didn't dare try to follow the already wary boy and girl to see if they'd lead him to the Ranger, so he went on into the general store to purchase the cloth.

He didn't trust them to give the Ranger the message to come find him, either. Maybe he could catch one of them alone later. The girl would be the easier of the two to force information from—just the threat of pain, he knew, and she'd sing out just what he wanted to hear.

Maybe there was an easier way, though. It sounded as if the Ranger—who might well also be his long-lost nephew—had gotten lucky and managed to hole up with a woman. From what the kids had been saying, he'd managed to charm kisses out of her, if not a whole lot more—damn his luck! Now if he could just locate that Miss Addy...

He picked out a gaudy red print for Mary Sue. He liked his women in red—red satin with spangles would even be better, but the hidden canyon camp was no saloon hall and that draggle-tail Mary Sue wasn't worth the price of satin.

"Buying a present for the missus?" the genial storekeeper asked with an understanding wink.

Fogarty resented the man's nosiness, but knew he

was just trying to be friendly. He nodded, forcing a grin.

"Your missus handy with a needle, is she?"

Fogarty shook his head, wishing the storekeeper would just let him pay and go.

"Don't reckon you'd have your missus' measurements," the storekeeper chattered on. "Too bad, 'cause there's a real good dressmaker on the edge of town, the Widow Kelly. Why, Miz Addy Kelly could whip up a real nice dress in just a coupla days. Did it for my wife once. But I reckon you're just passin' through, anyway."

Miz Addy? Could there be two women by that name in this one-horse town? There was one way to find out.

"Oh, I kin tell that dressmaker how big around my wife is," Fogarty said, smiling like a fond spouse and extending his spread hands out in front of him as if he were encircling a waist. "Why, she ain't no bigger 'n a minute. And it just so happens I'm going to be comin' back through here in less 'n a week, so if you'd be so kind as to tell me where to find that sewin' lady, I *will* go hire her to make my wife a nice dress. She deserves the best," he added magnanimously.

The storekeeper beamed and told Fogarty how to get to Mrs. Kelly's place on the edge of town.

On the edge of town—couldn't be better, Fogarty thought as he left the mercantile. No one would be apt to see if he had to employ...*persuasion* to get Miz Addy to talk.

"So I sez to him, 'Grady, you'd better remember the muffler I knitted you,'" Beatrice Morgan was telling Addy. "But do you think he did? Of course not, and within three days his sniffles turned into lung fever." Now Addy realized why the old woman always wore black.

"You still miss him, don't you?" Addy murmured, just before she snipped the thread and pulled the skirt from under the sewing machine.

"Miss him? Honey, I can't begin to tell you how much," Beatrice said with a heavy sigh. "Well, I'm sure *you* understand, as only another widow can. Not that Grady and I had been married yet, you understand, but we were promised..."

Addy stifled her own sigh. No, she didn't understand a widow's feelings, because she actually wasn't one, though naturally she couldn't tell Beatrice that. Then she thought about how she'd feel if something happened to Rede, and knew that despite the fact that no vows of love had yet been spoken between them, she'd truly know a widow's sorrow.

And where was Rede right now? He'd been gone for hours. Had he found an entrance into *El Óvalo?* Or had the outlaws found him first? Was he even now lying dead out there among the rolling, mesquite-and-cactus-dotted hills? She could feel no sense of loss within her, but she couldn't be sure she would instinctively know such a thing. Such an instinctual reaction sounded like something out of a novel.

Fogarty was glad he'd walked his horse the last quarter-mile up to the Widow Kelly's property. Since he had approached quietly, he'd been able to see the boy hightailing it out of the barn and over the back pasture fence in the direction of town—and the boy had not seen him.

Leaving his horse tethered to a tree just around a bend in the road from the isolated house and hoping nobody was watching the backyard from inside, he stole back to the barn. He didn't think he'd find Rede Smith in there in the middle of the day, but it was worth a look to see why the boy had gone in there.

He found the handkerchief and read its scrawled message—with difficulty, since he hadn't had much book learning: "Mistr Smith—ther is a man lookin fer yu who sez he's yur brother. He looks like yu but I dont beleeve him. Send fer me. Henry Jackson Jr."

Well, pup, you tried, but that's a warning he'll never get. Grinning, he pocketed the written warning before retracing his steps back to his horse, then rode up to the house as if he were a legitimate customer.

Stealthy-footed, Fogarty stepped up onto the porch, carrying the bolt of calico. A neat, hand-lettered sign in the middle of the window to the right of the door bore the words Mrs. Kelly's Dressmaking and Alterations—Reasonable Prices. He could hear someone talking inside through the open window.

Peering through the white lacy curtains, he identified the speaker, a thickset old woman. The other one, sitting at a sewing machine, was slender and young. That had to be Addy Kelly, but why couldn't she be alone?

He rapped sharply at the door, enjoying the way the younger woman jerked at the sudden noise. He couldn't wait to see how she would react to his resemblance to Rede! While she moved toward the door, Fogarty pulled his hat lower over his eyes and forced his features into an innocent expression.

She opened the door, a polite smile of inquiry on her face. Addy Kelly was a lovely filly, all right, with

thick brown hair and green eyes big as saucers—
which widened even further as she stared up at his
features.

"*R-Rede?*" she breathed, her brow furrowed in
confusion. "Why are you coming to the front—" she
began, nodding over her shoulder to indicate that she
was not alone. He saw the ranger blush as she realized that
the old woman behind her had to have heard her first
careless words.

He saw the moment when she looked at him carefully enough to see he *wasn't* Rede Smith. She
gasped and took a step back.

"I'm sorry, ma'am, didn't mean to startle you. Evidently I look a bit like someone you know. Edwards
is my name, John Edwards, outa Mason. I'm just
here to see if I could hire your services to make my
wife a dress." He held out the bolt of calico. "I have
her measurements," he added, patting the inside
breast pocket of his duster.

"C-certainly," Addy Kelly said shakily, her eyes
never leaving his face, as if she were mentally cat-
aloging the similarities and differences between himself and his nephew. "You're right, you *do* look like
someone—extraordinarily so—but just a bit different. Um…may I ask how you found me?"

"The general store owner was singing your
praises, ma'am," Fogarty said, keeping his smile
wide and fatuous. "He said you could make a dress
quicker 'n Houston took San Jacinto, if you know
what I mean. Oh, I wouldn't be back for several days,
though."

"I'd be happy to, since you have Mrs. Edwards's
measurements," Addy Kelly said. "Oh! I'm being
rude," she said, as the old woman rose from her

chair. "This is Miss Morgan, a friend of mine from town. Miss Morgan, may I present...um..."

"John Edwards," Fogarty supplied.

"Pleased to meet ya, Mr. Edwards," the old woman said, studying him for a moment before turning back to the dressmaker. "Addy, honey, I'd better be goin', since you got business to tend to. I didn't mean to stay so long, anyway. I'll just get on with my daily constitutional."

"I'm so sorry, I don't mean to interrupt anything!" Fogarty apologized falsely. If the old woman would hurry up and get out of here, he might just be able to get what he'd really come for.

Addy Kelly didn't seem to be in any hurry to be alone with him, though. "Beatrice, please feel free to stay," Addy Kelly urged. "It won't take long to write down the gentleman's wife's measurements and take a small deposit from him. Then we'll have a cup of coffee before I start laying out the pattern on that calico."

But the elderly woman could not be talked into sitting back down. "No, no, I need to get home and sweep my porch, honey. Don't worry, Mr. Edwards. You aren't interrupting anything. Miz Addy and me can visit anytime."

Fogarty could barely conceal his smile of satisfaction as the old woman made her way ponderously out the door and down off of the porch. As soon as she had reached the road, he turned back to Addy.

She was studying him, her green eyes thoughtful. "The resemblance is really rather remarkable," she murmured; then, as he was pondering whether to tell her that lie that he was Rede Smith's brother and a fellow Ranger, she was back to business. "Now then,

Mr. Edwards. Give me your wife's measurements, and then we can talk about what style to make the dress.''

Fogarty had no idea what to say, for his knowledge of women only concerned what they could do for his sexual needs. He gave her a charming smile, while he reached into his pocket and pretended to feel around for the paper with his fictitious wife's measurements, just so he could continue looking at the lovely, refined woman awhile longer.

He shrugged. ''Seems I've lost it, ma'am. But it don't matter much. Why, I reckon if you was to make a dress to fit you, it'd fit her, ma'am. Y'all are both tiny little things.''

She blinked, and a wary look came into her eyes. ''But mightn't your wife be taller or shorter than I?''

''No ma'am, she's just ezactly your height.''

Her face hardened and her eyes narrowed. She took a couple of steps back. ''You aren't *really* here to have a dress made, are you?''

Chapter Sixteen

Addy watched as the genial smile melted off the man's face, so like Rede's and yet not like his.

"No, ma'am. Guess ya saw right through me, didn't ya?" His expression was serious now. "Fact is, I'm not John Edwards. I'm Jack...Jack Smith. I'm Rede Smith's brother, and I need to find him. So's I kin help him—I'm also a Texas Ranger, ma'am," he added quickly. His tone was reassuring, but there was a coyote's cunning in his eyes. "Where is he?"

The prickling she'd felt going up and down her spine became an icicle. She hadn't trusted this man from the moment her eyes had first met his, *but why did he look so much like Rede?*

"How'd you know to come here?" she said, wishing again that Beatrice Morgan had not left, wishing her own hasty tongue hadn't given away her suspicion just yet.

"Rede sent a telegram, ma'am. To headquarters, lettin' us know he was stayin' with ya and needed help to round up them outlaws."

Addy's mind raced. He could have sent a telegram, either from Connor's Crossing or some nearby town, while he'd been out on Jessie—but wouldn't he have mentioned it to her?

She went past him and looked out her window. "Where's the rest of your help?" she said, pulling back the lace curtain and gesturing toward the empty road outside as she turned back to him. "You Rangers are famous for capturing outlaws, but surely they wouldn't have sent just one of you?"

He gave her that easy, reassuring smile again. "Th' rest of the boys are waitin' a ways outside town. We didn't want to attract no attention to ya, ma'am, by a large party of us seekin' ya out."

As casually as she could, Addy picked up her sewing scissors from beside the wheel of the sewing machine. They weren't much of a weapon, if her instincts were right about him, but it was all she had to hand. She had to find a casual way to get to the desk drawer.

"I'm sorry, Mr. Smith—or whatever your name *really* is. I'm not sure I believe you. If you were really a Texas Ranger looking for your brother, why would you need that cock-and-bull story about needing a dress made for your wife?" she said, gesturing with the scissors at the calico fabric he still held.

"But ma'am," he said, maddeningly patient. "I needed to find ya, but I wanted to protect ya from…shall we say…notoriety? You're a widow still in mourning—half-mourning, anyway," he said, with a nod toward her black-trimmed dove-gray dress. "I couldn't speak plain t' th' store owner, or in front of that old woman! What would the town *think* of a widow giving secret shelter to a man—*any* man, even a Ranger, not related to her, when there are plenty of other places he could stay?"

Addy felt herself growing angry at his insinuating tone. She wanted to say, *I don't give a hoot what they'd think,* but forced herself to smile apologetically.

"Perhaps I've been too hasty, sir. I can see that you meant well."

The man's hard face relaxed slightly. "Then y' won't mind if I wait here till Rede gets back."

"I'm sorry, but I'm afraid the best I can do would be to allow you to leave a note," Addy said with as much feigned regret as she could manage while she crossed the room to the desk.

"But ma'am," the man protested, exasperation and—was it anger?—tingeing his voice.

"You as good as said you understood the importance of being discreet," she said smoothly, opening the desk drawer. "I have a bride and her attendants coming here this afternoon for a fitting, so I'm afraid having you, a stranger, waiting around is out of the question. You can see that, can't you?" she added brightly, praying he'd believe the lie. No one was scheduled all afternoon. "I'm sure if you leave a note, Rede will be glad to meet you wherever you say."

He uttered something very like a growl and his lip curled, turning him ugly, and not like Rede at all.

"Here's some paper and a pencil," she said, reaching inside the desk drawer.

"Forget the note. I'm stayin' here."

Her hands closed around the cold butt of the pistol that had been her uncle's. Cocking it as she turned, she leveled it at the man's abdomen and prayed she would not be forced to use it. "No, you're not. You're going to drop what's in your hands, raise your arms over your head, walk out of my shop, and get off my property. And don't let me see you coming near here again, or I'll shoot you, is that understood?''

The man's eyes narrowed to cold slits and dueled with hers, and he hesitated. Addy quailed inside, knowing he was considering going for the gun he must have inside his duster.

''I said, drop what you're holding and get your hands over your head!'' Addy shouted. *''Immediately, or I won't hesitate to splatter you all over my shop!''*

Slowly, he dropped the cloth he'd been holding. It thudded against the wood planking of the floor with a most unfabriclike *clunk* as he raised his hands over his head.

A pistol, she realized. *He'd had a pistol within that folded cloth!*

''Tsk, tsk, Miz Addy, y' don't talk like no lady. Don't reckon y' got no reputation t' lose, after all.''

His words made her so furious she ached to pull the trigger, but she just repeated, *''Get on out of here right now, before I prove to you I don't shoot like a lady, either!''* She barely knew how to shoot a gun, but she knew she was angry enough to fire it anyway.

He turned, but as he walked, to the door, hands raised, he called over his shoulder, ''Since ya ain't no lady, mebbe ya won't mind knowin' yer precious Ranger ain't no Smith, either. He's a Fogarty, jes' like me. And this ain't over. When it is, you and Rede *Fogarty* are both gonna pay!''

She had guessed this man was an outlaw, but for a moment what he said about Rede didn't make any sense. She'd have to think about that later; for now, she had to make sure Fogarty didn't have any last-minute tricks up his sleeve.

"You just keep those hands over your head until you get to your horse!"

Fogarty stomped off the porch.

Addy waited, breathless with tension, as the man stalked out to his mount that stood grazing, ground-tied, across the road. He had just pushed his left foot into the stirrup and had swung his right leg over the horse's back when Addy, aiming over the outlaw's head, squeezed the trigger.

The horse reared, squealing in fright as the bullet splintered the bark of a nearby tree. Struggling to stay aboard, Fogarty grabbed for the horn and managed to shove his right boot into the other stirrup as the horse's forelegs returned to the ground. Then one hand grabbed for the reins, while the other dived inside the duster.

He was going for his other gun.

Before he could bring out the pistol, Addy fired again, this time at Fogarty's chest, but her shot went wide. His horse took off at a terrified gallop, and when the outlaw finally did get off a shot, the bullet embedded itself in the corner of the porch overhang.

The acrid haze of gunsmoke filled the air.

Addy wanted nothing so much as to collapse on the porch and curl into a sobbing, shaking ball, but she knew she couldn't allow herself that luxury just yet. Grimly she shut and bolted the door behind her, flipped her sign to indicate that the shop was closed, and ran to the back door to lock it, too. She shut all the windows and drew her shades, all but the one over the front window of the shop that faced the road. She pulled a chair up to that window, then crossed to the desk and reached for the wooden box of bullets. After replacing the two that had been fired, she took up her position at the window, grimly determined not to miss if Fogarty or any of his gang dared to try returning.

She wasn't so sure she wouldn't shoot Rede, too, just on principle.

He'd lied to her, she thought, as the tears of fright and rage began streaming down her cheeks. Not telling all the truth was a lie, wasn't it? She'd almost given herself to him, all the while not knowing who he really was!

She should have realized that the sound of gunfire would carry the short distance into town. Just as she was getting into a good cry she heard the sound of hoofbeats, and a moment later Asa Wilson and Deputy Brooks came galloping up and reined in to a skidding stop at her front door.

By the time Addy wiped her face and crossed the room, Asa was already pounding on the door, shouting, "Addy! Are you all right? Open up in there!"

She pulled the door open just as he was raising his fist to pound again.

"Miss Addy! Thank God! We heard shots—"

"I'm all right, Asa." she assured him, suddenly feeling exhausted. *Merciful heavens, how was she supposed to explain this without telling Rede's secret? Did he even deserve for her to keep it, after the secret he'd kept from her?*

"But what happened?" He glanced downward and his eyes widened.

Then she realized she was still clutching her uncle's old Colt. Even if he'd believed Addy Kelly, a widowed seamstress, had been indulging in target practice, her tear-reddened eyes would convince him otherwise.

But surely telling a part of the truth was a way to get Asa to leave, at least until she figured out what she wanted to do.

"It was Jack Fogarty!" she cried, allowing herself to tear up again. "He stopped here—for a drink of water, he said—then tried to rob me! If I hadn't been keeping Uncle's pistol handy..." She shuddered.

Asa seized her by the shoulders. "Dear God, robbery may not have been all he inten—" He shut his mouth abruptly. "Was he alone?"

Addy nodded.

"Which way did he go?"

She pointed in the direction she had seen Fogarty's horse head for, away from town.

"Brooks, let's ride!" he called to his deputy. "Maybe we're in time to catch him!"

He ran outside and threw himself into the saddle, keeping the excited beast in check with difficulty as he called out, "Miss Addy, you stay right here! Lock your doors and shut your windows! Don't let anybody in!" Then he and the deputy were off, a cloud of dust rising behind them.

Dear Asa. He was so protective of her, as if she were a delicate, brainless belle. What did he think she was going to do, take a nap in her front yard after such an event? Then she felt a pang of remorse for how she'd lied to him. But how could she tell him the whole truth before she'd talked to Rede? *And did Rede have a reason for not telling her the truth?*

The sound of voices made her stare down the road in the direction of town. Of course the sheriff hadn't been the only one who'd heard the shots. Half a dozen of the ladies of Connor's Crossing, led by a panting Beatrice Morgan, were bustling down the road.

It took an hour to give them all coffee, recount the story of Fogarty's supposed attempt to rob her, and fend off Beatrice's determined insistence that Addy must come stay with her in town until the Fogartys had been captured—or at the very least, allow Beatrice to pack a valise and come stay with Addy. It had taken all of Addy's tact to refuse the offer without hurting the old woman's feelings, and she was aware of Olympia Fickhiser's arched, disapproving brows.

"Oh, what a tangled web we weave," Addy quoted grimly to herself as she bid the ladies goodbye.

Now it was nearly suppertime, and she hadn't been able to make herself leave the chair in front of the window longer than it took to check out the back window to make sure that Fogarty wasn't trying to sneak in that way—or that Rede hadn't returned.

She wanted to hold on to her anger. She didn't want to admit to herself how much she longed to see Rede leading Jessie into the barn.

Where was he? Was he all right? What was he going to say when she repeated Fogarty's accusation?

Just as she went to look out the back window for the dozenth time she was startled by a knock at the front door.

Rede! Her heart, apparently, could not hold on to anger, even if her head could. But he wouldn't come to the front door and knock, she reminded herself.

Sure enough, it was only Asa Wilson. He was

standing with his back to the door when she reached it, telling his deputy to go on back to town, so she had time to compose her features.

"You—you didn't catch Fogarty, I assume?"

Asa shook his head. "No, I'm afraid not. We lost his trail in the hills."

She felt sorry for him. He looked so weary and disappointed.

"Why don't you come in and have some coffee, Asa?" she asked, despite the fact that she was more eager to watch for Rede.

He tried to smile, and said, "Thanks. If you have some ready, that is. I just stopped to pick you up and take you to Miss Morgan's. Then Brooks and I will meet back in town, get fresh horses, and go back out to search."

Not him, too! "Have you already spoken to Miss Beatrice somehow? She and some other ladies were already here, insisting I do the very same thing. I'm not—"

"Surely you see that it isn't safe for you to stay out here by yourself, Miss Addy?" he interrupted her to say. "A woman all alone? That bas— Excuse me, that *scoundrel* might come back at any time, trying to take you by surprise. And you bein' a lady, I won't say what he'd be after along with any valuables you might have! Come on, Miss Addy, it's the only sensible thing—"

It wasn't Asa's fault that she was cross with exhaustion. Or that he had unwittingly used the very same words her father had when he was trying to convince her not to marry Charles Parker after knowing him only a month, and then again when he had finally persuaded her to divorce him—*"It's the only sensible thing."*

"I'm sorry, Asa. I appreciate your concern, I really do. But this is my shop as well as my home, and I don't want to leave it. Miss Beatrice really has no extra room—"

Asa swung an arm in a frustrated arc. "Then stay with one of the other ladies, Miss Addy! The Fickhisers have plenty of room!"

Addy couldn't suppress an unladylike snort at the thought of Olympia Fickhiser being obliged to offer *her* hospitality. "No, I'm afraid that wouldn't do either, Asa. I'm staying right here. *I'll be all right.* That dadblamed outlaw isn't going to bother with me again—and I promise I'll come running into town if I see so much as a trace of him!"

He begged and pleaded, but she held firm.

"Okay, Miss Addy," he said at last, "but I won't sleep a wink tonight, worryin' about you."

She sighed as she watched him trudge back to his bay and swing up into the saddle again. Asa Wilson was a good man. Why couldn't she love him as he deserved?

Chapter Seventeen

The afternoon sky remained overcast, a perfect reflection of Rede's mood as he and Jessie wound between the mesquite-and-cedar-dotted hills in the direction of Connor's Crossing.

Why couldn't he find the way into *El Óvalo?* If it was big enough for men on horseback to pass through, it had to be sizeable!

Maybe he was just barking up the wrong tree, he told himself. Perhaps there was some other canyon around with a hard-to-find entrance.

If that was true, though, why had the odor of bat droppings in the abandoned chapel affected him so much? His gut told him he'd been there on the night his mother had fled with him from his father—but that need not mean they'd come *through* the chapel to get out of the canyon.

It was damn frustrating—that was a fact. He hated the idea, but was it time to wire his Ranger company captain and admit he needed help? He winced inwardly as he pictured the wiry, grizzled McDonald's skeptical reaction if he'd been there to discuss it with Rede face-to-face—"Smith, why are you so gol-darned certain they're hidin' out in that canyon? Hell, they could have a dozen hidey-holes!''

Of course he'd be right—and of course, Rede couldn't explain to his captain about his childhood memories of the place. Judas priest, he couldn't even explain to himself why he was so stubbornly sure the Fogarty Gang was still using the same place he'd been born in.

When he'd arisen this morning, he had pictured going into Connor's Crossing to telegraph his captain that he'd found the hideout and was ready for his Ranger company to come and help him capture them. Then he'd ride in triumph to Addy's house to announce his success. He'd imagined her beaming up at him in admiration. He'd be a hero, not only to her, but to Texas—and then maybe he'd be worthy of her at last.

Now the prospect of admitting defeat—admitting that at least, on his own, he could not find the hideout—left a bitter taste in his mouth. What choice did he have, though?

There was something else to think about, too. Ever since the ambush of the stagecoach outside of Connor's Crossing, Rede had known that someone in his company had betrayed him, either intentionally or not. He'd have to watch his back when the other Rangers arrived—in case the betrayal *had* been intentional, so the traitor didn't sabotage the capture.

But that was nothing he could do anything about today. All he could do now was ride into town and send that wire—and hope the telegrapher was a discreet man who wouldn't gossip about the message being sent.

Then he'd be free to go and admit to Addy he was

no wiser than he had been this morning. Deep inside, he knew just telling her about his frustration would make him feel better. Suddenly he couldn't wait to get there—to get *home*.

Topping a rise, he took a last look back at tiny *Nuestra Señora del Cañon* lying at the foot of *El Óvalo*—

—And saw the faint trail of dust rising up, heading for the abandoned chapel.

Rede whipped his spyglass out of his saddlebag and trained it upon the dust trail. Just as he suspected, it was rising from a galloping horse being ridden by a man who, just as Rede focused on him, spurred the horse on.

Instinctively he knew it was one of the outlaws, maybe even Jack Fogarty himself. Why else would he be riding hell-for-leather toward *El Óvalo?*

"Come on, Jessie," he muttered, reining the mare around in the direction they'd just come. "Let's see if we can catch up!" The mare wouldn't be able to gallop until she got down the hillside, but as soon as they were down on level terrain again, he'd bet Jessie had every bit as much speed as the cayuse Fogarty was riding.

The mare did her best, scooting surefootedly down the slope, then running her heart out, not needing more than his voice to encourage her to greater speed. Nevertheless, the outlaw had had a big lead and Rede and Jessie were still out of firing range when Rede saw the man ride the horse right into the old chapel.

Surely the horseman had been able to hear he was being pursued, but he hadn't hesitated. Maybe he planned to fire on Rede as he rode up to the church?

He left Jessie a hundred yards away and ran toward the side of the church in an oblique, zigzag pattern, so that if the outlaw was waiting at one of the windows with his gun, he'd have a tough time hitting Rede.

No shots rang out. Finally, Rede cautiously peered into the sanctuary.

Despite his holy surroundings, he wanted to curse.

The chapel was empty. The man and horse had vanished as if they had been a mirage.

Desperately, Rede dashed to the weedy yard, and then into the courtyard on the other side, vaulting over the crumbling wall and running to the square adobe building he'd been in before. Empty. There wasn't so much as a hoofprint in the still-damp ground outside.

Maddened, he ran into the sanctuary and stared at its emptiness until at last he had to give vent to the crazed laughter erupting from him.

Were the outlaw and his horse ghosts? How else could they just disappear like that?

Then he heard hoofbeats approaching—very near. He'd been too intent on finding the vanished horseman to have heard them coming. Two horses, by the sound of it. More outlaws, coming in to use the secret passageway?

Perfect—he'd hide in the priest's robing room and try to observe how they got in.

But the mare standing outside would give away his presence.

He couldn't wait in hiding now. He'd have to try to take them by himself, and hope at least one of them could be persuaded to reveal the secret.

Crouching at the side of the doorway, he took aim

at the approaching pair of riders. But before he could fire, he saw one of them was wearing a badge.

He could tell by the wary way they halted their mounts, just out of range, that they'd seen his horse.

"Who's in there?" called the lawman. "Come out with your hands up!"

Rede didn't have a choice. He couldn't continue to hide and risk the sheriff thinking he was one of the outlaws. He'd have to trust that this man really was a sheriff, an honest one who wasn't in cahoots with the outlaws. And if that much was true, maybe he'd be willing to help.

"I'm comin' out," he called back, holstering the Colt before he stepped out into daylight. "I have my hands up."

The man's hat brim was pulled low, so Rede had difficulty studying the lawman.

"I'm Sheriff Asa Wilson," announced the man. "And this here's my deputy. Who're you?"

So this was the man who hankered to court Addy. "Rede Smith. I'm a Texas Ranger. And sheriff, there's—"

"Is that a fact?" The man's voice as he interrupted Rede was loaded with skepticism. "What're you doin' out here?"

"Trailing the Fogarty Gang, same as I'm guessing you were," Rede said quickly. "A man rode in here," he said, indicating the interior of the chapel, "and he just vanished. I think there's a passageway in here somewhere, but I can't find—"

"Let me see your badge," the man interrupted, "but reach just your left hand down inside your pocket, real slow and easy-like."

"Sheriff, while we palaver about this, he's getting away!" Rede protested.

Sheriff Asa Wilson continued to stare at him, waiting, and didn't look the least impressed with Rede's urgency.

Rede couldn't blame him for his suspicion. In his place, he'd have felt the same. And he knew before Sheriff Wilson spoke that he didn't believe him.

"I don't have my badge," he began, and saw the sheriff's face harden. He was about to explain the whole story of how he'd put it on the dead shotgun guard when the deputy chimed in, "Asa, don't he look a mite like that wanted poster of Jack Fogarty? Leastways, from the eyes up—that's all you kin see of Fogarty on the poster since he's wearin' a bandanna over his nose an' mouth."

Wilson stiffened, staring at Rede, and Rede knew a sinking feeling. He'd have sold his soul at this moment to have taken after his mother's side of the family rather than his infamous father's.

"Yep, I reckon he does," he said slowly. "Smith, huh? Couldn't you have come up with a more imaginative alias, Fogarty?"

"I'm not one of the Fogarty Gang," Rede said evenly. "I'm a Texas Ranger, and I can prove it. Just let me telegraph my captain in San Antonio, and—"

"Yeah, sure. Whoever you are, you're under arrest. Keep coverin' me, Brooks, while I take his pistols."

"Right, Sheriff."

Rede knew there was no use arguing further that while they were taking him in, the real outlaw was getting away. He'd have to cool his heels in jail until Wilson wired McDonald and received his answer.

Resigned, he submitted to having his Colts taken and being searched for other weapons, then allowed himself to be handcuffed and led to his horse.

But when they drew near to Jessie, however, Wilson stopped stock-still.

"Hey, what're you doin' with Miz Kelly's mare? Horse stealin's still a hanging offense in Texas, Fogarty—not that we'd need another reason to stretch your neck after all the folks you've murdered. Folks in town are mad enough they might not want to wait for a trial, either."

Rede's heart sank. He had accepted the necessity of spending several hours, perhaps a day, in jail, waiting for his captain to vouch for him. The worst of it had been the lost time in pursuing the outlaws and knowing that Addy would worry when he didn't show up. He wanted to protect her reputation, even if it meant a night's worry for Addy.

But he hadn't reckoned with the extent of the small-town sheriff's affection for the widow Kelly. Of course he would recognize her horse. He'd made it his business to know everything about her.

And now to avoid the danger of a lynch mob, Rede was going to have to risk endangering Addy's good name and bring her into this sorry mess.

"I'm not one of the outlaws and I didn't murder anyone. Mrs. Kelly let me borrow her horse—"

If Wilson had stiffened before, he went downright rigid when Rede dared to sully Miss Addy's name by saying it, even formally.

"Sure she did," the sheriff growled, his eyes hard as granite. "You must think I'm a real simple fool, don't you, Fogarty?"

"I'm sure she'll tell you the same thing if you ask

her. And she'd also tell you I'm not an outlaw—
though I can understand if you want to hear that from
my captain first.''

''Well, ain't that gen'rous of him, Sheriff?'' jeered
the deputy.

''Uh…you'll be…*careful* when you talk to Mrs.
Kelly, right?'' Rede couldn't keep himself from asking. ''I wouldn't want anyone to hear about it and
get the wrong idea, know what I mean?''

Wilson's eyes held a murderous glare as they dueled with Rede's, but the sheriff was first to look
away. He turned his glare upon the deputy. ''I'm sure
Brooks won't say a word, *will you?*''

The deputy hastily agreed.

It was nine o'clock when the buggy pulled up in
front of Addy's house.

By this time Addy had been pacing the floor for
hours, alternating between the front window and the
back one, which looked out on the barn. She was
sure that Rede had encountered Fogarty somewhere
between here and *El Óvalo* and been killed.

She'd already decided to set out at dawn and
search for him—but how was she to succeed without
a horse? Or would her mare return riderless in the
intervening hours?

She stared at Asa coming up the walk, wanting to
see anyone but him right now. He'd come to tell her
he hadn't caught Fogarty, she thought. How could
she pretend interest in another fruitless pursuit when
the man she loved was lying out there bleeding, perhaps already dead?

''Asa, what—''

''Miz Addy, I waited awhile till it was dark and

brought the doctor's wagon—he doesn't know what I wanted it for, just that I wouldn't keep it long— so's nobody'd likely see you.''

"But why? What—?''

"I need you to come with me," he said, his face grim and tired.

"Asa, what's going on?''

"There's a man in my jail who was riding your mare. He says he had your permission. Is that true?''

Chapter Eighteen

All Addy could see as she entered the jail was Rede, who stood and curled his fingers around the bars of the cell, watching her approach.

She wanted to run to him, throw her arms around him through the bars, and sob with relief. At the same time she wanted to slap his face for his lie of omission.

"This is the man I caught with your horse, Miss Addy," Asa said. His voice was hard, clipped. "Do you know him?"

"I'm sorry you had to come down here," Rede said, while his dark eyes pleaded much more eloquently for forgiveness.

"Yes, I know him," Addy said, her eyes never leaving Rede. "He's Rede Smith, a Texas Ranger." She saw Rede give Asa a mild I-told-you-so look.

"How do you know he's a Ranger? Just 'cause he says so? Have you seen a badge?"

She'd never heard Asa sound so cynical. He's just doing his job, she reminded herself. It had to have been a shock to find a stranger riding *her* horse. He must wonder just what that meant.

"It's all right, Mrs. Kelly, you can tell him," Rede murmured. She blinked at his formal mode of address, since it seemed ages since she'd been more than just "Addy" to him.

"As a matter of fact, I have," she told Asa, turning to face him. "I held it in my hand on the day of the stage robbery. He told me to put it on one of the dead men, to make the outlaws think the Ranger was dead."

Asa's eyes went from Addy to Rede and back again.

"That was a damnfool thing to do—at least when you didn't let *me* know about it," Asa reproved Rede. "Miss Addy, you shouldn't have gone along with it."

"He had his reasons," Addy said levelly.

"And where's he been since then?" Asa said, his jaw jutting forward truculently.

She could hear the underlying hurt in his tone. *He knows,* she thought. *Somehow he can tell how I feel about Rede.*

"In my barn," she said, her gaze swinging away from the sheriff's, since it was mostly a lie. "Recovering from two gunshot wounds he sustained that day. He's lucky to have lived through them."

As she spoke, Rede unbuttoned his shirt and rolled up his sleeve, baring the healing wounds.

In back of them, Deputy Brooks whistled, but Asa snarled, "Another damnfool thing. You should've been seen by a doctor."

"And now that I've told you who he is," Addy continued, "aren't you going to open up that cell?"

Asa sighed. "I shouldn't. I *should* wait for word from Ranger headquarters in San Antonio. I wasn't going to release him, I was just gonna give you back your horse.''

''But—?''

''But I reckon he wouldn't have been shot up in that robbery if he was one of *them*—though I can't say your working methods make sense t' me, Smith.''

''Let's just say I've learned not to trust just anyone,'' Rede said. ''But now that we've met, I'm willing to work with you to capture the outlaws while we wait for my Ranger company to arrive.''

Asa's eyes didn't warm as he took the keys from the wall and stuck one of them into the keyhole, opening the cell door. ''We'll see. That telegraph message's already sent, Smith. This Ranger captain better vouch for you, or you're gonna find yourself right back in here, is that clear? And there's no need to be botherin' Miss Addy, now that I know about you. You can stay at my place.'' *Where I can keep an eye on you,* his eyes said.

Rede looked at Addy, a silent question in his gaze.

''It's best he goes back to my barn so the whole town doesn't hear about him,'' Addy said, and when the sheriff would have argued, she reminded him, ''You have a son, Asa. Little boys are apt to chatter.'' She'd given a logical reason for the choice, but it was a declaration of sorts, and all three of them knew it.

Rede cleared his throat and changed the subject. ''I'll say it again, Sheriff, there's a way into that canyon through the church. I just haven't found it yet.''

Asa gave a skeptical harrumph to that, then let

them out the back door and into the alley, where Jessie was tethered.

Addy and Rede were silent as they led the mare through the darkened streets and down the road to home.

By the light of the kerosene lantern she watched Rede unsaddle her mare and give her grain and water. When Addy would have left to go back into the house, though, Rede stopped her with a hand on her wrist.

"Thank you, Addy. Like I said, I'm sorry you had to go down to the jail to vouch for me. But Wilson seems like a good man. He won't flap his gums about you—and he won't let the deputy do it, either."

She whirled on him. "Is *that* all you think I worry about? I trusted *you* with my deepest darkest secret—the fact that I'm divorced. When were you going to tell *me* your last name isn't Smith, but Fogarty?"

He froze, which served as final confirmation of Fogarty's accusation. A light in his eyes died.

"I'm not an outlaw, Addy—I never have been," he said. "I take it you've seen that same wanted poster the deputy had, the one that shows Jack Fogarty with a bandanna over his nose and mouth?"

She shook her head. "No. *Your brother Jack* came calling on me this afternoon, looking for you." The fear she'd felt then fueled her fury now.

He stared at her. "He came *here?*"

She nodded in confirmation, briefly telling him about the way Fogarty had gained entrance with the supposed need to have a dress made for his wife, then given her that cock-and-bull story about also being a Ranger, and how she'd gotten out the gun and driven him off.

"Judas priest, Addy, he might have killed you!" he cried. "Or—"

She held up a hand, not needing to hear the same dreadful possibilities Asa had already alluded to.

"He's not my brother," Rede said. "James Fogarty was my father, and Jack is his youngest brother. My uncle. And I haven't been a Fogarty since I was a small boy, when my mother took me away from the outlaws before I could grow up in my father's footsteps. She gave me a new last name, so I wouldn't ever have to hang my head about being a Fogarty."

She couldn't let the poignant words mute her anger. *"Were you ever going to tell me?"*

His eyes looked like those of a soul in torment, but his shrug was casual. "I didn't figure you'd ever need to know. Soon as we catch them, I'd be riding on out of here, and you'd forget about me."

She winced to have him confirm the very thing she had feared all along.

"You mean you'd forget *me*," she whispered, feeling tears sting her eyes.

"No. Never," he said, his voice raw with pain. "But wasn't it bad enough you had to risk disgrace for hiding me here? You didn't ever have to know you were hiding someone with tainted blood."

Her jaw dropped. *"Is that how you think of yourself, Rede?* Of all the wrongheaded, damnfool ways of thinking! You thought I'd think less of you because of who your *father* was? I love *you*, the man *you* are, Rede Smith or whatever your name is. *But now I hate you for lying to me—and for wanting to leave me!"* she cried.

Addy didn't know when she had crossed the distance between them, but as she finished her lashing tirade, they were practically nose to nose.

And suddenly he had closed the inches between them and was holding her, whispering, "No, you don't hate me, sweetheart, no you don't…"

"Yes, I do!" she cried brokenly, sobbing against him, feeling her arms go around his neck as if they had a will of their own. "I hate you for lying to me and for thinking I'd forget you and for making me worry all day about you—"

"No, you don't," he repeated, tipping her chin up so that she was forced to look directly into his eyes. "Someone who hated me wouldn't bother to worry about me, or care whether I remembered you or not. Now, I admit we've both had some problems being honest with each other—and you're dead right that I should have told you about the family skeleton in the closet before this—but you *don't hate me. You love me.*"

His eyes demanded confirmation, even as he said it again, "You don't hate me, you love me."

It was the truth, and she couldn't deny it. She could only nod and admit it. "Yes, I love you, Rede. But it won't change anything. You're still going to—"

"*Just as I love you.* Shh," he murmured against her hair, when she would have gone on with her protestation. "Hush, sweetheart. It's going to be all right, I swear it is…."

And then she found herself raising her mouth to his and he was accepting it, swallowing all the hurt and rage and fear, and leaving in its place peace, and simultaneously, a fierce desire. A desire that made her believe his sincerity, yet want to brand him with her love, so that he could never leave her, would never *want* to ride away and leave her behind.

He rewarded her with a kiss that left her breathless. "Addy, sweet Addy," he murmured raggedly, "I don't know why you'd be willing to love me—" his forehead rested against hers "—but I'm going to take you at your word. And whether we stay here or go somewhere else when this is all over, we're going to be together—forever, sweetheart."

"Rede, make love to me," she said, gazing up at him in the dim light. She opened her mouth to him, and clung to him, and when she felt his hands on her, stroking her, cupping her, she gloried in them. It seemed they could not get close enough, quickly enough. His fingers were already working at the buttons of her bodice.

But this time, when she would have lain down and invited him to join her on his bedroll in the straw, he stopped her. "Oh, no. We're not going to be interrupted by lovesick kids or anything else. Not this time!" And before she knew it, he had bent over, placed an arm under her knees, and swung her up into his arms, carrying her with rapid, purposeful strides through the soft evening and into her house. Into her bedroom next to the kitchen.

Here he deposited her gently on the bed and drew the shades. Then he struck a lucifer against the sole of his boot, lighting the lamp and turning down the wick so that its soft glow spilled over them both.

"Unless you'd rather it was dark?" he said, gesturing toward the lamp. "But this first time we make love, I really crave to see you, all of you, my lovely sweet Addy...."

This first time.

Addy knew there were women who let their husbands touch them only in the dark, who never let their men see them naked. But she could not imagine being one of those women, not with this man. She wanted to see every inch of his glorious body, too, this time and every time.

"Don't blow the lamp out," she said.

Each of them began to undress, their gazes locked. But Addy had been wearing a dress with a score of tiny buttons marching down the bodice, so by the time Rede had shucked boots and pants and shirt and union suit, and stood naked before her, Addy had only managed to pull off her dress, petticoat, and corset cover and was still fumbling with corset hooks.

"Let me help," he whispered, pushing her shaking fingers gently aside. Gratefully, she let him take over.

But once he had reached the last hook and allowed the corset to fall to the floor behind him, he seemed in no hurry, kissing her and stroking her aching breasts through the thin barrier of her chemise. She arched into his caress, moaning at the jolting sensations racing through her. She could feel his manhood rubbing against her belly through the soft cotton of her drawers.

"Please," she begged against his neck, breathing in his scent, a scent made up of leather and horse and hot sun. She wanted him to hurry, to pull off the chemise and push down the drawers until she was as naked as he was.

He partly complied, pulling the chemise over her head, groaning in admiration as her full breasts spilled into his hands. He cupped them and suckled them, while she held on to his shoulders and struggled to remain upright on legs that seemed to be made of pudding.

"You're so damn beautiful, Addy," he breathed, and knelt before her. Then she felt the hand that had been stroking her right breast descend down over her belly, seeking and finding the slit in her drawers.

She almost fainted from the heat that flared through her as his fingers found their way through her folds and reached the exquisitely tender bud of flesh, his thumb sliding over it while a finger slipped inside her, stroking, withdrawing, stroking.... She could feel herself growing wet where his clever hand caressed her. Her heart raced with her lungs.

"Let yourself go, honey, let yourself feel," he urged her, his breath warm against her belly. "And then there'll be more, I promise...."

She thought she should be shocked, but it felt too good. It was all new to her, all wonderful. Her ex-husband had never, at his most indulgent, bothered to make her feel anything but invaded.

Then a rocketing surge of joy that was lightning and thunder and all the fireworks she'd ever seen back in St. Louis on Independence Day burst within her. She clutched at him as a little scream forced its way past her lips, then she sagged against him.

He held her against him for a moment, almost as if she were a child. "That's it, my sweet Addy, that was wonderful...*you* were wonderful...."

She wanted to ask him, to plead with him to lay her down right there on the rug in front of her bed, and bury himself within her, not bothering to remove her drawers, just using the same opening his hands had found. Didn't he need his own satisfaction? But she couldn't; it seemed, for an eon of time, she was incapable of speech.

It was really only the briefest minute, though, before he was lifting her onto the bed, standing over her and untying the bow at her waist and pulling down the last vestige of clothing. Then he lay down over her, kissing her lips, her eyes, her neck, her breasts.

"I want you, Addy Kelly," he muttered, as one of his hands stole around her buttock, pulling her closer against him. She could feel his knee inserting itself between her legs, parting them, even as he readied himself to enter her. She did not resist—on the contrary, she moved restlessly beneath him, wanting him inside her. It felt like she had wanted that all her life.

"I love you, Addy," Rede breathed, and then, in one swift stroke, he sheathed himself in her, filling her so completely she almost screamed again at the utter perfection of it, of the ecstasy of having him stretched out over her, skin to skin.

She had thought she could not feel anything better than that, but as he began to move inside her, slowly at first, then faster and faster, she became lost in a blazing vortex of sensation. Vaguely she was aware of his heart racing against hers, and his ragged breathing. But there was a precipice looming up ahead, and they were racing toward it, and it seemed more essential than her next breath that she throw herself over it at the same time as he did. He would catch her before she hit the ground.

He groaned then, and held her hips, thrusting wildly against her, and suddenly they were falling through space, holding on to each other.

Chapter Nineteen

Rede fell asleep holding Addy, more at peace than he had ever been. This woman knew him—*completely* knew him, even the shameful secret of his heritage. And she loved him still. He would be willing to die for her if it was necessary, but more importantly, he wanted to live to please her.

At dawn, they woke and took turns bathing in the copper hip bath, first Addy and then Rede.

"I wanted you from the first moment I saw you sashaying toward the stagecoach," he told Addy, savoring the feel of her hands in his hair as she knelt behind him and worked the soap into a lather. "I was walking behind you, and your bustle swayed back and forth so...." He stopped, lost for the right word. "I mean, I couldn't take my eyes off it—um, that is to say, you—your..." He waved his hands in the air, certain he had just put both feet in his mouth.

"My *derriere,* you mean," she supplied dryly, and splashed him for his effrontery.

He could tell she wasn't upset, though, so he splashed her back. "And then, when I sat opposite you in the coach, it was so hard not to stare. I didn't feel I had any right to be thinkin' what I was thinkin'—you bein' a lady and all, and dressed like a widow.''

Addy, clad only in her chemise and drawers, chuckled as she tipped his head back with her fingers before pouring a pitcherful of rinse water over his head. Handing him a towel, she confessed, ''I had the same problem, keeping my eyes off *you.* I thought you were an outlaw—so I was terribly shocked that all I wanted to do was look at you.''

Surprised, he swiveled in the water to look at her, but he could see she was telling the truth. ''I never caught you at it, so you must've been pretty careful,'' he said. ''Speakin' of lookin', though, I have to admit, it made me so angry when that bucket of bacon sitting next to you started makin' calf eyes at you. I wanted to knock him clean into next week.''

''Bucket of bacon? Calf eyes? Ranger Smith, I believe you are mixing your metaphors a bit,'' she murmured, but her amused smile quickly faded into a pensive expression. Rede knew she was remembering how the big man had inadvertantly saved her life by falling over her when he'd been shot during the holdup.

Rede didn't want Addy thinking about the massacre and feeling sad, and perhaps guilty because she had survived it. She'd spent too much of her recent life feeling those emotions.

He reached out a hand to caress her cheek, noticing at the same time how the water he'd splashed at her had rendered her chemise almost transparent.

''You'd have run off that stage at the first way station if you'd known what I was thinkin' as I sneaked looks at you,'' he said, his hand straying down her neck.

His attempt at distraction was successful. Addy shut her eyes, obviously relishing the caress. ''Oh, and what was that?'' she purred. ''I think it's safe to tell me now, don't you?''

''I reckon it is. Well, sweet Addy, I was thinkin' how I'd love to touch you here—'' he palmed her breast, his thumb circling the rosy circle of her nipple and feeling it peak against his touch, already warm from the bath ''—and here,'' he said, stroking her other breast. ''And *here*.'' His hand glided lower, between her legs.

She gasped, and her eyes flew open. ''You were thinking of touching me *there*—while we were on the *stage?*'' she squeaked, rocking back on her bare heels.

Rede felt himself grinning. ''Honey, a man doesn't need to be naked in a bedroom with a beautiful woman to be thinkin' things like that,'' he told her, rising from the tub and picking her up in his arms, ignoring the fact that he was dripping wet. She didn't seem to mind, either, so he laid her down on the bed. She'd used some rose-scented soap and she smelled so sweet and clean....

''You know what else I was imaginin' doin'?'' he said, pulling down her drawers and undoing the bows that tied her lace-trimmed chemise together in the front.

''I'm getting a fairly good idea,'' she said in a husky voice, her green eyes smoky with desire as he joined her on the bed.

''I wonder if you are,'' he drawled, his hand straying over her belly. From her astonished reactions to his lovemaking yesterday, he'd gotten a pretty good idea that the no-good scoundrel she'd been married to had never bothered much with pleasuring this wonderful woman. Everything Rede had done to make her feel good seemed new to her, so there was a good chance she'd never have experienced what he was going to do to her now.

He lowered his head as his hands parted the curls that guarded her womanly center.

"Rede, what are you *doing?*" she demanded as his mouth descended to that spot. *"Rede!"* she shrieked as his tongue laved her and stroked her, and then her fingers were tangling in his hair and she was moaning, writhing....

Moments after her explosion came, she tried to return the favor. But though he thought he would die from the pleasure of feeling her mouth closing about him, he could only enjoy it for a few heavenly moments before he had to be inside her, his love spilling into her like warm honey.

Later, she set his plate of eggs and bacon in front of him and sat across from him. It was already a hot summer morning, so she was clad only in her chemise and drawers. He had put on his denims, but he was still shirtless.

"Addy, I want you to do something for me because I love you," he began. This wasn't going to be an easy discussion, he had a feeling. He knew how much she prized her independence.

"I thought I just *did,*" she retorted, mischief dancing wickedly in those green eyes.

"You did, honey, and it was wonderful," he said. "But that isn't what I was talking about."

She quirked a brow. "Oh?"

"I still have to find and capture the Fogartys, but I'm worried about you, especially after you tellin' me my uncle came callin' on you yesterday. I can't be riding away from here, leavin' you here alone."

"Rede, I can watch out for myself," she protested, distress clouding her eyes. "I'll be careful, I swear. I'll keep my doors locked and stay inside, and if I do have to go out to the garden or the springhouse or something, I'll take my uncle's pistol—"

He shook his head. "Not good enough. You told me Miss Morgan offered to have you stay at her place, and I want you to take her up on that."

"But Rede, I can't run my business—"

"It's not forever," he reminded her. "Just till the Fogartys are behind bars or dead. My Ranger company ought to be joining me in a few days, and then we'll hunt them down. I'm not listening to any arguments, sweetheart. Your safety is too important to me. We'll pack up the essentials and I'm takin' you to her—unless you'd rather go stay with the mayor's wife?" He prayed he'd get her smiling again at the absurdity of that last suggestion.

Addy shuddered, then grinned. "I can't imagine anything worse than being beholden to Olympia Fickhiser. All right, I'll go to Miss Beatrice's." She sighed. "I know it's the wise thing to do."

"That's my sweet Addy," he praised, and raised up enough that he could kiss her across the table.

"But Rede, what about *us?*" she moaned, when his lips left hers. "I mean, while I'm staying with Miss Beatrice we can't...we won't be alone...." And then she blushed. "I sound like such a wicked, wanton woman, don't I? It's just that now that we...I..." She waved her hands, clearly floundering, as her flush deepened to crimson.

"Wicked," he agreed, grinning, "and wanton, but I'm not complaining. I know, sweetheart. Now that we've made love, I'm going to miss bein' able to sleep with you at night, to touch you whenever the notion strikes me." To prove his word, he reached out a finger and touched the top of one curving breast through her chemise. "But as soon as this is over, Addy, we can make up for lost time—"

At that precise moment a knock thundered at the back door, and a heartbeat later, the door was thrown open.

Addy yelped and jumped up from the table, staring wide-eyed as Sheriff Asa Wilson stepped over the threshold. Rede cursed inwardly, both at his carelessness in leaving the back door unlocked when he had gone to pump water for their bath, and at Wilson.

From the expression on his face, Rede could tell he'd seen the intimate caress through the window. Now he just gaped at them, his mouth open, taking in the sight of Addy standing there in frozen horror, clad only in her shimmy. Then his eyes slid over Rede's bare chest, and something in his face hardened.

"I was taught to wait to be invited in to a house, Sheriff—especially when it's a *lady's* house," Rede began in a warning voice. He didn't care if the man was the sheriff—he wasn't going to tolerate any disrespect offered toward Addy.

Wilson ignored Rede. "I reckon I knew this last night, Miss Addy. I just hoped I was wrong," he said at last.

As if his words had freed her, Addy fled into her bedroom, slamming the door behind her.

Wilson watched her go, then his eyes returned to Rede. "If you're trifling with her, Smith, I'll break every bone in your body," he growled.

"I'm going to marry her," Rede said evenly, "just as soon as we catch the Fogarty gang." In spite of the anger he felt at the sheriff's interruption, he couldn't help but feel sorry for the man. Rede could tell he'd been in love with Addy, but being an honorable man, he'd just been waiting for her supposed widowhood to end.

"You'd better do just that," the sheriff retorted, his voice low and threatening. Then, as Addy returned, now clad in a modest wrapper, added, "I tried the barn first. I just came to tell you that the wire came from San Antonio this morning, confirming that you're a Texas Ranger, and that your company would be leaving for Connor's Crossing today. They ought to be here some time tomorrow."

Rede nodded. "I'm taking Miss Addy to stay with Miss Beatrice till this is over," he told Wilson.

The hard glare in Asa Wilson's eyes softened somewhat. "I'll escort her there. Less gossip that way than if someone sees her with a stranger," he said.

It wasn't an offer—it was a command. And Rede guessed any renewed suggestion of working together to track down the Fogartys had better come from Wilson, not from him. A man had his pride, and the sheriff's had just taken a shot to the heart.

Asa insisted Addy ride his bay gelding while he walked alongside, but that courteous command was apparently the last thing he intended to say to her. So the silence, broken only by a mockingbird's call and the buzz of insects, stretched uncomfortably between them as she rode and he walked beside the horse toward town.

Addy's heart ached to see the stiff set of Asa's shoulders and the way he kept his eyes rigidly in front of him. *He was a good man, and she had hurt him without ever intending to.*

She would not for the world have changed what had happened between her and Rede last night, but now that passionate love had blossomed between them, she wished Asa could be happy, too. Surely there was a good woman out there for him!

"I—I'm sorry, Asa," she said at last, looking down at him from the gelding's back. "That you had to find out the way you did, I mean. I—I'd like to explain something," she added, intending to tell him about being a divorced woman, not a widow. She was not sure why she owed him this much honesty, but perhaps it might aid in healing his wounded feelings somehow.

"You don't owe me any explanations. Reckon you know what you're doing," he said, in a voice that did not encourage her to go on.

But she knew she had to. "Oh, I'm not at all that sure," she said quietly, looking down at her hands. "I just know I can't go on living a lie any longer. In doing so, I've made matters worse."

Addy felt his eyes on her now, but she knew she didn't dare meet his gaze or she would lose her nerve. She took a deep breath and said, "I have no right to the mourning I wear. I'm not a widow, I'm a divorcée. I divorced my husband back in St. Louis.

He was gambling away every cent we had, and he'd long since ceased being a husband." There. It was out.

"But…why?" Asa began, with a meaningful glance at the gray dress she wore with its bands of black.

Only a man—and especially one as uncomplicated as Asa—could have asked that question, she thought, stifling a bitter laugh.

"You've thought I was a widow, and treated me with respect—just as the rest of the town did. I probably shouldn't say as much, but you intended to court me when I put off my mourning, didn't you?" she dared to say.

Addy raised her eyes to his now, and it was Asa who looked away first.

"You're a widower with a young son, Asa. Would you still have planned to court me—honorably—if the town knew I was a divorced woman, and you saw all the ladies in town pass on the other side of the street just to avoid their skirts brushing mine?"

"Yes!" he stubbornly insisted, but his tone wasn't convincing.

"Asa, you know you would not have," she argued gently. "You're not the sort of man to have…less than honorable intentions, either, are you? And now you've found me acting…well, just as one thinks a divorced woman acts," she said, feeling the flush spread up her neck as she remembered Asa seeing her in her kitchen in her shimmy, being kissed by Rede.

His face turned as red as a brick, and he looked distinctly uncomfortable. "I don't know why you're telling me this, Miss Addy. You don't think *I'm* gonna gossip about it, do you?''

"No, I don't. It's just that…well, it was important to me that you didn't think I was the sort of woman who'd—'' Dear heaven, *why* had she opened this subject? But she was detemined to finish it. ''The sort of woman who would forget her late husband so soon.''

There was a long silence. They had reached the outskirts of town when he finally broke it. "You got a right to your happiness, I reckon," he said carefully.

"I love him, Asa. He loves me. We're going to be married as soon as the Fogartys are captured."

Now Asa's eyes were troubled and his expression dubious. "If he doesn't do right by you, Miss Addy, he'll have me to answer to."

His protectiveness warmed her. It was more than she had a right to expect.

She had thought they had said all there was to be said between them, but just as they reached Miss Beatrice's small house and she was preparing to dismount, Asa said, "I know you've made your mind up, Miss Addy, but maybe what you've told me about yourself ought to be just between us? I mean…it's going to be dangerous, capturing those outlaws. God forbid, but what if something happened to your Ranger? Then if you had already told everyone…'' His voice trailed off awkwardly. "Well, you know what I mean."

His words were a chilling reminder that Rede was not indestructible, and the men he sought held life very cheaply.

She gave a bitter little laugh. "You mean, I should

wait and see what happens, and not disgrace myself for nothing? Asa, I'm afraid if something happened to Rede, my reputation would be the least of my concerns.''

Asa looked crestfallen. ''I didn't say that right, Miss Addy, and now I've offended you. I just meant—''

''I'm not offended, Asa. It's just that I'm finished with pretending to be someone I'm not. No matter what happens.''

Chapter Twenty

When Asa and Addy entered Beatrice Morgan's small house behind the bank, the old woman was in the middle of frosting a chocolate cake. She was being "helped" by Billy, Asa's young son, who was holding the bowl for her and sneaking samples of the frosting when he thought she wasn't looking.

Beatrice didn't seem surprised when Asa announced Miss Addy had come "to stay with her until the trouble was over."

"Glad Asa finally talked some sense into ya, Addy. I know I'll sleep better, knowing you're not out there all by yourself. I'll enjoy having some company, too. Billy's gettin' tired of my old-lady stories, but he's too polite to say so, aren't you, Billy? Sheriff, this chocolate cake's for you—I'll be expecting you back here, come supper time. Won't that be nice, with you, me, Miss Addy and Billy, all together?"

Asa looked as if he'd swallowed a snake. "I...um...thank you kindly, but I reckon I'll have to make it another time—and I'll need to leave Billy here till bed time, if it's no trouble? Brooks and I are going to ride out with the posse again. There's a company of Texas Rangers due to arrive tomorrow and I'd sure like to have a jail full of Fogartys to hand over to them.''

Beatrice's wrinkled face looked troubled, but she said, ''Sure, he's no trouble—'cept he probably won't leave you any cake. You be careful out there, you hear?''

Asa nodded and left.

Beatrice waited until Billy had eaten his cake and gone outside to play before she said, ''You and the sheriff have a spat?''

Addy sighed and shook her head. ''Not exactly. Oh, Miss Beatrice, I've got something to tell you.'' At least it wouldn't be as hard to tell the old woman the truth about herself as it had been Asa.

''If it's about that Ranger who's been stayin' with you, I already know.''

Addy blinked in surprise. ''Did Asa—?''

''Naw, he's no chin-wagger,'' Beatrice said. ''But that Deputy Brooks is downright leaky-mouthed! He was settin' in front a' the saloon last night jawin' about you springin' the Ranger from jail when I was out for my evenin' constitutional. That gossipy fella was sayin' as he thought you was sweet on that Ranger—*more* than sweet, he as good as said—and I told him to hold his tongue.''

Addy sighed. She was sure Brooks held his tongue, all right—until the old woman had walked out of earshot.

''But I suspected somethin' was up ever since that stagecoach robbery. You've been actin' different— as if somethin' had woke you up, all of a sudden. There was roses in yore cheeks, girl. And there was that day Olympia Fickhiser claimed to 've heard a ghost at yore house. Well, I've been in that house frequently ever since your uncle built it, and it warn't never haunted b'fore.''

Addy couldn't help but laugh when she thought of Olympia Fickhiser's reaction, and Miss Beatrice joined in.

''Yes, that was Rede who made the noise, not a ghost. Oh, Miss Beatrice, I just know you're going to like him,'' Addy said, happy, like any woman in love, to be able to speak openly of her beloved. ''But I'm afraid there's more that Brooks didn't know....''

It came pouring out, all of it—the story of her disastrous marriage and eventual divorce, her subsequent decision to pose as a widow when she came to make a new start in Conner's Crossing, even Asa's embarrassing, unexpected arrival at her house this morning.

''So that's why Asa wouldn't come to supper,'' the old woman concluded.

''I feel so bad about this, Miss Beatrice,'' Addy admitted. ''But even before Rede came, I'm not sure I could have...*loved* Asa—as he deserves to be. And I don't think he would have found me all that admirable if he'd known the truth about me when I first arrived.''

''Good Lord, girl, you're not exactly Jezebel! But that man thinks he wants another plaster saint like his late wife, who was always carryin' around smelling salts and swooning. From Virginia, she was. He never did figure out all those delicate airs meant she just didn't have any gumption. It didn't surprise me none when the cholera carried her off. He hasn't figured out how much more interestin' a *real* woman is, even if she's had to make a tough choice or two like you have.'' She patted Addy's skirt-covered knee encouragingly.

"Thanks, Miss Beatrice, you're very kind," Addy said, touched.

"Shoot, girl. It takes an interestin' female to know one, doesn't it? The only man who ever figgered out how interestin' *I* was, though, was my late sweetheart. But I don't have any hankerin' to be the *only* interestin' female in town. Who would I talk to? You ain't gonna let Olympia Fickhiser run you off, are ya?"

"No, I'm not," Addy said, and she realized it was the truth.

Rede spent the morning and afternoon at *Nuestra Señora del Cañon,* walking over the grounds, poking among the moldering old books he'd found in a broken trunk in the priest's rotting cottage, exploring inside the chapel. Nowhere did he find any clue about the way into the canyon.

The higher the sun climbed, the more frustrated he became. He'd noticed on his first visit that there was no space between the exterior back of the chapel building and the canyon itself—yet the interior wall at the back of the chapel was smooth. And today, when he paced off the length of the building's exterior, and compared it with the inside, he came up with a difference of ten paces.

There had to be a secret passageway—just as he'd thought all along—but how did one get into it? He'd run his hands along the unlined adobe wall inch by inch, but nothing gave to the pressure of his fingers. How could a man on horseback have disappeared so quickly?

The floor was made of large blocks of adobe, and there were plenty of cracks in the mortar that joined them. Though Rede systematically pressed every inch of the slabs within two horse-lengths of the rear wall, he found nothing.

An inscription, carved in fading Spanish at the bottom of the headless, blue-robed statue caught his eye. ''The hand of Our Lady...'' he translated with difficulty. But the rest of the base was damaged, as if someone had deliberately chipped away the remainder of the inscription. Or perhaps merely time and neglect were the culprits.

Finally he strode outside and, tipping his head back and cupping his hands around his mouth, shouted, ''Hey, Jack Fogarty! It's me, Rede, Uncle Jack! I'm out here—come and face me, if you're not too yellow!''

He couldn't be sure his challenge had even carried over the high canyon walls, but just in case it had, he waited, pistol at the ready, for nearly an hour before deciding his uncle wasn't going to answer the challenge.

On the long ride home, he'd thought about going to see Addy, but realized he didn't even know where Beatrice Morgan's house was located. And somehow the idea of going to the jail to ask Wilson where Addy was just stuck in his craw.

He let Jessie turn off the road when they came to Addy's house and head for the barn. He was in for a long, lonely night.

It was all too obvious, when Addy and Billy joined Miss Beatrice on her ''constitutional'' the next morning, that word had gotten around town about the

Texas Ranger who'd been staying at her house. Married men who had previously been only respectfully courteous toward her, as the widow whose name was on their wives' dressmaking bills, suddenly seemed eager to engage her in conversation.

And it wasn't just the married men. Every male between ten and fourscore years seemed to suddenly find her a fascinating source of information, so that Beatrice and Addy could not make it down the street without being stopped multiple times. They asked her endless, eager questions about the robbery, the wounds sustained by the Ranger—and the expected arrival of the Texas Ranger company in Connor's Crossing today.

Being asked about the last subject bewildered her. It was as if she was suddenly expected to be omniscient. She knew no more than any of the rest of them about how many Rangers were coming, exactly when they were expected to arrive, and just how they would go about bringing the Fogarty Gang to justice.

"Yessir, things'll be better, now that them Rangers is comin'," one old graybeard opined—as if he hadn't seen Asa and his deputy walking their horses into earshot.

"Hi, Papa! I'm escortin' the ladies on their walk!" Billy cried.

"Hello, son. That's just fine."

The old graybeard hadn't the grace to look ashamed. "Bet you're eager to have the Rangers take that trouble off yer hands, eh, Sheriff Wilson?"

Addy saw Asa scowl. "Well, I don't plan to give up and wait around for them. My deputy and I are heading out to patrol the ranches and roads around Conner's Crossing. It won't do to relax our vigilance—and we just might be able to save the Rangers the trouble. Good day, Miz Morgan, Miz Kelly.'' He'd kicked his horse into a gallop and left them in a cloud of dust.

"Poor Asa," chuckled Beatrice in a low voice, once they'd moved on and Billy had been pulled into a game of marbles with some other boys. "Not only does he lose the lady he fancies, he's got to put up with being upstaged by the Texas Rangers. He's going to have a chip on his shoulder big as a log before this is through. Though it's hardly fair," she added, "to expect any small-town sheriff with one deputy and an occasional posse to be able to deal with outlaws like the Fogartys."

Addy could only nod in agreement.

The women they met, however, were as hostile as the men had been overly talkative. Addy and Miss Beatrice just happened to be passing the Baptist church when the Ladies' Missionary Society adjourned their weekly meeting. Led by Olympia Fickhiser, a vision of matronly virtue in olive-green faille—which Addy remembered trying to persuade her was not a good choice of colors, given her sallow complexion—the women sailed toward them.

"Uh-oh," breathed Beatrice at Addy's side. "Looks like Olympia's got a burr under her saddle. Don't let her browbeat you, dear."

"I won't," Addy promised. After the resolution she'd made yesterday to be herself, she didn't mind having a confrontation with the mayor's wife, but she was dismayed to see who was with her—none other than Mrs. Renfrew, the mother of the bride for whose wedding Addy was making all the dresses. She had already cut out the bride's dress and that of two of her bridesmaids, and if the job was canceled now, Addy would be out a considerable sum. And when word of *that* got out, no one would patronize her shop....

But there was no use crying over what was likely already spilled milk.

"Mrs. Kelly, I'd like a word with you," Olympia Fickhiser announced.

"Good morning, Olympia," Beatrice said, before Addy could reply. "Is that one of dear Addy's creations you're wearing? I can always tell. Talented fingers that sweet girl's got, eh?"

Olympia's face looked like she'd just been forced to kiss a horned toad. "Talented fingers, yes. And one hears those 'talented fingers'—" her lifted brows imbued the phrase with extra meaning "—have recently turned to *nursing* a wounded man. Very commendable, Mrs. Kelly."

"Thank you, Mrs. Fickhiser." Addy waited, wondering what was coming next. Olympia Fickhiser never gave out free compliments, and the glint in her narrowed eyes was not a kindly one.

"One wonders, however, why you thought it necessary to keep it—that is, *him*—a secret at your house and risk damaging your reputation. He could have been cared for equally well at the home of any of our married ladies without the danger of a scandal. Really, Mrs. Kelly, it shows a want of good judgment on your part! And when I think of how you felt it necessary to give me that faradiddle about a *ghost* in your house that day I was there patronizing your establishment, accompanied by my *innocent* daughter—"

All at once Addy spied Lucy Fickhiser at the back

of the bevvy of women, looking as if she'd like a hole to open up in the ground and swallow her up. The sight gave Addy a momentary grasp on her temper, which was fast slipping beyond her control. Carefully, she said, "I could not reveal something I was not at liberty to reveal, Mrs. Fickhiser. Mr. Smith had his reasons for secrecy."

Olympia raised her eyebrows still farther. "Indeed, Mrs. Kelly? And you had yours, I suppose—chief among them being the fact that you were still supposedly in mourning for a husband dead less than a year. You wish to portray yourself as a respectable widow, all the while enjoying the company of the dashing Ranger, isn't that it? Your dear departed husband must be rolling in his grave, my dear Mrs. Kelly, that you allowed yourself to be persuaded—"

Addy held up her hand. "That's quite enough, Mrs. Fickhiser."

"Now, Addy, maybe you shouldn't—" Beatrice began in anxious tones.

Addy ignored her. "I wouldn't want you worrying needlessly about my 'late husband's' feelings. It's time I confessed that there is *no* dear departed Mr. Kelly, good ladies—only a scoundrel of a man I divorced. Yes, that's right, I'm a *divorced* woman."

Chapter Twenty-One

There was a gasp from somewhere in the midst of the clustered ladies—had it come from Mrs. Renfrew, the mother of the bride-to-be? She couldn't be sure.

Olympia Fickhiser smirked in triumph. "I suspected it all along," she announced over her shoulder to the other ladies.

"But if you're expecting me to be exchanging my half-mourning for scarlet, Mrs. Fickhiser, you'll be sadly disappointed," Addy snapped, angry past caring what Olympia Fickhiser or Mrs. Renfrew or anyone thought. She'd move somewhere else, if need be, but she wasn't about to let a woman like the mayor's wife bully her. "I've lived quite respectably as an honest businesswoman—"

"Who *deserted* her lawful husband," the mayor's wife interrupted in an awful voice.

Addy itched to slap the smug woman's bony cheeks, but she knew she would just be helping Mrs. Fickhiser prove her point. But Beatrice Morgan was sputtering in distress, and Lucy looked miserable.

Then a rawboned, angular woman in a striped

nainsook dress spoke up. "Olympia, hush up. You're not being very charitable. Could be you don't know all the facts," she said. "Hello, Mrs. Kelly, we haven't spoken before, but I'm Molly Renfrew," she said, extending a hand toward Addy. "I've been meaning to come down to your shop and get fitted for my dress for my daughter's wedding."

Addy tried to hide her amazement at this unexpected champion.

"I don't know what you must think of me for not coming with Sally and her bridesmaids that day—I had to go to Austin to help another daughter with a new baby right after Sally got engaged."

Olympia's face took on a bilious cast. "Surely you don't mean to *tolerate* such a woman in this town, Mrs. Renfrew," she said, though her voice sounded far from sure. "I can give you the name of an excellent seamstress in Llano—"

Molly Renfrew didn't look at her. "Olympia, you claim to love the heathens on the other side of the world, but you sure have no compassion for your neighbors here in Texas," she said. "Mrs. Kelly's past isn't any of your business. Nor is mine, but I'm going to tell you anyway. It just so happens Mr. Renfrew isn't my first husband. He rescued me when my first husband beat me to within an inch of my life for the dozenth time. Are you saying I should have remained with my first husband?"

It was clear from the astonished faces of the other women she'd never revealed this to anyone before. They glanced at each other, but when they gazed at Addy again, their eyes held no hostility.

"I reckon none of us are perfect enough to throw stones," one of them murmured.

"Well, I never!"

But before Olympia Fickhiser could stalk off, the sound of hoofbeats reached their ears. Mrs. Renfrew pointed at ten approaching men on horseback trotting down the street toward them.

"Ah, those must be the Rangers now," she said, smiling. "Is the man you nursed back to health among them, Mrs. Kelly?"

Addy shaded her eyes with her hands and peered at them as they rode toward the group, but she did not see Rede among the many men who were mostly bearded, wearing wide-brimmed hats, dusty trousers, and every color of shirt.

Several of them tipped their hats and grinned as they passed the group of ladies, and the Connor's Crossing Baptist Missionary Society giggled and preened—all but Olympia Fickhiser, who stood still as Lot's wife after she had been turned into a pillar of salt.

But then a movement from the opposite direction caught her eye. Another horseman was loping toward them. Even from a distance, she knew it was Rede.

"There he is—that's Rede Smith, the wounded Ranger I nursed," she said, unable to keep the thrill of pride from her voice.

Olympia Fickhiser sniffed, but the other women stared with great interest as Rede met his fellow Rangers down the street.

Addy stared too, knowing he hadn't picked her out among the knot of women. She was aware of the ache of longing that had just reawakenened in her heart—the same ache that had kept her wakeful in her borrowed bed at Beatrice's last night, missing

him, wishing he could have held her as she fell
asleep.

She saw him point in the direction he had come,
and Addy guessed he was explaining about the oval
canyon and his belief that the outlaws' hideout was
there.

"My, isn't *he* a fine figure of a man?" drawled
Mrs. Renfrew as she continued to gaze at him. "Mrs.
Kelly—Addy—I *totally* understand why you felt
compelled to…aid such a man," she added. "He
quite puts me in mind of Mr. Renfrew when he came
galloping to my rescue that day so long ago!"

Addy felt herself blushing at the naked apprecia-
tion in the older woman's tone. Then she caught
Lucy's eye, and the plump girl winked.

Her mother had seen the little byplay, though.
"Come, Lucy. It's time we went home," she
snapped, grabbing the girl's hand and pulling her
along behind her.

No one bid the mayor's wife farewell. They were
all too busy taking in the spectacle of the Ranger
company wheeling as one and galloping off toward
El Óvalo.

"Sheee-it," Cletus Fogarty was lying on his belly
and peering down through a spyglass at the ground
in front of the chapel from Diamondback Mesa,
which lay just to the east of *El Óvalo*. He and the
other outlaws had just come from a successful raid
on a saloon in a neighboring town, and the saddlebags on their horses, who waited behind the mesa,
were laden with bottles of whiskey. "Some fellows
is setting up camp right in front a' the church. We
gonna ride in on 'em with guns blazin', Jack?"

Jack crawled up behind his cousin and gazed down too. "Son of a bitch. Gimme that glass, Clete."

Obediently the youth handed it over.

"No, we ain't," Jack said.

"We wait till they sleep, you mean, then mow 'em down?"

"Nope."

Clete's face was creased with disbelief. "But Jack—they've got us cut off from our hideout! Your wh— Mary Sue's in there!"

Jack gave him a nasty grin. "I ain't worried about that draggle-tail Mary Sue—whores are a dime a dozen. And you ain't worried about her, neither. What you mean is the loot's down there, don't you?"

A few days back, they'd robbed a stage heading toward Fort Davis with the army payroll, and none of them had had the chance to spend his share yet.

Cletus gave a sickly grin. "Yup, reckon I do. That's a consid'able sum, ya know. Even my puny stake would buy a helluva lotta tequila *and* a purty señorita to go with it. Why 're we just gonna let 'em camp there?"

"'Cause they ain't just a bunch a' saddle tramps, they're Texas Rangers, muttonhead," Jack said, but without heat. He could remember being a young hot-head like Clete.

"How d'you know?"

"'Cause I kin see my dear nephew among 'em," Jack answered, still peering through the spyglass. He'd told the rest of the gang about his accidental discovery that his long-lost nephew Rede was the very same Ranger who'd come all the way to Connor's Crossing seeking them. "And since they's Rangers, that means they ain't gonna just stupidly fall asleep without settin' a watch. We try riding down on them, and they'd hear us comin' in plenty a' time to be up and armed—and they's as many a' them as there is of us.''

Walt Fogarty, Cletus's older brother, had wormed his way up beside them at the edge of the plateau, and now spoke up. "But wh-wha-what if th-th-they fi-figger out th-th-"

"I swear, I ain't gonna wait here all day for ya t' finish a sentence, Walt," Jack Fogarty snarled at him. His cousin's stammer had always annoyed him. "What if they figger out the way in, is that it?"

Shamed, Walt hung his head and nodded.

"They ain't gonna do that. My nephew Rede— he'd be yore second cousin, I think—didn't, did he? Though he's been out here twice, puzzlin' over it. Naw, we're gonna have to ride a ways and camp out tonight, boys."

"I'd think you'd want to stay and gut-shoot yore damn nephew for bein' a Ranger when by rights he outa be ridin' with us," muttered Clete sullenly. "You said he's really a Fogarty, didn't ya?"

The remaining outlaws, holding the horses just out of sight below the flat tableland echoed Clete's dissatisfaction.

"Oh, yore cousin'll be pushin' up daisies soon enough," Fogarty assured them. "And it won't kill you to camp away from the hideout for one night, 'cause tomorrow's gonna make it worth it. We're gonna stage a *diversion*—then swoop down on the prize that'll let us live like kings when we head for the border right afterward."

"A d-di-diversion? Wh-wha-what's that?" Walt asked.

Jack Fogarty was so pleased with his plan he didn't even mind explaining. He motioned to Clete and Walt to join him back where the horses and the other men waited, then he went on. "See, they don't know if they've trapped us inside the canyon or not, so they think they're just gonna set there till they either starve us out or we attack 'em to get back to our hideout. So we're gonna stage an event a ways away—say, at Llano—that's gonna draw them off. They're gonna leave that camp an' come chasin' after us—or rather, where they'll think we are. Only by that time we ain't gonna be there."

"W-w-we ain't?"

"We're gonna get back inside the canyon while they're ridin' to where we think they are?" Clete asked. "How's that gonna make us rich?"

"No, of course we ain't gonna let ourselves get bottled up in that canyon, muttonhead," Jack Fogarty sneered. "I said we was gonna swoop down on the prize while they're racin' to th' wrong place."

"P-prize? What p-prize? Wh-wh-where?"

He told them, and soon all of them were grinning.

"And while we're at it, we might just take us some hostages t' ensure our safe trip across the Rio Grande," he added. He had one particular female hostage in mind—one whose taking would cause his nephew the Texas Ranger to go loco with rage. A loco man was easy to kill.

He might not even have to dirty his own hands with the killing, he considered. Once the man who'd betrayed Rede in exchange for Mary Sue's continued health got wind of what Rede was doing, he might just take care of the deed for Jack.

But wouldn't it be more satisfying to kill Rede

himself? James Fogarty would smile from hell, or wherever he was. He'd always been prouder of Jack than he'd ever been of the son who'd run out on him.

"So tell me again," George McDonald was saying, after the Ranger company had walked over the grounds and explored the chapel of *Nuestra Señora del Cañon* yet again without finding a way into the canyon, "Why are you so all-fired sure the Fogartys' hideout is in this canyon we can't even find a way into?"

Rede faced the grizzled captain. "Like I told you—I saw a man ride in here and when I got here, he had vanished, Captain."

McDonald ran a weathered hand over his chin and eyed the other men. "Reckon there's some logical explanation, Smith. He probably rode along the side a' the building, and you lost him in the shadows."

They were standing at the entrance of the chapel. "Nope, Captain, I saw what I said I did," Rede insisted. "I was close enough to see him ride *into* the building, and he was gone when I got here."

"And you're proposing to tie up an entire company of Rangers here till something happens?" McDonald's voice was scornful, and one or two of the other Rangers chuckled in amusement. "Hell, Smith, we don't even know if your hunch is right that this is the hideout, let alone if anyone is in there."

"It's more than a hunch," Rede said, meeting his captain's eyes, then knew he'd said too much when George McDonald's eyes narrowed.

"You want to explain that a bit further?"

"No. I just know it, that's all." There'd be time

enough to explain about his early years in that canyon after his lawless relatives were behind bars.

"Well, *I* think you've brought us here on a damn wild-goose chase," McDonald said. "I don't know why I didn't just ignore that telegram. I guess we were just relieved to hear *something* after so long without any word from you."

"I explained about the ambush, and getting wounded, Captain," Rede reminded him. He'd told McDonald and the others the whole story on the way out to the canyon—though he'd left out Addy's part in his recuperation after the stagecoach robbery, of course. There'd be time enough to tell them he was getting married and leaving the Rangers if he survived this expedition.

George McDonald spat a stream of tobacco juice on the ground and kicked dirt over it with the toe of his boot. "So you did. You feelin' up to scratch now?"

"Fine."

"All right, Smith, we'll camp here a coupla days. If them Fogartys don't show in that time, we're movin' out, understand?"

Rede nodded slowly. It wasn't much time, but it would have to do. He just wished he knew if the outlaws were in there, or somewhere beyond the canyon. "I'll take the first watch, Captain," he said.

Chapter Twenty-Two

"Mornin', Asa," Beatrice Morgan greeted the sheriff as she opened her back door to let Billy scamper inside.

"Mmm, cookies!" Addy heard the boy shout in a delighted voice.

"Yes, your favorite, sugar cookies with raisins and pecans," Beatrice said. "Asa, why not come on in for a cup a' coffee?"

"No, I reckon I'd better be goin'," Addy heard him say. She was sitting in the parlor pretending to crochet, as she'd been doing since shortly after dawn.

He wouldn't come in as long as she was still there. She regretted that Miss Beatrice was caught in the middle of the awkward situation. Just another reason to wish it was over soon.

"Is there any news?" Beatrice asked, before he could leave.

Addy moved quietly to the parlor doorway without being seen. She had to hear something or she would go crazy, she thought.

"Nope. The Rangers are camped out by *El Óvalo*.

I'm to get word to 'em if anything happens here. Damnfool waste a' time if you ask me.''

Well, we *didn't* ask you, Addy thought as she heard the door shut and his footsteps fade away.

My, aren't you cranky, she gibed at herself. No doubt her irritability was due to lack of sleep from missing Rede and not knowing what would happen, but she didn't like herself this way.

But when and how would it all end?

It was just after ten that morning when the rider came galloping hell-for-leather across the flat ground toward the Ranger camp.

Rede, who'd been cleaning his Colt while keeping an eye on the pot of beans that were cooking, recognized Asa Wilson even before he jumped off his lathered bay.

''The Fogartys struck Llano this mornin'—we just got the telegram!'' he shouted. ''They robbed an' killed a passel a' folks! The message said they rode south after that! You got t' get over there and cut 'em off afore they get across the border!''

McDonald, who'd been sitting next to Rede and unwrapping a chaw was already on his feet before the deputy had finished. ''All right, boys!'' he shouted. ''You heard the man! Mount up and let's ride!''

But Rede held up a hand. ''Whoa up just a minute, Captain,'' he said. ''Aren't some of us staying here to keep them from getting back in?''

''Smith, they've obviously picked a new hideout if this place was *ever* their hideout!'' McDonald said, his voice loaded with derision. ''And there ain't no damnfool use in anyone staying *here* if the Fogartys

are out *there!*'' He made a sweeping gesture in the
direction of Llano. ''Stop your jawin' and mount
up!''

All around him, his fellow Rangers were running
for their mounts. But Rede didn't move.

''*Did* anyone try to telegraph back to Llano?'' he
asked.

The sheriff snorted scornfully at the question. ''Of
course I did, Smith, but I got no answer! I figure the
wires are cut—either that or everybody's been massacred!''

Massacred. The word vibrated in the air. Though
he couldn't explain the feeling even to himself, Rede
couldn't shake the notion that something wasn't as
it appeared.

''I think it's a trick, Captain,'' Rede said, knowing
before he spoke that McDonald wasn't going to believe him. ''They're trying to draw us off here. Why
not send half the company to investigate and keep
half here?''

''Smith, the last time I looked I was the captain,
not you, ain't that right?'' snarled McDonald. ''Now
how's it gonna look if we miss the chance to catch
those bastards before they make it to Mexico? Mount
up, Smith—or consider yourself a private citizen
once again. Your choice!''

Glancing away from the captain's angry face,
Rede saw the sheriff watching both of them. *He'd
probably just love to witness me getting kicked out
of the Rangers.*

He sighed. Maybe his instincts were wrong. Judas
priest, he'd been wrong before. Maybe his stubborn
pride was getting in the way. ''All right, Captain,
I'm coming with you.''

* * *

"You really do need a parasol, walking out at this time of day," remarked Miss Beatrice as they left the house for Beatrice's beloved morning constitutional. "Here, take mine. It doesn't matter if my old face gets brown."

"No, you keep it," Addy said, gently pushing away the proferred parasol. "I'll be just fine with your old sunbonnet."

"Oh, that old thing doesn't keep the sun off nearly as well! Why don't we go look at parasols at the general store? Mr. Herman has some new ones in, I've heard."

"I have a parasol at home, so I really don't need one," murmured Addy, but neither of them was paying attention to her.

"*May* you get some candy, and the answer is we'll see, Billy. Why, look at all those horses tied up at the hitching post," Beatrice noted as they rounded the corner and crossed in front of the bank. "That's odd to see so many at once," she mused aloud. "And I don't recognize a one of 'em."

Odd, too, to see three men dressed like cowboys, just lounging in the alleyway, holding rifles down at their sides, thought Addy, but before she could think about their significance, a shot rang out from inside the building, followed in a heartbeat by a man's cry of pain and a woman's shrieks.

Now the cowboys outside had bandannas over the lower halves of their faces, and had raised their rifles so as to cover three other masked men running out of the bank clutching bulging canvas bags and waving pistols. Another man came out more slowly, his arms holding a female against his chest like a shield.

Addy gasped as she recognized the female as the mayor's daughter. "Lucy!"

The girl turned frightened eyes toward Addy as her captor maneuvered her toward a horse at the hitching post. "Miss Addy! *Help!*"

"Get on th' horse, missy, or I'll shoot ya in the back!"

"Oh, God preserve us," Beatrice moaned beside Addy, then fainted dead away, dropping the frilly parasol in the dirt.

"Stay with Miss Beatrice, Billy!" Addy said, dropping his hand and snatching up the parasol, then running toward the outlaw, who was still struggling to force Lucy onto his horse.

Addy launched herself at the masked man, beating at his back and head with the parasol, desperately hoping to distract him at least long enough to allow Lucy to escape.

With her second blow she knocked the bandit's hat off, and she managed to inflict a few more painful blows with the the parasol before the outlaw dived under the makeshift weapon and wrapped one burly arm around her waist while yanking the parasol out of her grasp with the other.

"Miss Addy! Don't you hurt Miss Addy!" came the childish cry as her wrists were pinioned behind her.

"Well, if it ain't Miz Addy Kelly! Thanks for savin' me the trouble of huntin' you up!" crowed one of the masked men to the side of her. It was a voice she'd heard before.

She whirled to face the new threat, but just as she recognized Jack Fogarty's cold eyes above the mask, a blinding pain crashed into the back of her head and her vision went black.

"Miss Addy!" The boy's shout was much closer.

Nooo! Not the boy!

"Take the kid too—he'll make good insurance!" Addy heard someone say as she staggered and tried to hold on to consciousness. *Don't hurt him....*

Then she knew nothing more.

The town of Llano lay some ten miles to the north-east of Connor's Crossing. As they reached the out-skirts, McDonald called a halt and announced they'd reconnoiter the town first, before heading south after the outlaws. To see what was what, as he put it.

It was a good thing they did. When they rode into the main street, the sheriff was standing in front of the telegraph office. He strode out to meet them.

"We just came from near Connor's Crossing," Captain McDonald called out to him. "Heard you had some trouble from the Fogarty gang here. How many were killed?"

The lawman looked surprised. "Nobody, far as I know," he said in a slow, twangy drawl. "Which makes it mighty hard for me to believe the telegra-pher in there," he added, wrinkling up his face in disgust as he jerked his head toward the building behind him. "He said it was the Fogartys, but I cain't hardly b'lieve they bothered to rob the telegraph of-fice—and no one else. He didn't have much cash around, seein' as how he'd just opened up."

"The Fogarty gang robbed a telegraph office?" McDonald repeated incredulously. "And that's all? We heard—"

"The money don't seem to be the main reason they came," he said.

Rede stiffened on the back of the sweating mare. He had a sickening feeling he knew what the man was going to say.

"He says they held a gun to his head and forced him to send a fake telegram to Connor's Crossing saying our town had been hit and they were fleeing south," the sheriff explained, "then a couple of them guarded him long enough for the rest to cut the lines in all directions."

"So he couldn't wire the truth after they rode away," McDonald concluded. "Which means—"

"That while we were headed here," Rede interrupted, "they knew that Connor's Crossing was unprotected except for a sheriff and a deputy *who thought the Fogartys had struck Llano and were going south!*"

"Damnation! That's *just* their game!" shouted a Ranger.

"We've got to get back to Connor's Crossing!" cried another.

Captain McDonald was thunderstruck. His eyes shot to Rede's, and they exchanged a look. There was a hangdog sag to the older man's shoulders.

Rede didn't waste time saying "I told you so." He was already wheeling the mare and spurring her back in the direction of Connor's Crossing.

Addy! All at once Rede knew there was something *personal* in the ruse the Fogartys had employed. Addy was somewhere in that little town, and Fogarty had a score to settle with her—and with Rede, through her.

The Rangers found Connor's Crossing like a red

anthill that had just been stirred with a stick. Towns-
folk had swarmed on Main Street, most of them
wringing their hands but not doing much of anything.
They stared with red-rimmed, shocked eyes at the
Rangers as they rode in.

The same apprehension that had made Rede spur
Jessie all the way back to Connor's Crossing now
clutched at his gut.

In front of the jail Asa Wilson was saddling a
horse—but it wasn't the bay he usually rode. A rifle
stood propped against the hitching post. A handful
of men sat on horses or stood nearby.

When he saw the Rangers coming, though, Wilson
stopped what he was doing and ran to them.

"Thank God you're back! They took my boy!
They took Addy, too! And the mayor's daughter! We
gotta ride after them!"

The nightmare words caused the scene around
them to fade for Rede. All he could see was the sheriff's anguished face.

"Addy? The outlaws have Addy?"

He was vaguely aware of a woman separating herself from a knot of females and dashing toward them,
barely avoiding being run down by another rider galloping in to join the posse.

The next thing Rede knew, someone was clutching
at his hand with frantic strength. He looked down to
behold a middle-aged, matronly woman. "You have
to save our daughter!" she shrieked, her face a red-
dened ruin of tears. "It wasn't enough that they
wounded my husband when they robbed the bank—
they've kidnapped Lucy!"

Chapter Twenty-Three

A dozen voices, all talking at once—those of Asa Wilson, the mayor's wife, an elderly woman whom Rede guessed was Beatrice Morgan, and others— supplied the details to the Rangers. The Fogartys had struck the bank an hour ago, wounding the mayor and killing a bank teller when they resisted. Lucy Fickhiser, the mayor's daughter, had been seized in the bank and used to force the deputy into dropping his gun. Addy, Beatrice Morgan and Billy Wilson, the sheriff's son, had just happened to be passing the bank when the bandits ran out of it, and when Addy spotted them holding Lucy, she had attempted to go to the girl's aid.

One of the outlaws hit Addy over the head with the butt of his pistol, knocking her unconscious, causing little Billy Wilson to run into the fray, fists flying, trying to help Addy. But the end result was that all three of them—Addy, Billy and Lucy—had been lifted or forced onto the outlaws' horses and used as shields as they galloped out of town.

Something didn't add up.

Rede rounded on the sheriff. *"Where were you,*

Wilson?'' he demanded. Why hadn't he done something to stop them? Rede knew he would have died before he'd have let a bunch of murdering outlaws take a child of his.

"Now, hold on, there, Smith—maybe there's something we ain't heard yet," McDonald began, laying a cautioning hand on Rede's shoulder.

Rede ignored it, watching as Wilson turned to him. His anguished face told the story even before the man spoke.

"I wish to God I *had* been here!" he cried. "My bay went lame on the way back to town after I rode out to give you the news about the Fogartys hitting Llano!" He pointed to the bay, which stood tied to a hitching post a few feet away. Sure enough, the beast was standing with his near foreleg cocked so that his weight wasn't fully resting on it.

"I had to walk him the rest of the way," Wilson continued miserably, "and didn't make it back till after the Fogartys had gone! You were right all along, Smith—it was a ruse! They just wanted to pull you Rangers away from the area so they could rob the bank. They robbed it, all right—and God help us, now they've got my *boy!* And Addy, and the mayor's daughter! You've got to help me—sweet Jesus, if anything happens to my boy..."

If anything happens to Addy...

"Please,'' the mayor's wife pleaded, weeping and sinking to her knees, frantically clutching at Rede's nearest leg. "Mr. Smith, please, please, save my daughter!"

Jessie sidled nervously, nostrils flaring, uneasy at the woman's hysteria. "Ma'am, we will..." Rede muttered. Impatient to be off after the outlaws, he was also mystified as to why the woman was addressing him instead of the captain, "but I'm not in command. Maybe you outa be speaking to Captain McDonald, here…." He tried to gently dislodge Mrs. Fickhiser, but hysteria had lent the woman a grip of iron.

"But you're Rede Smith, aren't you? It's *you* I must beg forgiveness of, before I can rightly plead for your assistance," the mayor's wife said, staring up at him with red-rimmed eyes. "I said such horrid spiteful things…about you and your Addy. Please forgive me and rescue our daughter…*please*…."

Wilson, ignoring Mrs. Fickhiser's melodrama, spoke to McDonald. "You'll need fresh horses," he said, with a gesture at the Ranger's lathered mounts.

No! That'll take too long! Rede's brain screamed. But glancing down at the mare's sweat-drenched sides and seeing that the other horses were in similar condition, he knew changing horses was the only answer. The mare had heart, but it wouldn't help Addy if Jessie collapsed in the attempt to save her mistress.

"Brooks, run down to the livery and tell Jackson we'll need to borrow all he's got in his corral," Wilson continued, "and we'll need hay and water for these." Then he turned back to the Rangers. "I'm coming with you."

"Me, too," said young Henry.

"I think she's wakin' up, Lucy," Addy heard a boyish voice say somewhere in front of where she lay.

She tried to open her eyes, but that first shaft of sunlight sent a blinding pain rocketing through her skull, so she squeezed them shut again and threw her arm over her face. Where was she, and why did she hurt so much in so many places?

"Shh...lie still, Miss Addy," Lucy hissed in her ear. "You've been unconscious."

Then she remembered. The outlaws. The struggle. She'd been trying to save Lucy. Now she was fearful of opening her eyes. "Wh-where are we?" she whispered.

"At the Fogartys' hideout—inside that oval canyon west of Connor's Crossing," Lucy whispered back. "They mean to hold us for ransom, Miss Addy!"

"Help me...help me sit up," she said, stifling a groan as a dozen places on her body screamed protests to rival the one in her brain.

"I can't," the girl said. "Our hands are tied."

Addy's eyes flew open. Needles of light jabbed at her brain, but she forced herself to focus.

Lucy sat next to her; Billy, in front of her. Both their hands were tied behind them.

"They didn't tie you because you were unconscious, I guess," the girl said.

Billy's eyes were round as saucers and gleamed with unshed tears. His lower lip quivered with the effort he was making not to cry in front of her, but tracks on his dusty cheeks testified that he hadn't always been successful at holding the tears back.

"Miss Addy, they said they'd keep us here till we die, if the ransom don't get paid," Billy told her. "I don't even know what a ransom is."

Addy's heart twisted at the boy's frightened expression. She sat up and opened her arms. "Come here, Billy," she invited. Then, as the child nestled against her breast, she added, "Don't you worry. It's going to be all right. Your papa and the Rangers will see to it.''

She only hoped she was right—*but they didn't even know where they were!*

"Have we been here long?" she asked Lucy.

"No, just a few minutes. Miss Addy, I'm scared too...." the girl admitted.

So am I. Addy injected as much calmness as she was capable of into her voice. "I know, Lucy, but try not to worry. Like I said, the Rangers and Sheriff Wilson won't let them get away with this."

"But they won't know how to get in," Lucy said, her voice sharp with fear.

Addy wished Lucy wouldn't speak so plainly in front of Billy, for her words were making the boy visibly more frightened. But Lucy was barely more than a child herself, and she had probably held her fears in check as long as she could.

"They'll figure out something...or we will," she said with a confidence she was far from feeling. "Uh...how *did* they get in? Rede hadn't been able to find a way."

Lucy told her, and Addy shook her head in amazement.

"It stunk in that ol' church, too! Didn't you think so, Lucy?" Billy added, holding his nose to demonstrate how bad. "I saw *bats* in there!"

"Pretty stinky, all right," Lucy agreed, as Addy shifted her gaze to study her surroundings.

At first, she saw no one. The canyon was about a quarter of a mile long, with a cluster of cottonwoods at the far end. The ground dropped away slightly just beyond the trees, and Addy saw the faint shimmer of water. As she watched, a horse ambled into her line of sight and headed for a drink. So the canyon had its own spring—no wonder the place made such an ideal hideout!

Off to the right, a pair of cows grazed placidly next to a small pen in which several pigs dozed in the sun. On the left stood a small, rude hut; in front of it, half a dozen chickens scratched in the dirt.

Midway between the canvas shelter and the spring was the campfire. A pair of stout, forked sticks supported a pole from which a pot hung suspended over the fire. Addy thought she could smell the odor of cooking meat wafting from it. Bedrolls were scattered around the fire at various angles. An untidy stack of tin plates and cups sat nearby. Not far from that, on the right, another makeshift canvas tent stood with its covers tied back, revealing a rough-hewn table with a roulette wheel sitting atop it, surrounded by a trio of half-consumed bottles of whiskey. A pair of spittoons sat on opposite sides of the table.

"All the comforts of home," she muttered.

A rustle in the grass warned her someone was coming toward them. Addy had the impulse to shut her eyes and feign sleep, but she didn't. She'd have to face them eventually.

It wasn't Jack Fogarty who stood staring at her, though, but a scrawny woman with stringy, tow-colored hair and wearing an incongruous dress of red grenadine.

"Hey, Jack, looky here! She's awake!" the woman called over her shoulder, before resuming her frank scrutiny.

The sly speculation in the woman's eyes made Addy uneasy.

"Who're you?" Addy demanded.

The woman let out a snort of laughter. "Ain't you the high 'n' mighty lady, though! *I'm* Mrs. Fogarty, Mrs. Jack Fogarty, that's who, an' you'd best mind your manners around me, iffen ya know what's good for you! Who're you?"

Jack Fogarty had a *wife?* "I'm Addy Kelly," she said, trying to hide her surprise. Could this woman somehow be motivated to help them?

"She ain't my wife."

Addy jumped. She hadn't heard Jack Fogarty approaching behind her; neither, judging from her suddenly fearful expression, had the woman. She shrank away from him, but not quickly enough to escape the outstretched hand dealing a slap that knocked the woman backward.

"I've warned you 'bout talkin' nonsense like that, Mary Sue," he growled. "We ain't hitched an' we ain't never gonna be. Don't let me hear you lyin' like that again or I'll stake you out for the red ants."

"I didn't mean nothing by it, Jack, honest." Mary Sue whimpered, and scooted away. Once she had backed out of his reach, she seemed to recover some of her courage. "What'd you bring *her* here for, anyway?" she asked sullenly, eyeing Addy with suspicion. "She looks a sight too prissy for you. And what about them other two?" she added, pointing at Lucy and Billy.

"It ain't none a' your concern, woman," Fogarty snarled. "Them vittles ready?"

"Sure, Jack, jes' like always." Her tone softened into one that was wheedling and pitifully flirtatious. "I know you 'n' the boys always come back from a raid hungry enough to eat a rustled steer hide, beller, an' all." She darted a glance at Addy. "And then,

once you've et, ya always want a little lovin',
don'cha?'' She nodded toward the hut. ''Right in
there on your pallet, Jack honey, whenever you're
ready.''

Painfully aware that an impressionable girl and an
innocent child were listening, Addy squirmed with
embarrassment at the woman's blunt speech. How
could the woman have so little sense of pride that
she spoke that way to Fogarty, especially after the
way he had just struck her?

The woman glanced at Addy again, and there was
a glint in her eye now. ''Say, I'll bet I know what
you brung her for—she's for the other fellas, ain't
she? So they'd have somethin' t' do 'sides listenin'
t' you takin' your pleasure on me, right? *Right?*'' she
repeated, her suspicion naked on her face now.

How could a woman have sunk so low as to be
jealous of a man like Fogarty?

Fogarty took the woman's sharp chin in ungentle
fingers. ''Mind yer own business, I said, an' do as
yer told, or it'll be worse 'n red ants. You'll join
Chapman over there,'' Fogarty snarled, pointing at
the far end of the canyon.

Addy followed his pointing finger, and spied a
low, raised mound in the weeds at the far end of the
oval. A thin plank of wood stuck out of one end.

Mary Sue's tight jaw slackened, then dropped
open as what little color she had faded from her pal-
lid cheek. ''You'd *kill* me, like ya did Chapman? But
Jack, honey, I lo—''

''Faster 'n you could blink,'' Fogarty interrupted.
''Now, go dish me up some stew, woman, and some
for our *guests,* too,'' he said, with an ironic gesture
toward the three on the ground. ''And don't even

think of offerin' Miz Kelly no sass, you worthless woman!''

Without watching Mary Sue walk away, Fogarty squatted in front of Lucy and took out his knife.

"Don't you hurt her!" Addy cried, tensing to launch herself at him. Lucy shrieked and cowered.

Fogarty guffawed. "Now, ladies, don't go jumpin' t' conclusions," he said, grabbing Lucy effortlessly and pulling her around so her back was to him. "If I wanted t' slit anyone's gullet, I'd've done it already. I jes' figgered now that you're safe in our little hideaway, it was time to let ya loose, so ya could eat an' all. It ain't like ya could leave, anyway." He laughed hugely, as if he had made a joke, while he sawed at the rope with the knife. Then he cut Billy's bonds, too.

Within five minutes Mary Sue had served up tin plates of stew to all of the outlaws, then filled three more and brought them to the captives. Then, taking nothing for herself, she scuttled into the little hut without so much as a backward glance.

Addy, too nervous to do more than play with her food, watched as Fogarty and the rest of the outlaws squatted or sat and shoveled the big hunks of meat and potatoes into their mouths. Lucy and she were safe until the bandits filled their stomachs, at least.

A few minutes later, Addy tensed as Fogarty laid his plate down and stood up.

"Boys, I'm gonna have me a little siesta," he announced with a grin. "There's to be one a' ya on guard at all times, just like always. Now, while I'm in there," he said, jerking his head toward the hut, "no one bothers our guests, ya hear me? That means none of you touches the woman or the girl, less'n ya want to die. You kin let 'em stroll around, get an idea how impossible it is t' get outa this canyon without our say-so.''

"Boss, what're we gonna do with them?" one of the outlaws asked, pointing at Addy, Lucy and Billy. There was something in the way his eyes slid over Lucy that made Addy fearful for the girl.

"We kin discuss that when I'm done with my siesta," Fogarty said, then ambled toward the hut.

Chapter Twenty-Four

"As soon as the fresh mounts are saddled up, we'll head southwest and try to catch up to them before they cross the Rio Grande. Their nags'll be tiring, so we've got a good shot, I reckon," Captain McDonald said. "And I don't think there's a snowball's chance in hell they'd go any other direction, but just in case, Wilson, why don't you have the telegrapher wire the other Ranger companies, and as many towns as he can in all directions?"

Asa nodded, and sent his deputy to carry out the order.

Rede started to open his mouth to protest, then closed it again. His feeling wasn't logical. No outlaw in his right mind would allow himself to get bottled up—in a canyon or anywhere else—if there was a chance of escaping. But his gut was telling him that after robbing the Connor's Crossing Bank, Jack Fogarty had led his gang right back into the *El Óvalo* canyon.

But *why?* If the Rangers guessed his intention, they could surround the canyon as long as necessary, until the outlaw gang was forced out by starvation.

Or was Fogarty loco enough to think he could hold the hostages for ransom there, then, when it had been paid, escape unscathed? It would be a simple matter for a few snipers to pick them off as they rode away.

But maybe Jack Fogarty had something more personal in mind, Rede thought grimly, a revenge aimed at *him,* the only Fogarty who had escaped the outlaw taint?

He shook his head. The horrible images he had of Addy at the mercy of the Fogartys—*wherever* they held her—must be affecting his brain.

"Somethin' you wanta say, Smith? You look like somethin's stickin' in your craw," McDonald observed, his eyes narrowed.

Rede looked away, aware that his fellow Rangers were watching him curiously. He himself had no respect for a Ranger who couldn't take orders, and he'd already challenged McDonald's authority enough. There was no point in irritating the captain further.

"No, I reckon not," he said at last. He pointed at the string of horses that were being led out from the livery stable. "I was just hoping that whatever horse I get is as fast as that mare I was riding before. I really want to catch those bastards, Captain."

McDonald snorted. "That's what the rest of us want too, Smith. Pick a mount and let's ride."

"Lucy, Billy, let's go take a look around," Addy said in a low voice, after Fogarty and his woman had been inside the hut for a few minutes.

"We gonna find a way to escape, Miss Addy?" Billy whispered excitedly, some color returning to his pale, worried little face.

"I don't know. Maybe," she murmured. Cautiously she got to her feet, all too aware that the outlaws had stopped what they were doing to watch them. "It won't hurt us to stretch our legs a little," she said brightly, raising her voice enough that it would carry.

They walked over to the spring first, and both women took advantage of the clear, fresh water to bathe their dusty faces. Addy took a handkerchief from her pocket and, over Billy's protests, sponged the dirt and dried blood away from the small cuts on the boy's face.

"You should have seen Billy back in town, Miss Addy," Lucy said. "After they knocked you out, he fought like a tiger trying to keep them from hurting you." Even as she praised the boy, she darted a nervous glance over her shoulder at the lounging men by the campfire.

"Thank you for trying, Billy. I'm so proud of you," Addy praised, dropping a kiss on the top of his head. *Dear God! He could have been killed!*

Billy blushed and beamed up at her. "Don't you worry, Miss Addy, Miss Lucy. I won't let those bad men bother you," he promised. "I'm gonna be sheriff some day when my papa gets old."

"And a fine one you'll be, too, Billy," Addy said, ruffling his hair. "For now, though, you mind what they say, all right? They've got guns and we haven't. But I know your papa and the Rangers will be rescuing us just as soon as possible," she promised again—and avoided Lucy's doubtful gaze.

Addy faced the boy and girl so that their watchers wouldn't be able to guess about her next question. "Lucy and Billy, I want you to show me where we entered the canyon. *Don't look at or point to it now.*

Let's kind of wander around, looking at everything else along the way, as if we're just exploring...." She didn't know if it would ever be possible to sneak out of the canyon, but at least she could study it.

They went toward the animal pens, and Billy made a great show of petting the soulful-eyed cow that came up to the fence, and Lucy pretended amusement at the antics of the sow's litter. Then, with seeming disinterest, they headed for the slight incline at one end of the canyon.

Instantly, a pair of outlaws got to their feet and jogged over, interposing themselves between Addy, Lucy and Billy and the canyon wall.

"I'm 'fraid ya can't be goin' over here, honey," one of them, a lanky youth with greased-back hair and a mousy attempt at a mustache, said with a leering smirk to Lucy, who had been leading the way.

Lucy shrank back against Addy, but then seemed to think better of it. "Oh, and whyever not?" she asked, and Addy was dismayed to see her flutter her lashes at the young criminal.

Oh, Lucy, don't think you can manipulate these boys like young Henry, Addy thought. She'd have to caution the girl about it soon as they were alone.

Just as Addy had feared, the result of Lucy's eyelash batting was immediate. The youth's smirk widened, and he licked his lips, then reached out a dirty hand and cupped Lucy's face, ignoring the girl's wrenching away.

"Boss's orders, sweetheart," he purred. "We don't invite *guests* all that often, but when we do, we like 'em to stay awhile. Aren't you a pretty one, though? Lucky for you, I like my girls with a little meat on 'em! What's your name?"

"Lucy Fickhiser, and I'm the mayor's daughter, so d-don't you dare t-touch me, you dirty thing!" Lucy sputtered. "When you're in jail my father will make you very sorry!"

Neither youth seemed at all frightened by Lucy's threat, of course, and guffawed in derision.

"I'm Clete Fogarty, and I'm Jack's cousin, Lucy honey, so I don't figger I'm too worried about your daddy. Wasn't he the one we let daylight into at the bank? I don't think he's gonna be chasin' after us any time soon, even if he don't die!"

Lucy gasped, and her plump cheeks paled.

The other youth, his face a dull red, his eyes riveted on Addy's breasts, poked Clete in the ribs.

"Oh, I'm fergittin' my manners," Clete mocked. "This here's Walt Fogarty, my brother. He ain't exactly got the gift a' gab, so he wanted me t' make the introductions. He likes skinny women that're a bit older 'n him, more experienced-like," he said, leering at Addy. "Sounds like *you'd* suit him just fine."

Clete stuck out a hand as if to put Addy's hand in Walt's, but Addy had anticipated the move and danced out of his way.

"Stop that!" she commanded sternly. "I believe Mr. Fogarty said you were not to bother us?"

The youth ignored her reproof—as Addy had known he would. "I already *know* yore name," he drawled. "You're Addy Kelly, ain't ya?" he drawled, letting his gaze roam deliberately over her, until she could almost feel it. "Why, I reckon Walt could span yore waist with those big hands a' his…."

Taking a deep breath, Addy reached out and seized

Lucy's and Billy's hands. "We're going to go back where we were sitting, and you're to leave us alone, or I will scream—is that clear? I don't think Jack would be pleased to be interrupted just now, do you?"

Clete glanced at the hut, and his face turned sullen. "Well, he might not be the boss forever," he muttered. "Things kin happen...."

He made no move to stop them from backing away. His eyes remained on them, though—and Addy could swear they were even colder than those of Jack Fogarty.

Addy knew Rede would move heaven and earth to save them, with the help of Asa and the other Texas Rangers. But in the meantime she had to try to figure out a way for them to escape if possible—and if it wasn't possible, at least decide how to keep the three of them safe while they were among the outlaws.

Fogarty had said the others weren't to "bother" the hostages—but she had counted eight of them besides the outlaw leader. What if one of them, such as the sullen Clete, decided to overthrow Jack Fogarty, promising the others they could do just as they liked with Lucy and herself?

She couldn't hope to win Clete Fogarty over to their side, Addy knew. Trying to make a deal with the sneering youth would be like dancing with the devil.

But it couldn't hurt to have Mary Sue as an ally, Addy mused, instead of one who viewed her as a potential rival.

It was dusk before the outlaw leader and his woman emerged from the shack, Jack scratching his belly and yawning, then giving Mary Sue a smack on the fanny—much as one would give a horse that had given its master a good ride, Addy thought, disgusted. Didn't she see how degrading her position was as Jack Fogarty's whore? And didn't either of them notice the resentful looks being cast at them by the other outlaws, who were slouched over their cards at the poker table?

Mary Sue preened at the gesture, but Fogarty, having satisfied one hunger, apparently thought it was time to satisfy the other type again. Addy saw him point at the chickens scratching in the dirt and taking dust baths nearby, then at an ax propped up against the hut. Mary Sue's thin features set into a pout, but Jack handed her the ax.

A moment later, Mary Sue had grabbed a squawking chicken by its neck and beheaded it, then began chasing another. Addy was glad that Billy had fallen asleep and didn't have to witness the horrible sight of the headless chickens running around until each finally collapsed in a bloody heap. The little boy had endured enough horror for one day.

"Lucy, stay with Billy," Addy whispered, gently easing the boy's head down off her lap.

"Why? What're you going to do?"

"See if I can make friends with Mary Sue." Winking at Lucy, she rose to her feet and went over to where the other woman had begun to pluck chicken feathers.

"Can I help?" Addy said, smiling encouragingly at Mary Sue.

The woman's face was hard and suspicious. "Why?"

Addy didn't wait for an invitation, but sat down next to her. "It's a big job doing all the cooking for all these men, isn't it? And now we've arrived—three more mouths to feed, right? No reason why I shouldn't give you a hand, is there?"

"No, I guess not," Mary Sue allowed, her features softening somewhat. "Keepin' these yahoos fed *is* a big chore, make no mistake. Seems like I no sooner get one meal done than they're ready for another."

"That's men for you," Addy agreed. "Here, I'm a pretty fair chicken plucker," she said, reaching out for a poultry carcass. "By the way, that stew you gave us earlier was really tasty," she added, and saw the woman try to suppress a smile. Mary Sue probably didn't get many compliments—or offers to help share her labor.

"Aw, that wasn't nothin'," she said. "Wait'll you taste my biscuits. While you're seein' to the chicken, I'll start mixin' up some dough."

By the time the sun had dropped below the western rim of *El Óvalo,* chicken was frying in a skillet on the fire, and the biscuits were baking in a dutch oven among the coals. And Mary Sue had lost much of her wariness.

"How long have you been here…with Jack and the other Fogartys?" Addy dared to ask, right after the outlaw leader had called over to complain that supper wasn't ready yet.

Mary Sue rolled her eyes. "Seems like forever, some days…but actually I just met Jack a coupla months ago."

"Where did you meet him?" Addy asked.

"I was workin' in a gen'ral store outside San Antone," the woman said, "and I was bored to tears, always doin' the same dull things, measurin' out cloth and flour and seein' the same married women with another squallin' brat on their hips every year. I was married, too, but I didn't want to turn out like those women, nosiree! I wanted me some excitement! So I started sneakin' out at night to the saloon around the corner, and one night this drifter came in and told me I was the purtiest gal he'd ever seen. That was Jack,'' Mary Sue said, nodding over to where Fogarty, unaware that he was the subject of her tale, was draining the last of the whiskey bottle at the poker table. "I thought he was the handsomest fella I'd ever laid eyes on, too. 'Bout that time my husband found out I was spendin' time with Jack, and he tried to tell me Jack was no good. Tried to keep me locked up at home at night, too, but Jack an' me always found a way to get together. I bet I'm shockin' you, ain't I?'' she said, poking Addy in the ribs.

"No, not really,'' Addy lied, feeling sorry for Mary Sue's poor, cuckolded husband, wherever he was. There was no way she could tell Mary Sue how sad the story made her without alienating her. Clearly Mary Sue thought her Jack was a daring, handsome lover, well worth leaving behind a good man and a safe home.

"Did you know Jack was an outlaw?'' Addy prodded, wanting to keep the woman talking.

Mary Sue nodded. "Sure I did. He'd even given me some jewelry he'd taken in a robbery. And when Jack talked me into running off with him, I did—and I was happy to go, 'cause I knew if I did, I wouldn't have t' be no housewife with half a dozen snotty-nosed kids. My husband found us, though, an' tried to talk Jack into sendin' me back, but Jack wouldn't hear of it. I been with him ever since," she finished with a proud toss of her head.

"And you're happy with him," Addy concluded for her. Hadn't Mary Sue realized the irony of her story? She had traded the honorable security of a husband and babies and a home for an uncertain future as an unpaid mistress and cook to a bunch of outlaws who probably weren't much less demanding than children. She wondered how Mary Sue managed to keep from getting pregnant by her outlaw lover, too. Had she just been lucky thus far? She'd heard there were ways of preventing conception, but Addy knew nothing about them.

"Sure I'm happy," replied Mary Sue with a touch of defiance.

"I just wanted you to know," Addy began carefully, "that I have no intention of coming between you and your man, Mary Sue. You *do* believe that, don't you? And I'm sure Lucy feels the same way," she said, nodding toward where the mayor's daughter was still sitting with Billy.

"Huh! I ain't worried about no sack-a'-lard *girl* replacin' me in Jack's heart," Mary Sue snorted.

"She doesn't want to, Mary Sue. She has a sweetheart back in Connor's Crossing. And I do, too, you see. In fact, there's nothing Lucy or I would like better than getting back our own men."

"And what do you think *I* got t' say about that?" Mary Sue retorted.

"Mary Sue, quit yer jawin' an' git supper finished!" shouted Jack irritably from the poker table.

Addy looked down and spoke in a low voice, hoping the fading light would keep the outlaw from seeing her talking. ''Oh, I know there's probably *nothing* you can do,'' she said in a voice loaded with sympathy. ''I just wanted to talk to you, woman to woman.''

Chapter Twenty-Five

Supper was over. By the light of the moon and a couple of lanterns they took with them to the spring, Addy had helped Mary Sue wash the tin plates. She'd had Lucy and Billy accompany them, not wanting to leave them alone by the campfire, where the Fogarty gang had brought out the whiskey bottles and cigars.

Now, as they trudged back toward the camp, Billy was rubbing his eyes and beginning to whine about missing his papa.

"Of course you do, lamb," Addy said, placing a protective arm soothingly around his narrow shoulders. "And I reckon he's missing you right now, too," she said, feeling a pang of guilt. *If the gallant boy had not tried to go to her aid, he wouldn't be here with her.*

"Do you think he'll come get us before we hafta sleep here, Miss Addy? I don't wanna sleep here," he said, his childish treble sounding perilously close to tears.

For a moment, Addy couldn't speak, and she felt her eyes stinging. *I don't want to sleep here either,*

Billy, she thought. *I wish I was safe at home in Rede's arms.*

"Oh, we'll make it fun, Billy," Lucy said encouragingly. "We'll lay out under the stars and see who can count the most, okay? How high can you count, anyway?"

"Twenty-'leven," Billy said, but he didn't sound too cheered.

"Don't you worry, boy," Mary Sue spoke up. "I'll fix you up a cozy nest a' blankets and you'll be snug as a caterpillar in a coccoon. And I'll have y'all sleep next to Jack's and my little house," the woman added in a low voice to Addy, "so's the boys cain't get up to no mischief durin' the night. All you'd have t' do is sing out."

Addy shot her a grateful look for her unexpected kindness to the child, but she wouldn't deceive herself as Mary Sue was doing. Jack Fogarty's eyes had been full of lust every time she'd caught him staring at her, and she knew he hadn't forgotten Addy getting the best of him back at her house. The fact that Mary Sue cared for him would mean nothing to the outlaw if he decided to force himself on Addy.

The outlaws had been drinking steadily while Mary Sue and the hostages had been at the spring, and their voices rose to meet them as they returned.

"What say we play a hand t' see who gets t' share a bedroll with our...uh, *guests?*" Clete proposed, grinning at the other outlaws as the women drew within earshot.

"Aw, we don't have to play fer the boy, Clete," jeered one of the other outlaws, his face demonic in the fire's glow. "You kin have him!"

Billy made a grab for Addy's skirts, shrinking

against them. "Miss Addy..." he whimpered. "Don't let him..."

The other outlaws guffawed, while Clete scowled and muttered, "Ya bunch a' chuckleheaded idiots, I wasn't talkin' about no *boy*."

Addy glared at the outlaws and put her arms protectively around the boy. "Shame on all of you for scaring a child!"

Evil sparkled in Clete Fogarty's eyes along with the flames' reflection. "Naw, I ain't cravin' no *boy*," he drawled, his narrow eyes shifting to the girl beside Addy. "I reckon the mayor's daughter'd make a nice soft pillow to lay my weary head on. Fact, she's got a *couple* a' soft pillows on her, ain't she? And them hips are nice 'n' padded fer me, too..."

Addy could feel Lucy tremble with rage and fear, and she edged as close as she could to Addy's other side.

"Now, Clete, you just hush your nonsense," Mary Sue admonished, but none of the outlaws were listening to Jack's whore.

"M-me, I w-w-want that Addy w-w-woman," stuttered Clete's brother Walt. "D-d-deal the cards, Lew," he said to the man shuffling the deck. "W-we'll settle this with a g-game."

"There ain't gonna be no card playin' fer th' wimmen tonight," snapped Jack Fogarty, rising from where he'd been stretched out with his head and shoulders propped up against his saddle.

"Why not?" Clete demanded, also getting to his feet, his jaw jutting forward belligerantly. "Thought the rule always was we shared what we took. Seems t' me it's only fair."

The air was thick with tension as the two faced

off over the fire. Neither was wearing a gun belt,
Addy noted, surreptitiously pulling Billy and Lucy
backward, but the younger man had a bowie knife
stuck in his belt, and she didn't doubt Jack had a
knife, too, somewhere on him.

"Just be a mite patient, boys," Jack said at last.
"You'll get to enjoy 'em, right enough, before we
send 'em back t' town. It just ain't gonna happen
t'night, that's all."

"Why the hell not?"

"'Cause I said so, that's why not. Once my
nephew the Ranger fetches th' ransom to us, we kin
tie him up and make a big party out of it. He'll have
to watch while we all take turns with 'em. Me first,
a' course, with Rede's li'l sweetheart, yonder—" he
said, pointing to Addy. "Yessir, I purely am goin' t'
enjoy watchin' his face while I take his woman, right
before I carve him up, piece by piece. I'll teach him
what happens to a Fogarty that turns his back on
family."

Addy's blood turned to ice in her veins as the image he evoked formed in her mind. But she didn't
dare let him see how much he'd frightened her. "I'd
rather be burned at the stake by Comanches," she
retorted, "but you won't ever get the chance to have
such a party. He'll kill you, Jack Fogarty!"

Jack Fogarty tipped his head back and laughed.
"We'll see, Miz Addy, we'll see."

Addy was vaguely conscious that Mary Sue, still
standing beside her, had gone rigid at hearing that
Fogarty meant to take part in the "party," but the
woman said nothing.

Clete was not to be ignored. "And in the meantime, what're we supposed to do? Go around with

stiff peckers, listenin' to you pokin' yer whore in there every night?'' he snarled, jerking his head in the direction of Fogarty's hut. ''It's been a long time since we bin let loose in a town, ya know.''

The others stirred restively, muttering among themselves. Fogarty had to throw them a bone, and everyone present knew it.

Dear God, let me protect Lucy somehow....

Fogarty smiled and scratched his belly as if he weren't being challenged for the leadership of the gang. ''Naw, I reckon you've earned a ree-ward, boy. Y'all kin borrow my Mary Sue fer t'night.''

''*Jack!*'' the woman screeched, throwing herself at him. ''Don't you be foolin' about somethin' like that, now! You know that Clete cain't take a joke—!''

Jack raised a clenched fist and shook it in her face. ''I *ain't* foolin', you silly bitch! You're gonna earn yore keep fer a change! Now go be nice t' my cousin, there, and then you spread 'em for the rest a' the boys—*if* they want yer skinny, used-up body, that is!''

Mary Sue threw herself at Jack's feet, sobbing. ''Jack, noooo, I'm *your* woman....''

But he just hauled her up by her hair and shoved her at Clete.

Addy stood, frozen with horror, but knowing she could do nothing to help the poor woman without endangering Lucy and Billy. Or herself.

Fogarty turned to the hostages. ''Now, you three come on—less'n ya want t' watch. You kin sleep in my shack tonight. Oh, don't fret none,'' he added, as Addy opened her mouth, ''I ain't gonna be in there, too. I'm a-gonna keep watch. I don't reckon yore lover'll be comin' t' call tonight, but it's my turn, anyway." He gestured for them to follow him.

Just at the door he stopped, though, and put his hand on Addy's chin, forcing her to look him in the eye. "You and the girl stay inside there all night, or I'll figger ya was too eager fer me t' wait till Rede comes, you hear?"

"You still look like somethin's stuck in your craw, boy," McDonald said as they stopped to water the horses at the Guadelupe River. "You worried about the woman? Can't say as I blame you there."

For a moment, Rede wondered how his captain had gotten wind of his feelings for Addy, then remembered the mayor's wife's revealing words in the aftermath of the bank robbery.

Rede nodded, studying the grizzled old Ranger. "If any of them have...*harmed* Addy Kelly any further," he began, not wanting to put his fears into exact, ugly words, "I'm not going to wait for a trial, Captain." He knew McDonald wouldn't be shocked by the sentiment.

"Don't reckon anyone could blame ya for feelin' that way, Smith," he said. "Won't nobody stop you, either."

His words encouraged Rede to express what had been nagging at him all afternoon. "Captain, I just can't shake this feeling that we're heading the wrong way. No one we've talked to has seen the outlaws passing, we've seen no sign...."

McDonald stiffened slightly. "You think they went straight south, instead of southwest? It's possible, I guess, but why would they take a longer route to Mexico? Naw, we just haven't caught up to 'em yet. I'm not surprised no one's seen 'em—they're probably skirtin' the main roads."

"No, that's not what I mean. I know you don't agree, but I can't help thinkin' they went back to *El Óvalo*. I want to head back that way. I'll go alone if you'd rather not send anyone with me." He was careful to keep his voice low, so that only the captain could hear.

McDonald's jaw went rigid. "It ain't like you to run from a fight."

It was an accusation.

Rede stiffened. "I think you know that's not how it is, Captain."

McDonald gave a big sigh and turned away, but not before Rede saw something haunted in his eyes. "Yes, I do know. You've been a good Ranger and a true one...better than most, for sure. I can't stop you if you want to resign from the Rangers, Smith. But when we catch up with those outlaws, there's going to be a fight, and dammit, I'm gonna need every man."

He stared across the river in the direction of a pair of liveoaks for a moment, then shifted his stance slightly. "Rede, I gotta say I admire your grit, stickin' to this like you have, even after you got wounded and all. You're like this terrier I used to have when I was a tad. Whatever critter he was after, he wouldn't give up. And when he caught it, he'd latch on and just shake it to death. He did fine until one day he took a notion to catch our bull. He caught him by the nose and hung on. That bull shook him all the way to the fence, doin' to him what the dog had been doin' to all those rats."

Rede knew there was a warning in the words.

They made camp just outside of Kerrville that night. There was no use trying to track the Fogartys when the dark hid any possible signs of the outlaws' passing.

Fatigued by hard hours of fruitless pursuit, many of the Rangers were already snoring in their bedrolls before tinned beans could be heated up over the fire, but there was no sleep for Rede. How could he sleep with Addy out there somewhere, a captive of the worst desperados ever to terrorize Texas?

Asa Wilson had volunteered for the first watch. He probably knew he wouldn't sleep either, Rede mused, getting up from his bedroll at last and taking the sheriff a cup of coffee.

"Much obliged." Wilson's face was set in hard, haggard lines. The man was in hell every bit as much as Rede was. The Fogarty gang had his only child, and they were men for whom the lives of others had no value at all.

For a while Rede just stood with Wilson, drinking coffee.

"Uncle Asa, Mr. Rede, do ya think we'll catch up to 'em tomorrow mornin'?" young Henry asked from his bedroll nearby.

Rede let the sheriff reply. "Dunno, son. I hope so," Asa said.

"I'm so afeared for Lucy. She's got t' be awfully scared. They won't hurt her, will they, Mr. Rede?"

Rede was careful not to look at the youth, afraid that even the shadows wouldn't hide his doubt. "No, they won't hurt her. They took her to hold for ransom, so they won't want anything bad to happen to her. Besides," he added bracingly, "I've met your girl, remember? She doesn't strike me as the kind to put up with any nonsense.''

He had expected Henry to laugh, or at least smile. But the youth didn't look comforted. ''That's just what scares me for her,'' he said. ''Sometimes she don't know when to let someone else get the last word.''

After Rede's turn on watch, he finally fell into a restless sleep, only to dream of the chapel of *Nuestra Señora del Cañon.* In his mind he roamed again over every square foot of the ruined sanctuary, only to be spoken to by the statue, who had somehow magically regained her head.

The Virgin's eyes, as blue as her robe, were filled with endless compassion. ''Rede Fogarty, what is written on my pedestal?''

He shook his head, unable to remember.

She looked at him with pity. ''You know the part.'' Her words echoed as she said them. ''The hand of Our Lady helps in times of trouble....''

Chapter Twenty-Six

Addy had dreamed, too, when she had finally fallen asleep sometime close to morning. In her dream she was walking down the aisle of the Connor's Crossing Baptist Church, dressed in a bridal gown which she had sewn, a creation even more splendid than the one she had worn in her first wedding, which had been attended by the cream of St. Louis society....

The whole town was in attendance, even Olympia Fickhiser. Addy was walking toward Rede Smith— Rede Fogarty—who looked very dashing in a dapper black frock coat with a string tie, a big smile on his face and love shining in his eyes. Asa and a couple of Rede's fellow Rangers stood as the groomsmen; Lucy Fickhiser and Beatrice Morgan were Addy's. Her mother was beaming at her from the first pew. Addy had her hand on her father's arm, and he was smiling approvingly at her, and murmuring, "This is the man I wanted for you all along, honey. This is the right man for you, so the only sensible thing to do is marry him, isn't it?"

Her hand was placed in Rede's steady, warm one,

and then the preacher began the familiar, "Dearly beloved…"

But it wasn't the right voice. She looked up into the face of the man standing in front of them, and instead of the kindly face of Preacher Crenshaw, she saw James Fogarty's mocking features….

Addy thought she screamed. Jerking bolt upright, she blinked and looked around her.

Her wedding to Rede had been but a tantalizing dream. They were still captives, and Rede was doubtless still heading for the border with the other Rangers, thinking he was riding to her rescue.

The faint light stealing through the rickety door told her it was only dawn. Beside her, Lucy and Billy still slumbered on a ragged blanket on the dirt floor, for last night, neither she nor Lucy had wanted to sleep on the bed with its dingy sheets, knowing that Fogarty and Mary Sue had just used them. Billy, in his innocence, had not understood, but he hadn't argued, falling asleep between them in seconds.

Wiping the nightmare-induced beads of sweat from her face and peering through the cracked door, Addy saw Mary Sue stirring up the coals of the campfire and setting the coffeepot on to boil. She seemed to be the only other occupant of the canyon awake; all around the campfire Addy could see the huddled forms of the sleeping outlaws. There was no sign of Jack Fogarty.

After using the smelly chamber pot the outlaw leader had left for them, Addy joined her.

Mary Sue looked as if she had aged ten years overnight. One eye was nearly swollen shut. Her hand trembled as she lifted the coffeepot from the coals and poured the hot liquid into a dented tin cup. She did not look up as Addy sat next to her.

"Are you...are you all right?" A silly question. How could the woman ever be "all right" again, after what she must have endured, not only last night, but ever since Fogarty had taken her away with him?

"Don't waste yore time frettin' 'bout me," Mary Sue muttered, not looking at Addy. "I'll be jes' fine, less'n one a' them bastards left a brat in me. Then I'll kill myself, I swear I will."

Addy wanted to put her arms around the woman and hold her, and assure her nothing like this would ever happen to her again. But how could she make such a promise, unless they got free? And she didn't think Mary Sue would thank her for her pity.

"Mary Sue, if we ever get out of here, I'll help you get home, I promise I will," Addy told her.

"My husband won't take me back. Can't say as I'd blame him, neither."

"Then I'll help you start a new life," Addy said recklessly, even as she wondered how she was going to do that. She was in disgrace herself back in Connor's Crossing. They all knew now that she was divorced, and even with the approval of Molly Renfrew, the rancher's wife, she'd be a pariah.

"Can you sew?"

A quick shake of the head. "Not more 'n how to mend a rip, and not very good at that."

"I could teach you a few things, then you could set up a seamstress shop in some other place."

"Jack won't ever let me go," Mary Sue said gloomily. "Damn him. He's plumb crazy, you know that?"

Addy could only nod. She'd seen the glint of insanity in the man's eyes even before last night. The only surprising thing was how long it had taken his woman to see it.

"Plumb crazy," Mary Sue repeated. "He's so determined to get revenge on that Rede Smith—that Ranger who was born a Fogarty—that he's gone blind t' everythin' else. Like the way the others are resentin' stayin' here jes' so Jack can get even for his brother James bein' hanged and Rede desertin' the gang an' all. Why, most of them barely remember James, and they're figgerin' they could be nearly t' Mexico by now after that bank robbery. Instead, they're holed up here, waitin' fer that Rede t' come back fer you. He's sweet on you, ain't he?"

For a moment Addy could only stare. Then she nodded. "We love one another, yes."

Mary Sue looked at her now, and her watery eyes were filled with envy—but it was mixed with sorrow. "Then I'm sorry fer ya, Miss Addy, 'cause Jack'll kill him if he comes back here. Or if he don't figure it out in time, the others'll get restless, and they'll…well, they'll make you wish you was dead." She hung her head again.

"Then you must help me, Mary Sue."

"What in hell kin we do?"

"Do you know how to get out?"

Again, Mary Sue shook her head. "He wouldn't never show me. I know there's somethin' over there you have to pull on t' git that secret passage door to work, but that's all I know."

"Secret passage door? Haven't you looked at it when they've all been gone?"

Mary Sue shrugged. "A' course. They're all gone from here a lot a' times. But I reckon I'm stupid."

Addy daringly reached out and put her arm around Mary Sue. "You're not stupid, you hear me, Mary Sue? You just haven't figured it out yet. Maybe if we put our heads together..."

"Jack won't give us no chance to try. Now that he's taken you hostages, he ain't gonna be leavin' this canyon till somethin' happens. I heard the boys talkin' last night, and they said Jack left a message in the chapel fer your Rede."

"A message? What do you mean?" Addy asked.

"Dunno."

Addy wished she could do something more to stir the woman out of her despairing lethargy, but the odor of coffee had woken a couple of the outlaws, and they were stumbling toward the campfire.

"We'll have to pray we get a chance to do something...to escape," Addy whispered quickly, before the others could come within hearing distance.

"Pray? T' who? I don't believe in God no more."

Normally, Rede didn't remember his dreams, but last night's images wouldn't let go of him. Even as he rode southwest with the rest of the Rangers, he kept seeing the statue with her pitying smile, and hearing her words—*"Rede Fogarty, what is written on my pedestal?"*

He'd gladly give up his soul to recall the partial inscription at the base of the statue, and the rest of what she'd said—something about help and trouble.

The white, dusty trail and the figures of those galloping ahead of him and beside him blurred while he racked his brain. He'd never been a religious man, but now he prayed. *Help me, God. I'm trying to save the woman I love—and she's a good woman, Lord—*

as well as a girl who's just growing up and an innocent little boy who's the apple of his papa's eye.

They stopped to rest the horses at noon in the dusty little town of Medina. They were still at least a day and a half from the border. As they stood around, watching the horses taking turns drinking from a watering trough, a man strode over to them.

"I'm the sheriff here, and I got yore telegram," the man said in a twangy drawl. "I haven't seen a passel a' fellows ridin' through, but is there anything I kin do to give you a helpin' hand? Provide ya with sandwiches or something? Won't take but a few minutes to rustle some up at the saloon over yonder...and I could ride along with ya to help, in case you catch up to 'em this side of the Rio Grande."

A helping hand.

Rede felt like he'd just been hit by a bolt of lightning.

The hand of Our Lady helps in times of trouble. That was the entire inscription at the base of the statue! He couldn't figure what difference his remembering made—all he knew was that he had to get back there.

"Captain, I'm going back," he said suddenly, interrupting the Medina sheriff in middrawl. "I'm sorry, but I think I might've just thought of something that could get me into that canyon."

A vein throbbed ominously in McDonald's temple and his lips thinned. He was probably embarrassed that Rede had chosen this moment, in front of another lawman, to go loco. "Smith, you heard the man. With a little hard riding and luck, we could make it to Mexico by noon day after tomorrow.

There's plenty a' time for your crazy notions after we try and trace 'em across the river.''

Rede shook his head, his eyes dueling with McDonald's.

"I wasn't going to tell you this," McDonald said in a low voice that only the closest could hear, "but there's a captaincy opening up in a Ranger company farther west. I was going to recommend you for it."

Once, such a prospect would have been a very tempting apple to dangle in front of Rede. Imagine, the son of a famous outlaw being a Ranger captain! Now, however, he didn't hesitate.

"I thank you for the thought, Captain. But I'm going to have to resign from the Rangers."

Rede was surprised by the sadness he saw in McDonald's face. He'd never thought that the veteran captain had felt any extra personal liking for Rede, any more than for the other Rangers, but maybe he'd been mistaken.

"So be it, then, Smith. I can't stop you, but you're makin' a mistake. There ain't nothin' or no one in that canyon, even if you do find a way in."

Rede was aware of his fellow Rangers staring at him, many of whom he'd ridden alongside while they fought Comanches and pursued raiding *bandidos* as well as American outlaws. Some of them looked sympathetic; others, disdainful.

"Go with God, Smith." That came from Asa Wilson. The two men exchanged a look, but the Connor's Crossing sheriff made no move to join him. *Probably he thinks I'm as loco as McDonald does.*

"I'll go with you, Mr. Rede," Henry offered, but his face was furrowed with doubt.

"No, you better stay with your uncle, Henry,"

Rede said. "I'm just followin' a wild hunch, and I could be completely wrong. They've got the best chance of catching up with the outlaws and the hostages. But I appreciate the offer." He didn't know what he was going to find—maybe nothing, or maybe danger, and if it was the latter, he sure didn't want the boy mixed up in it.

Raising his hand in farewell, Rede wheeled his mount back in the direction from which he had just come. He had never felt more alone.

Chapter Twenty-Seven

"If they was comin' they'd've come by now," Clete muttered the next morning later as the outlaws squatted or stood around the campfire. "How 'bout if one of us rides inta town and leaves a ransom note some place it's sure t' git found?"

"You young idiot! After we took the mayor's daughter an' the sheriff's son, that town's on the boil," Jack retorted with a contemptuous sneer. "They probably got th' posse ringin' the town, or if they don't, ya can bet they're on the alert for any strange face. What good would it do us if you git took an' put in jail? An' if ya think we'd come break you out, think again, cuz."

Clete's face, always morose, flushed with anger. "Just how long were you plannin' for us to sit here like flies in a corked bottle, dammit?"

There were murmurs of agreement from the others, especially Clete's brother Walt.

Addy, who'd been sitting on a low boulder nearby drinking coffee, now sank behind it, glad that Lucy and Billy were talking to Mary Sue while she did the wash over at the spring. The Fogarty Gang's internal dissension worried her. As much as she'd love to see Jack defeated, his actions had kept them relatively safe inside the canyon while they waited for the Rangers—or at least Rede Smith—to figure out the hostages were being kept there. If tempers exploded among the gang, there was always the chance Lucy, Billy, or herself could get injured in the crossfire— not to mention what could happen to them afterward.

"It's b-b-been a who-whole d-d-day—" stuttered Walt.

"A whole day since we took 'em, Jack," Clete finished for his brother. "Jes' how long were you intendin' to give 'em? While we're stuck waitin' here, we cain't go out and hold up any stages or banks, or raid any ranches. Why, we're down to our last stock to slaughter," he added, with a nod toward the animal pens. "And our last bottles a' whiskey."

"You pups are always too impatient, that's what's wrong with ya," Jack snapped. "Yore never gonna make old bones iffen ya don't learn some persistence. This is a *game,* boy, like the chess game I tried to learn you once when you was a kid, but you were too impatient then, too. You don't win big less'n yore willin' to wait it out."

"I thought chess was boring," Clete taunted. "An' ya know what else I think? I think you jes' like to stay safe, like a turtle keepin' his head in."

Addy, who'd been unable to stop herself from peering around the boulder, hadn't even seen the gun leave the leather holster, just the bright flash of the bullet as it burst from the muzzle and knocked the coffee cup from Clete's hand.

Clete yelped and rubbed his palm, which had been grazed by the bullet.

"Turtle, am I?" hooted Jack Fogarty. "Reckon I'm still faster 'n you, Clete. See that ya remember who's boss a' this outfit from now on." He turned and stalked into the shack without a backward glance.

"This ain't over, cuz," Addy heard Clete mutter. The others stared after Jack, then back at Clete.

"Well, what're ya lookin' at?" he snarled at them. "Don't ya have anythin' else t' do?"

Walt glanced at the shack, his face clearly anxious, then said in a low voice, "I—I'm with y-y-you, b-b-brother."

"Yeah, we want t' bust outa here. To hell with them hostages," said a balding shifty-eyed fellow called Tench. "It was a bad plan from the start. I think we oughta have some fun with the women, then let 'em loose while we head for the Badlands."

They chorused their agreement.

Clete eyed them each in turn. "All right," he said with a shaky grin. "But I say we wait till tonight. We'll get ol' Jack liquored up, then I'll plug 'im. Assuming we ain't had no Ranger visitors by then— haw, haw!"

Addy whipped her head back around the boulder so they wouldn't see her.

But too late, apparently. Something—her sudden movement, or the edge of her skirt sticking out from the side of the boulder—must have caught Clete's eye, for the next thing she knew he was standing over her, then dragging her out by one arm to show the others.

"Well, looky here. Looks like we got us a spy already. Ya know what they do to spies, woman?"

His hand snaked out, and fastened itself around her neck as if it were a noose.

Numbly she nodded, closing her eyes, imagining her limp body dangling from one of the cottonwoods by the spring—the only trees tall enough for the purpose. "I—I won't say anything," she managed to choke out. "I swear."

"Ya better not—not to that girl or Mary Sue or nobody—or it won't be you that pays with a rope around yer neck—it'll be the kid, understand?"

Frozen with horror at the threat to Billy, she nodded again. She didn't resist when he shoved her to the dirt at his feet.

She went through the day in a daze, dreading the setting sun for what nightfall would bring. She hardly spoke to Lucy or Billy or Mary Sue, for she was too afraid that any speech would lead to telling them the plot she had overheard, and result in Billy's death.

For Clete Fogarty would win, she had no doubt. He was younger and would have the element of surprise on his side. What chance did an older, drunk Fogarty have against a younger, more treacherous one?

Addy watched the whiskey being brought out that evening with a sense of inevitability.

She got up and motioned to Lucy and Billy. "Come on, I think it's time we turned in for the night," she announced. Inadvertantly, she looked at Clete as she went by him, and he had the gall to wink.

"G'night, Mary Sue," Billy called. He seemed to have joined in the project of cultivating the goodwill of the outlaw's woman with great enthusiasm.

"Night, punkin," she replied, ruffling his hair as he passed.

Fearful Mary Sue might become an unintended casualty during the attempted coup, Addy said casually, "Mary Sue, why don't you come with us? Maybe you could tell Billy a story. He's heard all mine."

But the woman just shook her head. "I don't know no stories that child should hear. Reckon I'll sit out with the boys for a while."

Addy sighed, unable to think of another excuse to call Mary Sue away from Fogarty's side that wouldn't warn her something was up. She dared not gamble with Billy's life.

She lay down with Lucy and Billy and pretended to sleep, but even after the others' breathing assumed the regular rhythm of slumber, she lay staring up into the darkness, waiting, listening to them getting louder and louder out at the campfire....

Until at last she heard shouts, Mary Sue's screech, and the twin reports that signaled Jack Fogarty's death.

Billy woke up screaming at the sound of the gunfire; Lucy, wild-eyed, demanded, *"What was that?"*

Addy held Billy to soothe him while she told Lucy what she had overheard this morning—leaving out the part about the outlaws' plan to "have fun with" the two of them. There was no use frightening Lucy until it actually happened, and if they were lucky and kept out of sight, they might be rescued before the drunken outlaws remembered their plans for the female hostages. And of course, now that Jack was dead, there was no need to mention Clete's threat to harm Billy.

"*No*. Let's just stay quiet in here," she said, when

the girl would have gone to lift the buffalo hide flap and look.

Then she heard swift steps coming toward the shack, and her heart began a slow, painful ache within her chest. *Oh, Rede...*

"Addy! It's me, Mary Sue! I'm comin' in."

In one quick motion Addy jumped up and yanked the rickety door open.

"I'm sorry," she told the woman. "I'm so sorry..." She hoped she wouldn't have to admit she had kept knowledge to herself that might have saved Jack Fogarty's useless life.

Mary Sue looked at her strangely. "What're you talkin' about? I ain't sorry," she said. "He got what he deserved, the low-down, sneaking little coward. I just figured you'd heard the shots an' came to let you know what happened, so's you'd know."

"Wh-who got what he deserved?" a trembling Lucy asked.

"Clete, of course," Mary Sue said grimly. "Jack had a notion they was plottin' somethin' this mornin' when he saw 'em with their heads together out there. He jest pretended to drink deep, so his hand was as steady 'n' fast as ever when Clete went fer his gun. Clete's dead, and the other boys're fallin' all over themselves assurin' Fogarty they're still loyal."

Rede rode like a man possessed, barely stopping to rest, changing horses in another small town when he sensed the mount beneath him was flagging. He had to get back to *El Óvalo!*

Had his dream had any real meaning or was it just the product of wishful thinking? It didn't matter. He had to save Addy, even if it cost his life. That was what his full name, Redemption, meant, didn't it? To buy something, or someone, back?

Exhausted by the strain of the last few days, he'd fallen asleep on his next horse, waking only when the willing beast stumbled on the shadowy moonlit road and almost threw him. He stopped then, hobbling the horse and wrapping himself up in his bedroll under a venerable mesquite whose low boughs would shield him from sight—not that anyone but coyotes would be apt to wander by.

He'd only sleep an hour or so, he thought, so he could be at the ruined chapel by dawn. He'd love to catch the Fogartys still asleep, so the first full rays of the sun would blind their eyes....

He awoke, however, to the sound of a mockingbird singing from one of the branches overhead and the sun dappling its face through the sparse foliage.

"Damnation!" he shouted, flinging the blanket back and startling the horse grazing a few yards away. Within minutes they were again galloping northeastward.

It was late afternoon by the time he reached Connor's Crossing. He skirted around its southwestern edge, not wanting to be slowed down by answering anyone's questions or fending off offers to help. It was dusk when he got to the chapel in front of the canyon.

It was nearly dark inside the chapel, but not so much so that he had trouble seeing the note scrawled on a ragged piece of brown paper, the kind storekeepers used to wrap purchases in. It was tied around the waist of the headless statue by means of a piece of twine looped through a hole at each top end of the paper.

He pulled it off and took it outside, hoping he still had some lucifers in the small tin in his pocket.

He did, but there were only three. He struck the first against the rough adobe of the chapel exterior.

The message was ill-spelled and hard to decipher, but the meaning was clear enough—"Howdy Nefew! I new youd be back. If you aint alone, send ennywun else away. Yore sentence is deth fer desertin yer kin. I will let yer Addy Kelly go after yer ded."

There was more, but the match was scorching his fingers. He dropped it and watched it sputter out on the ground.

In spite of the circumstances, Rede wanted to laugh. How could he be accused of deserting the Fogartys when he'd only been a child, unable to distinguish between good and bad?

Thank God he'd had a mother who'd known wrong from right and had chosen a better life for him. Because of her, he had grown up knowing what *honor* meant. Even if he didn't live through the meeting with his uncle—and the odds were great that he wouldn't—he couldn't wish Emma Fogarty had chosen any differently.

He struck the second match, and once the flame had flared into life, read the rest of the note—"I will know when you cum, so dont try nothin. I will let you inside at noon no matter wich day, Yer Uncle Jack"

Noon was some fifteen hours away. But if his guess about the dream had been correct, he wouldn't have to wait that long.

He could try it now, but he was guessing it would make at least *some* noise when it worked, possibly alerting them. Chances were the outlaws were still awake, and they might even have some sort of light by the canyon exit. A light would outline his body as he emerged on the other side of the passageway—making him a perfect target.

He'd try it at dawn. With any luck, the camp would be asleep then, except for perhaps a lookout. *Hold on, Addy,* he thought, and hunkered down to wait for the sun to rise. There was no chance in the world he'd fall asleep now. He was too eager to get the showdown over with and free Addy, whether he was alive to hold her afterward or not.

But waiting in the darkness for hours and remaining fully alert proved impossible, as tired as he was. If he wasn't asleep, he was in the next stage to it, hours later, when the click of a pistol being cocked just outside the chapel startled him into full alertness.

"Who's there?" he demanded in a harsh whisper, only to see, in the early light, the last person he'd ever expected.

"Relax, Rede. It's just me," said McDonald.

"Captain?" Rede said incredulously. "What are you doing here? I thought—"

"I—I couldn't let you just go off like that," the older man said, smiling slightly at Rede's astonishment. "I had to see what made you so sure you should come back here."

"The others—?" If the whole Ranger Company was outside, the odds had just improved about a thousand times!

McDonald shook his head. "No, I told them to go on as planned. They still mostly thought you were…uh…misguided. But I'm here."

Rede reached out and clapped the Ranger captain on the back. "It means a lot that *you* came, anyway,

Captain. I was right—the hostages *are* being kept inside the canyon.''

"How do you know?''

"I—I found a note saying so.'' He wasn't going to show McDonald the note in which Fogarty addressed him as ''nephew''—there'd be time to explain *that* later, please God. He'd tell McDonald all about why wanting to arrest the Fogartys had been such a driving force in his life.

"And I think I've guessed the way to get in,'' Rede continued. "That's why I had to head back here.'' Rede glanced at the pearling sky just over McDonald's shoulder. "Looks like it's time to try it,'' he said, striding over to the headless statue.

McDonald's features sharpened. "What are you going to do?''

"I've decided the way into the canyon has something to do with the hands of the statue, there. I think if I pull on one of them it'll somehow open a passageway into the canyon.''

He expected his captain to look skeptical, perhaps even laugh—but instead, McDonald appeared sad. As if he'd been afraid Rede would say just what he said.

"How did you figure it out?'' McDonald asked. His tone sounded like he already knew Rede was right.

Still puzzling over that, Rede sent a silent apology to the apparition in his dream. Heavenly visions were another thing he wasn't ready to try to explain to the weathered old campaigner yet. Later, he promised, when all were safe.

Rede shrugged. "Let me see if it works before I do any braggin'.''

"Stop right there, Smith. Don't touch the statue." And suddenly the pistol he'd had in his hand was pointing at Rede.

Rede froze. *"What are you doing, McDonald?"*

"I—I can't let you go in there," the captain said. "I can't let you—can't let *anyone*—see her like that. Drop your gun, Rede."

His words didn't make any sense. "See her?" Rede echoed, mystified. "Are you talking about my Addy? Captain, I *know* those bastards might've... might've forced her by now, but I love her! It wasn't her fault, and I have to save her—and the others! Now, don't point that pistol at me."

"No, not your Addy," McDonald said, almost impatiently. "My—my wife. Mary Sue. Drop your gun and raise your hands. *Now.*" He cocked the pistol as if to underline his seriousness.

Numbly, Rede obeyed. The *clunk* of the Colt hitting the stone floor echoed in the empty chapel. *"Your wife's in there? Fogarty kidnapped your wife?"*

"He didn't...kidnap her," McDonald said, his voice thin with tension, like a wire that had stretched so thin it was about to snap. "She went willingly. She's been his whore, Smith. Naturally, I can't let you see her like that. And now that you know, I'm afraid I'm going to have to shoot you, son. I'm real sorry, but that's the way it has to be. I can't have her good name...dragged through the mud."

The man was insane.

"I wouldn't tell a soul, Captain, you can trust me," Rede said evenly, keeping his eyes on McDonald's for any indication he was about to make a move.

McDonald shook his head. "You wouldn't mean to, but you'd have a few too many whiskeys, and out it would come. Don't you think I know how it happens? That's how Fogarty found out you were comin' for him, Rede. I was drinkin' with him, tryin' to make him let her go...or at least let me see her...I was tryin' anything to get him to agree. And the next thing I knew, I was tellin' him about one a' my Rangers comin' to Connor's Crossing in disguise to catch him and his gang...."

Chapter Twenty-Eight

Rede reeled as he realized the enormity of the betrayal. "It was *you* that informed," he breathed. "*You're* the reason I got ambushed...." *And the reason several innocent people on that stage were murdered.*

"Yeah, it was me. I'm sorry about it, boy, but there's no use cryin' 'bout spilt milk. Don't you see, that's why I can't take a chance with you talkin'? This is the way it has to be." The pistol wavered, then he steadied it.

No use cryin' 'bout spilt milk. Those were *people* he was talking about! Rede was more furious than he'd ever been, killing-furious, but he couldn't afford to show it. Not now. "Captain," he said, "don't you want to take her out of there, take her home? I'd be willing to bet she's had time to see the error of her ways."

McDonald shook his head. "Naw, Fogarty says she don't want to come back."

"He could be lying." While he spoke, Rede was deciding which way to feint to fight for his life. If shots were fired during the struggle, the Fogarty

Gang would probably hear it and be warned, but it couldn't be helped. If he didn't overcome McDonald, he couldn't rescue Addy and the others.

"Now turn around and raise your hands in the air."

Rede complied, warily. Would he have time to act before McDonald sent a bullet into his brain?

"Now back on outa here with me. I'd just as soon not shoot you in a house a' God."

Rede almost laughed at the madman's scruples.

He waited until they were nearly to the door. Suddenly he lunged to the left, then came around with a roundhouse punch that knocked McDonald backward and sent the gun sliding across the floor.

Desperately, both men leaped at the pistol, but McDonald was closer, and grabbed it. Rede knew his own gun was still lying on the floor a few yards from him, but it was too far away to save him.

McDonald smiled a terrible smile and got to his feet, his form silhouetted by the rising sun at the doorway behind him.

"Maybe you should kneel with your hands folded. Only don't cover your chest, Smith."

Rede remained in his crouching position. "Go to hell, McDonald."

All at once McDonald was springing at Rede—no, he was falling, with all the boneless grace of the dead.

Too late, Rede saw the figure standing in the doorway, holding the butt of the gun with which he'd hit McDonald over the head. How had Fogarty gotten out of the canyon and sneaked around in back of them? Or had he been outside *El Óvalo* the whole time?

I'm a dead man, Rede thought. *For sure this time.* He was unable to see his nemesis clearly since the rising sun placed the man in shadow. Then the figure spoke.

"Damn, I thought you were a goner," said Asa Wilson. "I was ready to shoot him if I had to, but the way he was standing in front of you, I was afraid it'd go right through and hit you, too."

Weak-kneed with relief, Rede gazed at the sheriff. "But why are you here? I thought..."

Asa shrugged. "I thought you were wrong, that there was no chance the Fogartys would come back here," he admitted. "But then McDonald sneaked outa camp in the middle of the night when he thought everyone else was sleepin'. I figured he was up to something. Then, when I realized he was comin' here..." He shrugged. "I realized he must know somethin' we didn't."

"You heard...what he said to me in there?"

Asa nodded. "Everything." He watched as Rede leaned over the recumbent McDonald and placed a couple of fingers on his neck. "I didn't kill the sidewinder, did I?"

Rede shook his head.

"Too bad, in a way. He deserved to die. Now he'll have to stand trial—and we're gonna have to make sure he keeps quiet in case he wakes up while we're in there." He nodded in the direction of the canyon.

"You're assuming I'm right about the way into the canyon."

Again, Asa nodded. "I've got a rope on my saddle out there—"

"I'll guard him while you get it."

Five minutes later, with the still-unconscious

Ranger captain lying bound and gagged, they had stepped up to the headless statue.

"Be ready," Rede said, jerking his head toward the chapel wall close to the canyon wall. Asa cocked his pistol and stood poised in that direction.

Rede reached out and took hold of the stone right hand of the statue. If he'd expected any magical tingle, he didn't experience it. The carved stone merely felt cool in his hands. He pushed.

Nothing moved.

Please, Lord. He tried the other hand.

Nothing.

Lord, there's two innocent women in there—one of whom I love more than my life, and a child.

Desperately, he interlaced his fingers with those of the statue's right hand and pushed upward. "*Please...*" he prayed. He begged.

And then it came to his ears—that slow rumbling in the ground beneath them. Inch by inch, so slowly that he thought at first he was just seeing what he wanted to see, the wall abutting the canyon began to slide back, revealing a narrow passageway, just tall enough and wide enough to admit a man on horseback if he ducked low against the horse's neck.

"Well, I'll be..." Wilson muttered softly, staring at the opening that had not been there before. "Those old padres musta devised that mechanism in the days of the old Spanish mission, so they had a place to hide when the hostiles were on the warpath. Amazing. Later on I'd like to see if I can figure out how it works."

Rede peered into the darkness of the passageway. He could hear nothing on the other side to make him think anyone was yet the wiser for his discovery.

Addy, I'm coming...

* * *

In her dream, Addy saw Clete being shot over and over, from all angles, dying again and again. The first gunshots seemed but an echo of the nightmare. Then she heard another report from somewhere outside the shack.

Lucy had already jumped off their pallet and was kneeling in front of the low buffalo hide flap window. And Billy was scrambling to join her.

"What's going on? Lucy, come away from there! And Billy, you stay put here on this pallet!" she cried, making a grab for the boy's shirttail. "It isn't worth being hit by a stray bullet just to see which of them is killing which other of them this time!"

Lucy obediently came back, but her face was excited. "They aren't killing one another, Miss Addy! They're being attacked! Someone's gotten in—I can't tell just who yet, but I saw the one guarding the entrance—I think it was that nasty fellow called Tench—go down! And I can see two other outlaws just lying on the ground out there, not moving—I'm pretty sure they were hit, too."

"What?" She had to see for herself.

Replacing Lucy at the window, Addy was in time to see a pair of outlaws go racing past. Just then there were twin loud *cracks,* and one outlaw flung his arms wide and fell, a spreading crimson stain dyeing the cloth between his shoulder blades. The other was still running, heading for the cover of the trees, but he didn't make it before he was felled, too. She looked in the direction of the shots, but couldn't see anything through the smoke of gunfire.

But the voice was familiar enough. "This is Rede

Smith of the Texas Rangers. Your sanctuary's been invaded! Give yourselves up! Come out with your hands up, and we won't shoot the rest of you.''

Addy's heart flooded with gladness, and simultaneously, with fear for him. *Dear God, what if he had found his way in, only to be killed in the attempt to save them?*

"What for, so you can lynch us?" jeered Jack Fogarty. It sounded to Addy like he was calling from right in back of the shack. "No thanks! 'Sides, they's only two of you—you an' that sheriff! I saw ya come in! No use tryin' t' make believe yore a whole Ranger company—there's more than enough a' us here t' take care of th' two a ya!''

Billy was galvanized by Fogarty's words. "My *papa's* here?" He made a dash for the door.

Addy snatched him back. *"You stay right here, down on the floor, or you could get shot!"* she whispered urgently. She thought quickly. There was still Walt, the stuttering Fogarty cousin, and a couple of others. Four to two. But there was also Mary Sue—and Addy had no idea if she would help either side.

"No one's going to be lynched," Rede called back. "I can promise you'd stand trial, Jack."

"Mighty comfortin', that is! I kin die chokin' at the end of a rope *after* a trial, instead a' b'fore. Like yore daddy did! An' that's *Uncle* Jack to *you*, nephew. Let's show some proper respect, eh? Did you tell yore sheriff pard yet that you were a Fogarty, same's me?''

Silence met his question. Addy could imagine Asa staring at Rede in astonishment—the same way Lucy was staring at her now.

"Ya didn't, did ya?" Fogarty taunted. "I ain't surprised."

"None of that matters now, Fogarty." The voice was Asa's this time. "You and your men come forward with your hands up."

The smoke had cleared somewhat, but Addy couldn't see Rede or Asa. From the direction their voices had come from, however, she thought they were crouched behind a large boulder right next to the entrance. Apparently the remaining gang members had all taken positions of cover, too. But where was Mary Sue?

Don't take any chances, Rede!

"Naw, I don't think we'll be doin' that," Fogarty said. "I think you know we got us three hostages here. So iffen ya want them to stay healthy, I'd suggest ya back on outa here, Sheriff. I'm willin' t' release them females and yore boy without any more money than what we already took from yore bank—ain't that generous? But my nephew has t' stay when ya leave. He 'n' I have a reckonin' that's long overdue."

Addy and Lucy stared at one another, stricken. The price of their freedom was to be Rede's life?

"No! Don't do it, Rede!" she screamed out the window.

There was no answer. All of a sudden there was a blur of motion coming toward her from outside, and Fogarty dived through the window, pursued by three bullets that whizzed over their heads as he came up beside her, holding his still smoking pistol and grinning evilly.

"That was mighty careless of ya, nephew! Yore

woman and the girl and the sheriff's boy 're in here!
Why, ya mighta hit 'em, jes' now!''

Again, silence on the other side of the acrid
smoke.

And then the sound of running feet—and more
gunshots, both from the rocks and from the direction
of the trees. Addy heard a thud, and a single, terrible
cry. A death cry.

"Two of your boys just died, runnin' in t' join
you, Fogarty!" Rede shouted. "How many does that
leave? You must be getting pretty lonely!"

"R—" she began, but before she could call out a
warning that there was still another outlaw left inside
the canyon besides Jack Fogarty—and Mary Sue—
Fogarty had clamped a brutal, dirty hand over her
mouth.

"Now, don't go givin' away all our secrets, Miz
Addy!" he said, waggling a finger of his other hand
in front of her face. "No more a' that, or the boy
dies, right here 'n' now."

Addy saw Billy's wide, terrified eyes a second before he buried his tearful face against Lucy's breast.
She shook her head, indicating her silence. He took
his hand away.

"I kin see it's time for me to convince yore sweetheart I mean business. C'mere, boy. It's time t' earn
yore keep."

Billy whimpered and tried to burrow into Lucy,
but Fogarty yanked him away by the neck of his
shirt. "Stop yore whinin' or I won't let yore pa have
ya back. I'll make ya stay here an' be an outlaw."

"I *won't!*" Billy yelled, swinging his fists at Fogarty.

"Billy, be still and just do what he tells you!" Addy pleaded.

Obediently, the boy stopped struggling and allowed Fogarty to pick him up so that he was held, face forward, against the outlaw's chest. Fogarty moved to the door, then turned back to look at Addy and Lucy in turn. "You females stay right in here, ya understand? Either one a' ya tries anythin' funny an' the boy dies."

Numbly, Addy nodded, and saw a white-faced Lucy do the same. But she could not suppress a moan of fear when she saw Fogarty pull his pistol back out of his waistband and place the muzzle against the child's temple. Billy whimpered as he stepped to the door and pushed it open.

"You kin see I got the boy here!" he shouted. "Come out from behind that rock with yore hands up before I count t' ten, nephew, or I'll shoot him, I swear I will!"

Addy thought her heart would stop.

"One! Two! Three…"

"I'll come, Jack!" Rede called back. "But you have to release the ladies!"

Jack's laugh was harsh. "Reckon you ain't in any position to make conditions, nephew! Oh, *you* might not care if I kill the sheriff's boy, but I reckon he'll shoot ya hisself iffen you don't do as I say! *Four! Five!"*

Addy, helplessly staring out the low window in an agony of fear, saw Rede come out from behind the sheltering boulder and raise his hands skyward, then walk toward Fogarty.

"Now, that's real sensible," Jack approved. "And jes' t' show ya my good faith, I'm gonna let the mayor's daughter go free. C'mon out, Miss Lucy!'' he called over his shoulder.

Addy turned away from the window to find Lucy gazing at her with anguished eyes.

"Miss Addy..." Lucy's eyes gleamed with unshed tears in her pale face. "I don't want to leave you here...."

"*Go*, Lucy," Addy said. "I'll be all right, you'll see. This'll all turn out all right." Now, if only she could believe it, she thought as the girl went through the doorway and sprinted toward the rock, and safety.

"I'm doin' what you want, Fogarty," Addy heard Rede say as he crossed the distance from the boulder to Fogarty. "Let the boy and Miss Addy go, too."

But Fogarty shook his head. "Naw, I'm keepin' yore woman as insurance, ya might say. I'll let her go after the sheriff leaves the canyon with his brat and the girl—and after I kill you." He kept the gun trained on Rede and the boy clutched firmly against his chest. "Walt, c'mon out from wherever yore hidin' and fetch some rope t' tie our new *guest* up."

Chapter Twenty-Nine

With a growing sense of resignation, Rede watched as a gangling young man came loping out from behind a tree, made a stop where the saddles and saddlebags were piled, and ran toward them, carrying a coiled rope.

"Mary Sue! Where are you? Come out here and take my nephew's pistols!" Fogarty barked.

He didn't see where she had come from, this bony, washed-out woman in her faded red dress, but all at once she was by his side, pulling his pistols from his holsters and handing them to Fogarty, who stuck them in his belt.

So this was the woman whose desertion had made a good Ranger go crazy. She didn't look like much now, but she must have once been very pretty. Fleetingly, her eyes, dull and dispirited, met his.

He turned and gazed at the ramshackle hut he had heard Addy calling from. Could she see him right now? Was she all right? He didn't mind dying if this was the only way he could save her, but he couldn't help feeling melancholy for all the happiness he and Addy might have had together.

"Okay, I've done what you demanded," he said to Fogarty as the outlaw called Walt tied his hands behind him. "Let the boy go."

Fogarty chuckled. "Let him go? I let him go while his papa's still in the canyon, and I've lost my ace in the hole, haven't I? Sheriff," he said, raising his voice, "toss yore guns on out from behind that rock. My cousin Walt will pick 'em up, and see you 'n' the girl leave. He'll send yore boy through the passage just b'fore he locks it so's you cain't barge back in, understand?"

"I understand!" Wilson called back, and a moment later, two guns flew out and hit the rocky ground with twin *clunks*.

Walt jogged over and picked them up, shouting back, "I g-g-g-got 'em, J-J-Jack!"

"Then let the sheriff and the girl go through the passage!" Fogarty called back.

Rede saw Asa stop and look at him. From this distance, he couldn't discern the sheriff's expression, but he hoped he wasn't hesitating. Deliberately, he nodded toward the entrance to the canyon. *Go.*

Asa Wilson, his arm around the mayor's daughter, went. A minute later, Walt called out. "H-he's on th-the other s-s-side!"

"Damn stutterin' idiot!" Rede heard Fogarty mutter under his breath. Then he raised his voice, "Walt, I'm lettin' the kid go! Make sure he gets ou—OW! Damn you, you little demon!" he cried, as Billy, free at last, kicked him in the shins before running for the entrance.

Walt and Billy disappeared into the dark passageway.

"Walt, you come on back soon's the kid's out!"

Fogarty called after him. They waited, and then Rede heard the distant rumble of the hidden door closing.

They waited, but Walt didn't reappear.

"Walt?" Fogarty called, then lowered his voice to a mutter again. "Now what could be keepin' that damnfool simpleton?" He took a few steps forward, still keeping his gun trained on Rede, and cupped his other hand around his mouth. "Hey, the fun's about t' begin, Walt!"

Rede saw out of the corner of his eye that Mary Sue was staring at him curiously.

"Mrs. McDonald," he said in a whisper, inclining his head politely, as if they were meeting in the street.

"How'd you know my name?" she demanded, whispering back.

"Your husband's out there," he told her. "He told me about you. He's waiting for you, Mrs. MacDonald. He loves you. He's missed you." *Lord, please let her believe it.*

"Now what the Sam Hill..." Fogarty muttered, and Rede thought he'd been overheard. But Fogarty had started walking toward the direction Walt had gone. "Watch the Ranger, Mary Sue. Give a holler if he tries anything."

She stiffened and stared after the outlaw resentfully. "Talks to me like I was a damn dog."

"Actually, he treats you worse than a dog, Mary Sue," said Addy in a low voice from the window of the shack. "And he's the one who gave you to the others the other night, remember? Just as if you didn't have any feelings."

Rede wanted nothing more than to gaze at Addy,

and go to her, but he had to keep working on the outlaw's woman while he could.

Mary Sue turned back to Rede, her face pale. "George McDonald hates me…he has to, after what I done."

Rede shook his head, keeping the woman's gaze locked with his, and pressed his advantage. "No, ma'am. He doesn't hate you. He forgives you." *God forgive me—I don't know what's in McDonald's heart toward his wife. But I have to use anything I can to save Addy and myself.*

"Forgives me?" the woman repeated, her eyes staring at the entrance to the canyon now.

"Sure. I could take you to him, if you'll help me get loose."

The woman stared dubiously at him. "I don't know…."

"*Do it*, Mary Sue," Addy urged, clambering out the window. "*Please…*"

"Addy, honey, stay in there!" he begged. "Just in case…" *In case Fogarty turns around and starts shooting.*

"But how?" Mary Sue asked, staring at the knots in the rope. "Jack'll be back b'fore I could work them knots loose."

"Don't you have a cooking knife over by the fire?" Addy called in a hoarse whisper.

Mary Sue's tired, hopeless face brightened. "Happens I do!" Keeping an eye on Fogarty, who was still striding toward the entrance in search of Walt, she edged over and picked it out of a rusty pot full of utensils.

Stashing it in her apron pocket, she sidled back to Rede.

"You're a good woman," Rede whispered, as he backed up to her, and felt her starting to saw at his bonds.

"Ain't no one said that to me in the longest time," Mary Sue said, her voice thick with unshed tears.

"Hey! What's goin' on there?" shouted Fogarty, who was running back toward them. "Mary Sue, what're you up to?"

Mary Sue sprang away from Rede, her hands waving. "Nothin', Jack! Just checkin' the ropes, that's all!"

Rede had carefully kept his hands behind him, as if he was still bound, but he saw Fogarty stop a few yards from them and his eyes narrow, and knew he had spotted the cut rope that lay in the dirt behind him.

"Damn you, bitch!" he screamed, and took aim.

Mary Sue screamed as the bullet found her. She went down in a flurry of red skirts. Rede heard Addy screaming, too, but he couldn't concentrate on that, because now Fogarty had shifted his aim and was about to shoot *him.*

He threw himself to the side, knowing it would only buy him a moment of time, and felt the bullet whiz over his head. The roar of the gun echoed around the canyon. He knew in the next second Fogarty would reaim, and this time, he was unlikely to miss, even though Rede was rolling in the attempt to make himself as difficult a target as possible.

I love you, Addy...

"Fogarty!" The challenging shout made Fogarty whirl around, as it was meant to. Rede raised his head to stare.

Captain McDonald stood on the slight incline at the entrance to the canyon, a rifle leveled at Fogarty.

"This is for Mary Sue," he said, and fired.

Fogarty shot, too.

The men fell simultaneously, but it was clear from the way Fogarty fell that he was dead before he hit the ground.

Rede raced to the captain, and out of the corner of his eye, he saw Addy running toward Mary Sue.

McDonald's eyes were already glazed when he reached him, but Rede knew the man recognized him. "Had to avenge my...wife," he said, the words coming with difficulty. "Sheriff said...okay..."

"You avenged her, Captain," Rede told him, as he cradled the dying man's head in his lap.

"Had t' make it up to you, too."

"You did," Rede assured him. "You saved my life, Captain. Much obliged."

"O-owed you..."

"George!" cried a woman's voice overhead, and Rede looked up to see that Mary Sue, with Addy's help, had hobbled over to them. She was clutching her shoulder. A darker red splotch spread below her hand, but Rede guessed it was a wound she'd survive.

"George!" moaned Mary Sue again. "I'm here, George! Hang on!"

"M-Mary Sue...love...you..." George managed to gasp, and then his head rolled limply back into Rede's lap.

"Go with God, Captain, and thank you," Rede murmured, and shut the dead man's staring eyes.

Gently he set the captain's head down. While Mary Sue's keening wails filled the canyon, he went to Addy and held her while she wept with relief.

Chapter Thirty

"Rede tells me your husband will be buried with the full honors of a hero, Mary Sue," Addy told Mary Sue, as she bandaged the grieving woman's shoulder with strips torn from a clean, if threadbare, petticoat Mary Sue had stored in an old trunk in the shack. Finding bandaging material had been a good excuse to prevent Mary Sue from seeing Rede and Asa wrapping the captain's body in a canvas tarp. "And he'll see to it that you get his pension as his widow."

Mary Sue lifted her tearstained face. "It don't hardly seem like I deserve to have it," she said mournfully.

"Nonsense. The captain would have wanted you to have it, I'm sure. He must have loved you very much, or he wouldn't have dared to come charging into the canyon to rescue you like he did," Addy said.

Rede had told Addy the whole story, though—out of earshot of Mary Sue, of course—of how McDonald had shown up and would have killed him if Asa hadn't followed him.

"Anyway," she continued, leading Mary Sue back into the sunlight again, "that pension will help, but once your shoulder gets better, you'll need to start a new life. I meant what I said about teaching you how to sew, Mary Sue. And you're welcome to live with me—with *us*," she corrected herself, blushing, after her eyes flew involuntarily to the tall, lean form of the man she loved.

Mary Sue smiled wanly, following her gaze. "Oh, I don't want to get in the way a' newlyweds," she said, "but I *would* like to learn the trade. Maybe there's some way I could rent a room in town, and come to your house and take lessons?"

"I'm sure we could work something out," Addy said with a smile, already planning to ask Beatrice Morgan if she'd let Mary Sue stay with her. Beatrice would probably welcome the regular company—and with any luck, she and the rest of the town would believe that Mary Sue McDonald had truly been kidnapped and held by the Fogarty gang against her will.

If Mary Sue mourned at all for her erstwhile paramour, Jack Fogarty, she gave no evidence of it. She'd never even glanced back at his body or at those of the other outlaws. Addy knew a detail of men would have to come out from town to see that the dead outlaws were decently buried—which was certainly more than the vicious outlaws had ever done for their victims.

Walt, Jack's stuttering cousin, was not one of the dead. He had cravenly surrendered to Asa just as soon as he got out of Jack Fogarty's sight. Not foreseeing that Jack would be killed in the canyon, he had probably hoped to turn state's evidence and testify against his uncle to save his own neck. Instead,

he would be marched back to town in front of Asa's
horse and jailed until it could be decided just which
town would get to put him on trial.

"I'm ready to go *home,* Lucy! Aren't you?" Billy
called to the girl. Both were mounted, as Addy was,
on horses that had belonged to the outlaws, though
Billy's horse would be tied to his father's.

"I sure am," Lucy said. "Can't we leave soon,
Sheriff Asa? I'm really worried about my papa."

Addy felt guilty that she had hardly spared the
wounded Mayor Fickhiser a thought while she'd
been held captive in *El Óvalo* Canyon. Why, they
didn't even know if Lucy's father had survived the
wounds he'd sustained during the bank robbery.
Please God, let him be alive. There had been enough
dying.

"Are you ready to go home, sweetheart?" Rede
said, looking worn and weary as he mounted the
horse beside hers and gathered up the reins. He
would also be leading the horse McDonald had ridden to the canyon, which was now carrying his body.

She smiled tenderly at him, and spoke softly so
the others couldn't hear. "If you're coming with
me."

He grinned back, the weariness fading from his
features. A devilish glint danced in his eyes, the same
devilish glint Addy remembered from those first days
when he'd been lying in her bed, recovering from his
wounds. "I'll come by after dark," he said. "We
don't want to offend the town's sensibilities any
more than necessary, do we?"

She felt a moment's rebelliousness at this need to
even pretend to observe propriety. She'd had a belly-
ful of it, and now that she and Rede had survived

life-threatening danger at the hands of the Fogarty gang, she wanted nothing more than to be openly at Rede's side every hour of the day—and night.

He laughed and placed a teasing finger against her pouting lower lip. "It's just for a short time," he whispered, "'Cause I want to marry you by the end of the week, Miz Addy Kelly. I know you'll want a nice dress and a proper church wedding...but I'm not waiting too long to call you my wife."

His hot gaze promised untold pleasure later tonight when he came to her. But in the meantime, she thought of a certain beautiful dress she'd made ages ago and never worn. It lay folded between sheets of scented paper in a trunk in her attic. She'd believed in dreams then, and now she had reason to believe in them again. All it would take was a little pressing with a hot iron—and she could probably accomplish that before Rede arrived at her house tonight.

"If we can get the preacher to cooperate, I believe we could get married tomorrow," she said with a saucy wink. "Only...what name am I taking on, Rede? Smith or Fogarty?"

He sobered and stared off into the distant lime-stone-studded hills. "I once thought I'd like nothing better than to call myself Rede Fogarty and know that I had washed the name clean of dishonor." He shrugged, and looked back at the chapel door as if he could see all the way through into the oval-shaped canyon that lay on the other side of the seemingly magical wall. "I don't know that the stain can ever be erased, though. The name of Fogarty is going to be associated with outlaws and robbery and murder long after you and I are dust, Addy. I don't want our children to bear it."

She felt all warm inside at the certain way he said "our children."

"I think I'll stay just plain 'Smith,' if it's all right with you," he said.

"It's fine with me, Rede, honey. And I'll be just plain Mrs. Smith."

Just beyond Connor's Crossing, the little cavalcade encountered Brooks patrolling with two men of the posse—for the deputy had taken seriously his duty to protect the town in the sheriff's absence. After Asa had explained what had happened, Brooks and one of the men agreed to take charge of Walt Fogarty and McDonald's body, while the other man galloped ahead to alert Connor's Crossing that the missing ones had returned.

It was quite a welcoming committee, therefore, that lined the main street of Connor's Crossing to cheer the "conquering heroes," as one old graybeard called them. It seemed that the town's entire population had turned out to clap and cheer. Beatrice Morgan stood right in front of her house, crying happy tears. The mayor, leaning on his wife, his arm in a sling, had summoned the brass band made up of veterans of the Civil War, which usually played only on Independence Day. They were playing a rousing, if slightly off-key, version of "When Johnny Comes Marching Home."

Lucy jumped off her horse and ran to her father and mother and was caught up in their embrace. Then the mayor made an impromtu speech extolling the heroes, including Asa Wilson and all the Rangers, including the fallen Captain McDonald. At the end of it, he especially thanked Rede Smith for his heroic incognito efforts that had led to the end of the Fogarty gang.

"I'd be proud to have you stay on in Connor's Crossing as another deputy, Smith," Asa Wilson said. "This town is growing, and pretty soon we'll need more lawmen to protect it."

Rede's gaze locked with Addy's while he replied. "I don't know, Wilson. Addy and I haven't talked about…where we'll be living…after we're married."

Addy said, "I imagine you could go right back to your Ranger company. They'd be happy to have you." She was careful to keep her voice low so that Mary Sue, who was already being fussed over by Beatrice Morgan, wouldn't hear. "They'll need a new captain. Is that what you want, Rede? If it is, I'll understand…but I want roots. I *need* roots."

He needed them too, he knew. He'd never really had a home of his own—one couldn't really call a boardinghouse room home, and so much of the time he wasn't even there, but sleeping next to a campfire on the hard ground.

Addy's house had become home to him.

"I'm not going back to the Rangers, Addy," he said. "I joined the Rangers to prove something—to myself, I guess. That I was the furthest thing from being an outlaw. And I wanted to accomplish something." He took a deep breath. "I've done that now. The Fogarty gang doesn't exist any more. My home is with you, Addy. I'd be happy to stay here, if that's where *you* want to be. But—" he glanced meaningfully around him at the townspeople—especially at the mayor's wife. "Do *you* want to stay here?"

"I have a business here, Rede," Addy said. "And a house I love because my aunt and uncle left it to me. I'm planning to stay right here, since it's all right with you.''

She still looked hesitant, though, and he saw her eyes stray involuntarily to Olympia Fickhiser.

The mayor's wife looked up just then, and met her gaze straight on, but her eyes were brimming with tears.

"Please say you'll stay, Miss Addy," Olympia Fickhiser pleaded. "Lucy tells me you've been a good friend to her, and have taught her much. Things I should, perhaps, have been teaching her—by example. I'd be honored if you'd consider yourselves our friends—and if you'd let us host your wedding reception, whenever it will be." She broke off because her daughter was whispering something into her ear.

"And yes, Lucy, you may invite young Henry as your escort to the party. Henry's one of many subjects I've decided I was wrong about, you see, Addy. I imagine he and the Rangers will be arriving back any time now...."

After beaming at her daughter and at young Henry's father, the livery owner, Olympia turned back to Rede. Her face suddenly held an uncertain expression again.

"That is...I gather nuptials *are* pending?"

Rede grinned at her, then at Addy as he held her close. "Yes ma'am. They're pending right quick." He looked at the sheriff. "And I reckon I'll take you up on that deputy job, Asa—to start with, at least until I decide what my place in Connor's Crossing is."

He lowered his voice and spoke into Addy's ear. "Besides being your husband, that is."

* * * * *

Travel back in time to America's past with wonderful Westerns from Harlequin Historicals

ON SALE MARCH 2001

LONGSHADOW'S WOMAN
by **Bronwyn Williams**
(The Carolinas, 1879)

LILY GETS HER MAN
by **Charlene Sands**
(Texas, 1880s)

ON SALE APRIL 2001

THE SEDUCTION OF SHAY DEVEREAUX
by **Carolyn Davidson**
(Louisiana, 1870)

NIGHT HAWK'S BRIDE
by **Jillian Hart**
(Wisconsin, 1840)

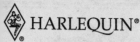

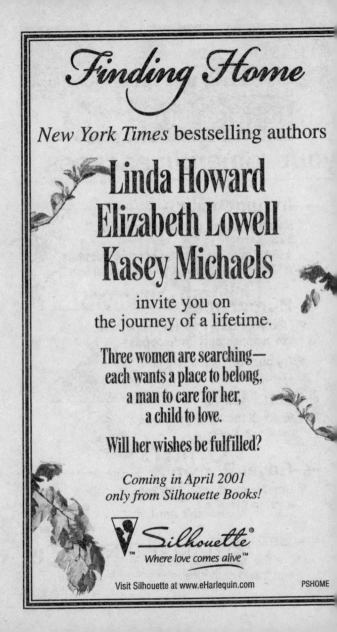

REGENCY ROMANCE

Visit the elegant English countryside,
explore the whirlwind of London Society
and meet feisty heroines who tame roguish
heroes with their wit, zest and feminine
charm, in...The Regency Collection.

Available in March 2001 at your favorite retail outlet:

TRUE COLOURS
by Nicola Cornick

THE WOLFE'S MATE
by Paula Marshall

MR. TRELAWNEY'S
PROPOSAL
by Mary Brendan

TALLIE'S KNIGHT
by Anne Gracie

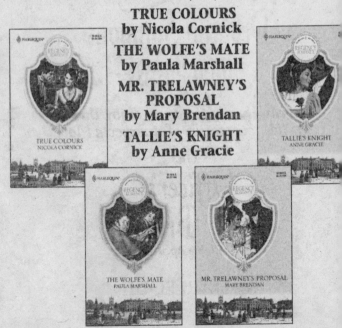